Praise for The End of Sleep

'A raucous, brilliantly funny ride through Arab culture and the colourful streets of Cairo' *Scotland on Sunday*

'Everything about Somerville's debut made me hungry: hungry to visit Cairo, but above all hungry for whatever this author chooses to serve up next' *Sunday Telegraph*

'Brimming with a love of Arab culture, this madcap tale follows Cairo-based Fin as he searches for his friend Farouk, a quest that takes him through gallons of whisky, tea and Nile water!' *Sainsbury's Magazine*

'A heady adventure tale' *The Shortlist*

'This freewheeling novel is a love letter from one happily shambolic country to another' *Mail on Sunday*

'Glorious passages of description' *Daily Telegraph*

'A life-affirming story of a man looking for a beginning, a middle, and most importantly, an ending'
Belfast Telegraph

'A brisk page-turner' *GQ*

'A riotous, humorous, careering and life-affirming story, *The End of Sleep* introduces a brand-new voice . . . a hymn to life and the world in which it's set' Patrick McCabe

Rowan Somerville was born in the West End of London in 1966. He was educated by Jesuits and took an honours degree in Literature from the University of Edinburgh. He has worked in film, television and radio and he now lives in the west of Ireland. *The End of Sleep* is his first novel.

the end of sleep

Rowan Somerville

PHOENIX

A PHOENIX PAPERBACK

First published in Great Britain in 2008
by Weidenfeld & Nicolson
This paperback edition published in 2009
by Phoenix,
an imprint of Orion Books Ltd,
Orion House, 5 Upper St Martin's Lane,
London WC2H 9EA

An Hachette UK company

1 3 5 7 9 10 8 6 4 2

A CIP catalogue record for this book
is available from the British Library.

ISBN 978-0-7538-2343-9

Typeset by Input Data Services Ltd,
Bridgwater, Somerset

Printed and bound in Great Britain
by Clays Ltd, St Ives plc

The Orion Publishing Group's policy is to use papers that
are natural, renewable and recyclable products and
made from wood grown in sustainable forests. The logging
and manufacturing processes are expected to conform to
the environmental regulations of the country of origin.

www.orionbooks.co.uk

Acknowledgements

First thanks are to beloved Lauren.

None of this would have happened without the sagacity and compassion of Stuart Macfarlane. Nor the mystical half-Christmas present from you, dear Kate McCreery, which germinated the peculiarly accurate predictions of Katy Noura and the subsequent hospitality and valued wisdom of Hisham Gamel. Thank you my friends. I am deeply grateful to those who gave me a place to live during the long adventure of this story's birth: the Swiney family; the Freeland family; Sir Christopher and Jenny Bland; Venetia and Gambas Scott; Gillian Anderson and the Helene Wurlitzer Foundation of New Mexico. I am grateful to those who gave their time, taste and intellect to the manuscript as it took teetering steps into literature: Marcelle d'Argy Smith; Darren Watterston; Crispin Somerville; Lee Brackstone; Clare Conville; Louise Lamont; Peter Straus; Justine Prestwich; Cécile Hohenlohe; Lauren Abdel Razak; Nicola Harrison; Hardy Blechman; Douglas Barrett and Peter and Brigid Hardwick (whose inspiration goes back twenty-five years). Please know, my dear brother Lorne, that I am still so touched by your extraordinary act of generosity in 2006. I send love and gratitude to my friends on Denman Island: Keith; Wendi; Sam and Wind; Larry; Ferris; Gecko; Ella;

Tulku Karzang and the Venerable Lingtrul Rinpoche. Thanks and love to my compadres in New Mexico: Hannah Cole; Michael Knight; Jackie Keating; Peggy Goldstein; Charlie and Emily Henry (bless you for your love, hospitality and p/u truck) and my friend and editor, that great American man of letters (and left-wing feudalist), Tom Michael Collins. Love and thanks to the princesses, buccaneers, farmers, pirates and fishermen of North Cornwall: Simon; Gemma; Ayrton; Pelé; Steph; Chris; Alex; Harold; Johnnie; Rose; Trehane; Mark and Wendy. Thanks to my dear friends in Ramelton, Co. Donegal: Annie; Anita; Don; Kenny; Marcel; Martin and Sean. Thank you to all those international morale boosters of London town who have supported me in so many different ways. Thank you to Julian Ozanne for wisdom, generosity and profound friendship. Heartfelt thanks and love to Michael and Claude Davies. Great thanks to the beloved Byngs, E & J, who have helped me like the dearest friends and promoted me like one of their own most fortunate authors. Thank you so much Kirsty Dunseath and all at W&N for your faith and labour. Special thanks to Natasha Fairweather my brave and intelligent agent. Finally a message of love to my incomparable familiar, Moss. I don't know where you are, or if you are – only that you are for ever in my heart.

This novel supports the Chain of Hope, an international medical charity dedicated to alleviating the suffering of children with heart diseases in developing and war-torn countries. Its mission is to provide access to medical care for such children whilst developing cardiac units in the developing world. For more information please visit www.chainofhope.org.

Dawn does not come twice to waken a man.

Bedouin proverb

For
Crispin
Lorne
Kate
Jane
and
Walter

$\mathbf{1}$

*Skinhead Saïd! To the village of Mena a feckless
dreamer, to Farouk a dear and old friend.
Skinhead Saïd! Born with the affliction that he was
destined for greatness and, if not greatness, glory.*

EXCERPT FROM VILLAGE SONG
ATTRIBUTED TO THE YOUNG URCHIN HASAN

Fin still sleeps. There can be a moment, if Fin has just the right number of drinks, when everything is OK. Sleep is like this for Fin, but soon sleep will end.

Fin is hurt. On his leg is a bruise which began like an angry red birthmark but has bloomed into a multicoloured stain while he slept.

'Again, you have been involved in drunkenness,' his boss had said on the telephone, waking him late into the morning of yesterday. 'A fight no less, with an American. Not just any American, but one connected to the embassy of the United States. It is—'

'Look,' he had replied pathetically, 'it wasn't exactly a fight.'

'For Christ's sake, don't interrupt me,' she snapped. She

was a Christian, a Copt. After a few years in Cairo Fin had learnt that people's religion was most quickly revealed in their blasphemy. 'It is news to no one that how you look and how you behave has, in the past six months, become more and more' – she coughed – 'louche.' Fin wondered how long she had been waiting to try out this word. 'The truth is, I have only put up with your indifferent attitude because ... well, you're cheap. Now, I've had calls from people, important people, and to be a frank person, I'm embarrassed and you are' – the light cough again – 'dismissed.'

Fin was hungover. He had felt too ill to reply so he put the phone down, but not so ill that he didn't care, so he visited enough bars, drank enough cocktails and had enough vapid conversations to overcome the urge for self-pity and collapse into the lenient arms of unconsciousness, where now he tosses and turns.

Fin still sleeps. There are only moments before dawn, when the name of God will be called out from the three thousand, two hundred and eighty-four minarets of Cairo, some built more than a thousand years ago and some yet to be completed, but all resting on the ruins and cracks, on the fragments and wreckage, on the debris of other worlds, other religions, other dreams.

There are only moments before dawn but it has been three years since Fin came to Egypt to occupy the post of senior reporter on the *Cairo Herald*, the second-largest English-language newspaper in Egypt.

The position was a disappointment. He'd hoped there would be meetings in the shadowy corners of souks. He'd hoped there would be smoking of hand-rolled oval cigarettes and the wearing of crumpled linen suits. He'd hoped there would be the tapping out of stories-that-mattered on shiny black typewriters late into the night. He was always typing in these fantasies. Typing, wearing linen suits and smoking. Not that he owned a typewriter, or even smoked cigarettes.

Across the city the men who still call out the *Salaat el-fajr*, the prayer that follows dawn, move about in three thousand two hundred and eighty-four ways. Some search in metal ottomans for a preferred galabeya; some sip tea from tiny glasses too hot to hold; some flush or tip water into just-used latrines; some massage life into old cracking limbs; some prepare baths having made love to a new wife or a wife of many years; some trace verses of the Holy Koran in the early light; some throw grain to cooing pigeons; some peel an apple, some search through sand-storms of static for the radio news.

Most of the men who will wake the great city are no longer moving about. Their voices have no body, and if there is such a thing as a soul, they have no soul. They have been caught in a machine, months or years before, and they will repeat the prayer in flawless verisimilitude until the machine jams or the tape snaps.

Fin still sleeps. Liberated for a few more moments from the tyrannical awareness that life has not yet become the glorious movie of his imagination. Liberated from the reality that his working hours have been spent keeping the expat community abreast of the latest old boys' cricket match or quietly trawling the Internet for stories to dress up as news. Liberated from the knowledge that, although he had been senior reporter for the *Cairo Herald*, there were no junior reporters. Indeed, until the boss's nephew arrived with a journalism degree from an expensive private

3

university in Pennsylvania, there were no other reporters at all.

Fin did own a linen suit. It lies half on the bed, as crumpled as the best of them, sloughed off like an old skin. The suit had gone some way towards rescuing Fin from drab reality, but it had not saved him. And perhaps it was part of the problem. But what, he would ask himself nightly, squinting at the world through the opaque disc of an emptying glass, was the problem? He was healthy enough, young enough – older than he looked, older than he behaved – but young enough. He had a job. He'd had a job. And then of course, a fight.

If Fin were not in the last stages of damp and troubled sleep, he might plead for a different word. 'Fight' was unfair or at least imprecise. 'Scuffle' might be a more appropriate term but still not, as he would say, *le mot juste*. 'Attack' would be Fin's word. Fin had been attacked by an American. A cold and muscular man with a thin-lipped high-protein smile, who had claimed upon introduction to be a consultant attached to some dubious office at the US embassy but had said nothing as he struck Fin's leg with a telescoping metal cosh.

Fin still sleeps. Soon he will be torn from his sleep by a visitor, but now he is sleeping. Sleeping and mumbling – perhaps to Munkar or Nakir, two angels of Islam who sit by the dead and tally up their sins. Perhaps Fin is feeling the aftershocks of the recent violence. Perhaps he is moaning as the dull pain in his leg advances and recedes like the tide of the Red Sea at Sharm el-Sheikh.

Soon Fin will wake, but now he sleeps.

When Fin arrived in Cairo it filled him, allowing no room for dark mists and abstract thoughts. It was as if the dust that covered everything, and that seemed on first glance to have sucked the colour out of the city, provided no surface on which his desolate moods could find purchase. After a few months fate provided an Egyptian friend, Farouk, who showed him that underneath this dun blanket was an exotic palette of possibilities. Cairo was on the surface a city of filth, chaos and ruins. But to those who were able to sink into it, Cairo was al-Kahira – the Triumphant, teeming with people, ebullient, enveloped in the past, kinetic, yielding, collapsing and constantly rebuilding itself out of the debris. With its alleyways and courtyards, its ruins built on ruins, Cairo was a city of nooks and passages, a place which seemed to promise that possibility, perhaps even deliverance, would be waiting round the next corner.

Dawn has almost come, and those who will call Cairo to prayer are purifying themselves in the name of God. Hands and wrists are being washed; water gargled and sniffed; faces, ears, heads and necks splashed and wiped with wet hands; feet and ankles washed from right to left, from right to left, and again from right to left. Three thousand, two hundred and eighty-four people, one action.

Hours before, Fin had zigzagged through his front door, injured and jobless, desperate for relief. He had limped the ambit of his apartment, searching in each room, forgetting what he was looking for before stumbling into the next room in the hope it might be there. Another hour of pacing while suckling at the remnants of a bottle and Fin no longer needed to think about what to do. He had called Farouk.

As the telephone had connected he hoped that Farouk

had forgotten, or not even noticed, the way Fin had broken off contact. He had felt oppressed by Farouk, by his single-mindedness, his certainty, his criticism, his impatience, his demands for money, his unwavering opinions. In the end, he was no longer sure if Farouk was the most mendacious person he had ever met, or the most honest. All Fin knew was that he had wanted to be free of him.

Farouk was a fundamentalist, that is what Fin had concluded, although not in the political or even religious sense. No, Farouk, was a fundamentalist by nature. He was a man with no tolerance for other opinions; a man who would ruthlessly suppress any dissent; a man assured of the absolute truth of all his views, however much they might contradict themselves or change with his moods. In short, Farouk was a one-man totalitarian state.

And yet, here he was calling him, he did not know why. Perhaps because his options were so few.

'Farouk, hello, can you hear me? Is that Farouk? It's your friend – Fin.'

'Yes.'

'It's FIN. You know.' Fin could hear a horse whinnying in the background. Despite drunken vows and pledges of friendship he hadn't called Farouk for a couple of months, perhaps more. Farouk said nothing.

'It's Fin, Fin the infidel. Don't you—'

'I know who you are, *habibi*. What is it that you want?'

'What do you mean WANT? I just wanted to say hello . . . Are you busy at the moment? Sorry I haven't called . . . What's going on with you – are you around?'

'You do not need to call. I am always in Mena village. My house is your home. I will send Waled. Tomorrow.'

'No, no, don't worry – no need for Waled . . . I'll grab a

cab in the morning and be with you . . . by lunch?'

'I am not worried. Waled will come. He owns his taxi now.' *Click*.

Fuck, Fin had thought. He didn't need Waled in his life. Not for transport, not in Fin's condition. He was fond of Waled. Very fond. Waled pulsed with benevolence. He was hashish's greatest achievement. But as a taxi driver he was unacceptable. Waled had no grasp of time in increments shorter than twelve hours, and this could mean a lot of waiting. Fin was not good at waiting. He hated waiting. Forced to fill intervals of time without preparation, Fin felt condemned.

It was always this way, he thought. Farouk seemed to make him do things he did not like, uncovering the fault lines of Fin's aversions and then ploughing him deeply into them. It had been a relief to stop seeing Farouk, but now he was returning. However, Fin knew there was little purpose musing, because Farouk brooked no argument. The matter was settled. '*Ellei faat maat*,' as his Egyptian friends would say – 'What is past is dead.'

The sky is bruising. Dawn has past. The imams are climbing the towers step by spiral step, climbing to God, to Allah. A man's finger hovers over the doorbell. Fin is at the end of sleep.

SALAAT EL-FAJR

2

The doorbell punctured Fin's dreams, becoming the screams of Shia flagellants beating livid flesh with sacks of broken glass. Fin pitched into consciousness, snapping his eyes open but still wedged in the punishment of his dream by the relentless shrieks of the bell. He could not move his legs. They were caught, trussed up. It was the American, he thought, careering into panic. The American had tied him up and was now ringing his doorbell, banging and ringing with violence on his mind. Fin flailed for the light switch and caught an already cracked tumbler half-full of water, which spilled onto a pile of books but seemed, with surreal rationale, to arrest the screeching bell. He stretched forward and slid his fingers down the cool cast-iron stem of the lamp.

Light changed everything, brought reason and with it the first prayer calls of the day. Fin looked down at his legs; his bonds were no more than bed sheets, twisted around like a sloppy mummification. He might have laughed had his head not threatened to shatter.

The bell returned, pulsing aggressively on-off, on-off, on-off, on ... Fin bound a sheet around his waist and limped towards the front door, creased cotton trailing behind him like a Japanese ball gown. On the way he passed a claw hammer and a framed map of the Middle East abandoned with a scattering of picture tacks on the concrete floor of his narrow hall. Fin crouched down and seized the hammer. If it really was the American, he must be ready. He pulled open the door, jaw clenched, weapon cinched.

Every other morning when Fin opened the door of his apartment on the short alleyway that was El-Mahahdi Street the same sight lay before him. The ground would be dry and dusty but solid, not quite paved and not quite dirt. A small shop would display household items and sweets, pink, red and bright green boxes, orange plastic brooms and sunny yellow dustpans. Colours that, for Fin, had been locked away in the nursery until he came to Cairo. Opposite would be Abnedi's barber shop, dirty white with alternating red-and-blue Arabic script on either side of the doorway. Fin kept meaning to ask Abnedi whether the symbols described hairstyles on offer or quoted the Holy Koran. Outside the shop Fatty Abnedi himself would sit, day and night, in tight grey trousers and a drab dark-green sweater. At the end of the alleyway was a mobile phone shop guarded by a four-foot inflatable phone with cartoon feet. The blow-up telephone was patched with black insulating tape after a boy, with the bread for El-Mahahdi Street balanced on his head, had crashed into it on his bicycle.

This is what Fin should have seen from his first-floor vantage point when he flung open the door. But not today. Today there was nothing but flat white blankness. Fin blinked, trying to pour sense into this absence. The blankness moved and a border appeared around it, a periphery, which became a frame, quickly thickening with the world he had expected to see. In an instant, Fin realised the optical shock was no more than a white card held in front of the face of a man wearing a long parchment-coloured galabeya. Fin could see that written on the card, in the shaky pencilled lines of one unaccustomed to the Roman script, were the three letters of his name:

FIN.

The man did not move, but his galabeya billowed gently in the morning breeze, wafting jasmine essence towards Fin like curious antennae. Fin felt the cool of the early morning ripple across his chest, break gently against his armpits and melt into the staleness of his apartment. He heard every sound in the neighbourhood – a car door closing, a child crying for milk, pigeons cooing on his roof, late prayers. Fin loosened his grip on the hammer, feeling the rubber on the handle give in to his hand.

'What do you want?'

The man did not answer but with the theatrical slowness of a belly dancer allowed the card to descend. A bushy knoll of silvery white hair appeared, a broad forehead as brown and shiny as gravy, bright eyes that had not slept for days and, at the end of a long and regal nose, a wide and beatific smile. Waled.

'Waled?' exclaimed Fin.

Waled threw open his arms, grasped Fin by the shoulders and kissed him three times on his scowling face before pulling him into an extravagant embrace. Fin pulled away angrily as his back was raked with the sharp corner of the card. Waled, uninvited and indifferent to everything but his own delight, oblivious to the chaos of bottles, half-eaten *shwarma* and notebooks, oblivious to Fin's mounting fury, stepped into the apartment, crossed the hall and sat down in Fin's study, beaming contentedly.

'Waled, it's five thirty in the fucking morning. What are you doing here?'

Waled gazed up at Fin and held the card out in front of him. He rocked it from side to side like a steering wheel, and with an expression not too far from rapture, proclaimed, 'Waled-cab!'

Fin glared at Waled. He wanted more explanation, if only to fuel his fury, but Waled had exhausted his English and explained the situation with an economy that was his natural mode of expression. Fin hobbled out of the room and into the hall, memories of the previous night's telephone call surfacing like stunned fish. There was no point attempting sleep again, he thought.

'Fucking Waled,' Fin muttered, limping through the hall, avoiding the picture tacks and framed map on the stone floor. He had bought it in the Khan el-Khalili bazaar after noticing that the map described the territory the British had promised to the Arabs after the First World War. He had been intrigued by it, captivated by its historical narrative. For a while he talked of little else. Now it lay face down, untouched for ten days since Fin had knocked a fist-sized clump of crumbling plaster out of the wall with his first clumsy nail. Fin entered the kitchen. 'Fucking Waled,' he repeated, yanking open the refrigerator door with unnecessary force. It was an old appliance possessed by a thousand rattling demons, but through some dark miracle it continued to work. Even the internal light still functioned. Thick wisps of cloudy condensation tumbled out as Fin opened its heavy door, and the golden glow of the interior shone into the pale blue of the morning. Fin smiled for there, as he had hoped, in the middle of the middle shelf was an ice-cold bottle of Sakkara, Egypt's finest lager.

Fin examined the generous bottle, the representation of the ancient pyramid on its label, the proud lettering, the ever mysterious Arabic script and the true, true words, 'Egypt's Quality Beer'. Egyptian Stella, Meister, Heineken – they all had their qualities – but for Fin the greatest of them all was Sakkara. And there it stood, glistening and inviting, floating on billows of condensation. It was a treasure, and Fin wanted it. His dehydrated and battered body yearned for it more than anything short of salvation. But Fin was courteous and had been among the Arabs long enough to absorb some of their ways. He knew what he must do. He grasped the bottle by its cool neck, pressed it to his aching forehead, closed the refrigerator with his knee and launched himself back into the study, where Waled sat at the desk, pleased as a man in love.

Fin proffered the icy bottle to Waled, but he smiled and looked away, shaking a hand in polite refusal. Fin knew this move. It was part of the daily dance of giving and receiving in Egypt, but he was in no mood for it. Fin wafted the bottle in front of Waled and reminded him that it was Sakkara and it was cold and it was specifically and uniquely for his dear friend Waled. Waled looked away, waving both hands forcefully.

'*La', la', shokran.*' No, thank you.

Fin put the bottle on the desk in front of Waled and

popped off the cap with a plastic lighter. Waled turned away dramatically and Fin's patience ran out.

'Oh for fuck's sake, Waled. Just take it.' Fin thrust the bottle into Waled's lap.

'La', ana Muslim!'

Waled stood and pushed the bottle away. Fin flushed. It was haram, forbidden. Alcohol was haram for every Muslim. Of course Fin was aware of this; with the exception of three Coptic friends and his now ex-boss, all the Egyptians Fin knew were Muslims. However, in Fin's experience abstinence from alcohol seemed to lag behind other duties, such as giving alms and making a trip to Mecca. Most of the people he knew drank occasionally.

Fin shrugged and studied the bottle. He noticed how it was glistening provocatively with those tiny drops of condensation he found so attractive. He looked at Waled and saw that he wore the sad, resigned expression of a disappointed parent. Fin apologised, begging forgiveness, touching his heart with the palm of his hand as he had learnt and including the appendage *wallahi*, the precise meaning of which he was unsure, though he had an idea that it multiplied or concentrated anything that was said. Waled's smile returned. He kissed the back of his hand, turned it and kissed the front, before throwing the kiss into the air and the problem out of their lives.

Content once more, Waled resumed his place, rummaging through the pockets of his galabeya and stacking the contents neatly on the desk. Car keys, a packet of Ambassador cigarettes, an old cracked biro, a battered box of matches, a toothpick, a handful of toasted pumpkin seeds, an elastic-bound wallet crowded with low-value banknotes. Waled surveyed these objects with an evident lack of satisfaction, then dug into both pockets with a concentration that soon became unease. He emptied his pockets, turning them inside out so that they hung down like lop ears and, frowning, began frisking himself with light pats. As he reached his left ankle a broad smile erupted across his face and, with the pride of an English gardener displaying his prize-winning marrow, he produced from his sock a large egg of sandy-coloured hashish.

Fin picked up the Sakkara and took three deep gulps, feeling the crisp bitterness flood his system with a delicious sense of comfort. Waled licked at the lump of hashish with the flame of his lighter, crumbling a thick ridge of the warmed resin onto a newspaper article that lay on the desk. It was a piece Fin had written a few months before and the only work he had ever bothered to save – a few hundred words on the curious cluster of world-class kebab shops on the King Faisal Road. His boss, who rarely read the news in her journal, had for once bothered to comment to Fin, informing him that the writing was 'inappropriately passionate' for its subject matter.

Waled broke a cigarette into the rubble of hashish and, solicitous as always, looked up at Fin for confirmation that the newspaper was acceptable wrapping for a joint. Fin regarded the scrap of paper. To him, its roughly torn edge suggested a butterfly's wing, and he thought with detached amusement of the reverse metamorphosis that Waled was about to enact – a precious butterfly twisted into a potent little caterpillar of hashish. Fin sighed. His article about kebab shops on the King Faisal Road was nothing special. It was merely a document of his frustration. He nodded to Waled and shuffled unevenly to the bathroom for a shower. At least his article would make someone smile.

3

Wet but not cleaned by the unsatisfying dribble of his shower, Fin looked around for his dressing gown. He could not see it and would never see it again. It was six miles across town, hanging on the back of his maid's door – stolen and presented to her husband as a birthday gift three weeks before.

As with so many things, Fin did not understand the absence of his dressing gown. He snapped out the twisted knot of a bed sheet, feeling a flash of calm as it filled like a sail in a warm breeze and floated down with something like serenity. The sheet was stained with zebra patterns of sweat in the pleated creases of off-white cotton. There was a sort of unexpected beauty there, somehow created by him, unrepeatable. Fin rested the sheet on his shoulders like a cape and sat on the bed.

He glimpsed himself in the mirror, his thick curly hair untouched by brush or comb for many years, impossible now to neaten, his shoulders and chest slim, almost boyish, but his belly . . . He looked away. There was a small but definite pot. A girlfriend had told him that it was endearing, that it emphasised the finesse of his hips. He did not know what she had meant, but he had stopped pulling it in for a while. He shook off the sheet and stood up, naked, grunting as the blue-black bruise on his thigh woke like a dull firework.

Fin pulled on his crumpled suit and cleanest dirty shirt, and entered his airless study. It was layered with pale blue veils of smoke and Waled was back on full beam. Fin unearthed his wallet from under a volume of medieval Arab cookery and crammed his notebook into his jacket pocket. He considered heating up the crusted bowl of *foul medames* he had seen lurking behind the beer. It was the perfect dish for beginning a day and Fin was superstitious about embarking on a journey without eating. In fact he felt it was inadvisable to begin anything without a meal. He looked at Waled's eyes, blood-red with hashish, and decided that it would be wise to maintain momentum.

'*Yallah*, Waled,' he said, checking that no part of his desk was on fire. Waled rose as if levitated by angelic forces. Exhaling the last three inches of the joint, he floated through the hall, radiating benign intensity, oblivious to the ground beneath him, over the map and tacks and out of the front door. Fin limped after him, astonished by Waled's fragrant slipstream of jasmine and hashish.

Fin followed Waled down El-Mahahdi Street, and all was as it should be. Abnedi was walking slowly towards them rubbing his eyes with the finger and thumb of his right hand.

'*Sabah el-'asal*,' said Fin, never tiring of Cairo's poetic greetings, where a morning was not merely wished to be good, it was wished to be full of honey.

'*Sabah el-noor*,' answered Abnedi, looking far from the morning of light he wished in return.

'How are you?' Fin asked passing.

'*El-hamdelillah*,' replied Abnedi, throwing up the metal shutters.

Waled's car was parked at the end of El-Mahahdi and, as Fin caught up, Waled was already under the bonnet, pushing and poking at the engine to negotiate the delicate matter of starting the engine. Half an hour later they were on their way, rattling and weaving through Cairo's static traffic in comfortable silence. When driving, Waled eschewed all sensate skills in favour of intuition, and he returned the beeps and astounded curses of other drivers with a smile of unfailing benevolence. Fin fell into a teetering slumber, his head knocking against the still cool glass of the car window until the cessation of the rattling engine woke him, announcing their arrival in Mena village.

Waled left Fin outside Khayam's tea house, assuring him with delighted gesticulations that Farouk would meet him in the amount of time represented by the chink of space between his thumb and forefinger. Fin had haggled over the fare before settling on a price marginally higher than the local tariff. He paid double anyway, because he was grateful to Waled for allowing him the dignity of the local price, and because, even though the greater part of the population strived and sweated to meet their basic requirements, things were cheap for a Westerner.

Waled drove off, kissing the air, leaving Fin standing in a village he had come to know well.

Khayam's was the only tea house in Mena village and the villagers had been taking tea there for hundreds of years. It faced an uneven semi-paved road with a large pile of gravel and the back of the barber shop, behind which, at this particular moment, a camel was tethered. The tourist cafés up the road served Coca-Cola and lethal Western food, and looked on to one of the most famous sights of the world, but Khayam's tea house was the social nucleus for all Mena village. Half the village, Fin reminded himself, gazing at the clientele. Fin did not know where the women went.

Fin's bruised leg still pained him, and he limped past a table where men were playing dominoes and took a seat against the tea house wall. He called to the waiter and surveyed two men talking over tea, the older in a grey businesslike worsted-wool galabeya, the younger man in jeans and a bright sweater. Both wore red headscarves wrapped loosely around their necks. A man with a suavely trimmed moustache and a baseball cap wrapped in white muslin stood beside them. Fin supposed they were talking about him.

His tea arrived – a chipped teacup and a dusty tea bag floating in a bath of warm water. Fin shook his head and gave it back to the waiter. He wanted *shay* – mint tea, not tourist tea. The waiter took it away without comment. Fin looked around him. Behind the camel, the walls were the colour of apricot baby food and the shutters were the green of the Irish Sea in summer. An old man was seated on a fallen stone, his arms thrown behind him, supporting him like a deckchair, surveying the road in quiet absorption.

The first time Fin had visited the village, he arrived without knowing he had done so. His destination, like that of most people, was the Giza Sphinx and pyramid complex. It had not occurred to him that the chaotic rows of houses and stables that huddled round one side of the Pyramids were known to their inhabitants as Mena village. And yet, if he were to get in a Cairo taxi and ask for Mena village, the driver would not know where to take him. If he were to look for Mena on a map, he would not find it. A few older Cairenes knew the area as Nazlit el-Semman, the Place of the Quails, but Fin had never seen or even eaten a quail here, despite the fact that, as well as goats and rabbits, the flat roofs of all the houses in the village were alive with every other domestic fowl including chickens, geese, ducks and pigeons. No, only the inhabitants of Mena village knew it by its name – they and their friends.

The waiter walked past with five glasses of mint tea, none of them for Fin. When he passed again, Fin reminded him about the tea and requested that someone be sent down the road for tahina and toasted pitta.

Fin wondered when Farouk would arrive. He was almost looking forward to seeing him. One could not deny that Farouk was extraordinarily generous, quick-witted and clear-seeing. And furthermore, like all the men of Mena village, he was a horseman of sublime talent.

Had the village of Mena been famous, it would have been famous for its horses. On certain auspicious nights the horses, festooned with silver jewellery and prancing like quadruped ballerinas, were led into the desert to the accompaniment of passionate and longing music. The horses danced while the men gambled on the beauty and boldness of their performance. They were valued beyond all possessions – at least that is what Farouk had said.

Fin gazed at the point of the Great Pyramid, rising like a fiction behind a dusty row of buildings. Like everyone who is not an Arab, when Fin had first thought of Cairo he had thought of the Pyramids. But within weeks of living there he could see that Cairo was no more 'about' the Pyramids than Paris was about the Eiffel Tower or Washington DC, the White House. Cairo was defined by the people who lived there: the Arabs, Copts, Berbers, Mongols, Turks, Ethiopians, Albanians, Slavs, Greeks, French and British.

Even in landscape Cairo was not dominated by pyramids but by the curved domes and minarets of the city's mosques, which rose in spirals, tapers, smooth curves and perfect octagons and were sandwiched between garish advertising hoardings and high-rises of cracking concrete.

Fin had been in Cairo for a month when he'd had his first sight of the Great Pyramid. Exhausted by the concentrated experience of the city, worn down by the dirt and noise and what he mistook for aggressiveness in the people, he'd hardly noticed when his taxi had crossed the Giza Bridge. The Pyramid had shimmered through a urea-yellow haze of car fumes like an arrow pointing to God. A shiver like a xylophone riff rushed down his spine. Never had he seen such scale and clarity. The silhouette – two converging lines – expressed the totality of the edifice and, in a reverse of logic, its mystery intensified as Fin drew nearer.

The driver had interrupted Fin's reverie, demanding a fare that would have taken them to Sudan. The rest of his wonderment abseiled in the glare of an American-style fast-food emporium offering 'Pyramid Fried Chicken'.

Outside, a crowd of mostly Egyptian tourists queued for a twenty-first-century experience that promised climate-controlled as-seen-on-TV fare and, if certain combinations of protein, fat and sugar were ordered, a bright plastic toy.

The queue for the pyramid complex had been shorter and faster-moving. Fin had paid the entry fee and made his way towards the Pyramids along a blistering tarmac road. He had spent the next few hours dodging the fevered attentions of touts, guides and sellers of fake antiquities. He had squeezed himself into claustrophobic tombs that smelt of urine and tramped around the smaller Pyramids, increasingly dehydrated but unwilling to buy water because of the stress of negotiation. He had left the complex dazed and dry, and wandered through the lefts and rights of the village until the clamour of people offering him perfumes, tours and treasures had faded and there before him was a café, the same café where now he sat waiting for Farouk .

That afternoon, two years ago or more, he had drunk one cup after another of strong sweet tea while he came to terms with the profound disappointment of the last remaining wonder of the world. The Pyramids, he had realised, as the third warm wet bush of mint had tumbled from his glass onto his sun-cracked lips, were better viewed from afar.

Fin recalled paying for his tea and drifting through the village in search of a meal. It had been the relentless heat of late afternoon, so there were no food stalls and the dusty streets were almost empty. Fin had kept walking until he found himself at the edge of the village where the buildings ceased and the desert began. Here, camels were tethered and a rumpless horse wandered freely looking for a place to die. Further out, towards the first mound of sand, was a tent, deep green felt against the washed-out yellow of the ground. Fin had approached it, crunching across the arid stones, drawn to its colour and fairy-tale shape. As he neared he could hear men and women inside, their voices muffled by the thick cloth. Gold braid covered the edges of the material and a gust of dry wind revealed a flash of red lining. Fin had tried to peer through a narrow opening in the tent flaps, but all he could see were indefinite shapes and flashes of low light. An intoxicating aroma of cumin and roast meats flowed through the space, and Fin had closed his eyes, breathing in, tasting the atmosphere within.

A small, slightly built man with fierce dark eyes exploded out of the tent brandishing a mobile telephone in mid-squeal. Fin leapt back, trying to look as if he had just arrived. The man observed him for a moment before turning and answering his telephone. Fin edged back, but the man snapped away the phone and placed himself in front of Fin.

'*Salaam aleikum,*' the man said, tapping his forehead with the fingers of his right hand.

'*Wa'aleikum essalaam,*' Fin replied, coughing un-necessarily.

'What do you want?' the man asked in English with a directness Fin found hostile.

'Nothing,' Fin replied, smiling weakly. 'I don't want anything. I'm just killing time.'

The man shook his head. 'Only the dead wish for nothing. And I tell you, my friend, you cannot kill time. It is time that kills you.'

The man turned, lifting the tent flap to enter.

'What's going on . . .' Fin stopped himself.

The man, whose directness and air of certainty were uncompromised by his physical fragility, allowed the heavy material to fall back.

'It is the wedding of my niece. The daughter of my sister. Come, I invite you.'

Fin backed away, embarrassed to have forced an invitation.

'No, no,' he spluttered. 'I have to get back to Cairo.'

'You have time in Cairo you must kill?' the slight figure had asked with a smile.

Fin shrugged and the Egyptian's face darkened into a scowl.

'You think my heart is black?' he demanded in a low voice. 'You wish to insult my family? My village?'

Fin shook his head and hands, spluttering apologies.

'Good,' said the man. His scowl transformed into a grin so quickly that Fin wondered if he'd ever been serious.

'I am Farouk al-Mabsoud bin Faisal.' He lifted open the flap of the tent. 'Follow me'.

Fin had followed.

When Fin emerged from the tent, he had eaten, talked, listened and danced until the last of the sun's warmth had faded from the desert sands. He had acquired a new family, been rebaptised in Arab hospitality and now knew for certain that he would remain in Egypt.

The arrival of the waiter with his tea – toffee brown, mint fresh, beyond sweet – brought Fin back to the present. Khayam's tea was at the very extreme of this beverage. Shrill sweetness balanced intense strength, and a fistful of mint banished scarcity. It was a drink that could change a mood, alter a day, sharpen a lance.

Fin scalded his mouth. Where, he wondered, was Farouk?

He looked up and down the street. A man walked towards the café, his head swathed in a headscarf, moving slowly in the mounting heat. He stopped at the camel, untied it and led it quietly away, denying an old cat its shade. The creature mewed in protest, stretched one leg, splaying its paw like a star, then padded across the road to find shade on the pavement by a fallen-down wall and its pile of rubble.

Fin allowed his gaze to fall to his feet where a narrow fissure divided the left foot from the right, flowing on to the café wall where it branched into a thousand tributaries. He examined the wall's nervous cracks, stretching from corner to corner, defining its future, defining, Fin thought, all our futures. The buildings of Mena were, he recalled, renowned within a rather local radius, for occasionally, but suddenly, collapsing. Strange, he thought, because the village's centrepiece, the Pyramid of Khufu or Cheops, known as the Great Pyramid, had remained standing for the best part of four thousand, six hundred years, and was built of the same stone. But whereas the houses of the village were built on sand underpinned by a network of ancient and unexplored tunnels, the Great Pyramid was thought to be built at the exact centre of the earth's land mass, on a subterranean mountain of solid granite.

Despite the inconvenience and danger, citizens of Mena village were proud when a part of their family home collapsed. They felt, Farouk had claimed, speaking with absolute confidence for all the inhabitants of his village, that it was proof of their direct connection to the greatest of the world's wonders, a testament to the auspicious historical value of their village.

The cat mewed again. Fin reminded the passing waiter about his breakfast. He watched as two women walked by, talking at each other, heads covered with banana-yellow scarves gathered tightly under their chins. A horse ambled unhurriedly up the road as if it were making house calls. A man passed the solitary beast heading towards the café. There was no mistaking him, it could be none other – Farouk al-Mabsoud bin Faisal, hunched up like an old thin crow, sucking white heat out of the end of a cigarette and walking in the middle of the now solar-grilled road.

Farouk saw Fin and began nodding his head as if confirming a long-held suspicion. Fin stood and, squeezing between tables, he hobbled towards his friend. They embraced, kissing three times in the traditional manner. Farouk looked intently into Fin's eyes.

'You look old, and why do you walk like this? Like a woman who is pregnant.'

'I had a fight . . .'

'A fight?'

'I was in a bar—'

Farouk cut him off with a wave of his cigarette. 'It does not matter. We go now. We must see the Old Sheikh, important business. You have met him?'

'No. Perhaps, yes . . . I mean, why don't you go on and I'll catch up with you. I've been waiting for breakfast.'

Farouk shook his head. 'We will eat later.' Taking a step away from the table, he threw a coin and a few hissing words towards the waiter. Fin didn't like missing breakfast, but he followed his friend. What else could he do? he asked himself, kicking up a cloud of dusty sand.

4

Farouk and Fin sat outside the Old Sheikh's house on an ancient wall heavy and crumbling like perfect fudge. This far on the outer edge of the village the roads were smothered in the deep sand of the desert, dampening the effort of travel and softening the clatter of shoes and wheels. Despite the urgency of their departure the Sheikh was still sleeping, and although Farouk would have been welcome to wait in the shade of the house or courtyard, he insisted to Fin that it was more respectful to wait outside, in the full glare of the morning sun.

Fin sat sweating, his throat as dry as the mortar between the uneven blocks of wall, the skin on his wrists and hands visibly darkening. He was grateful, he explained to an uninterested Farouk, to the shipwrecked sailors of the Spanish Armada who, finding themselves stranded on Irish turf in 1588 and discovering pliant Catholic maids, did the decent thing and bred some colour into an otherwise pasty race.

Farouk sat inattentive, motionless as a sarcophagus. The heat became brutal but he did not remove his navy blue V-neck sweater, which incongruously bore the logo of a

Scottish golf club. He said nothing. For Farouk silence between adults was a simple thing.

'What about your new wife, Farouk?' Fin asked finally.

'Why do you speak of my wife?'

'I'm just asking.'

'And you, English, are you now married?'

Fin was not, of course. Not English, and not married – not even close. Inevitably, there had been sorts of love. He had met and dated women – expat doctors, foreign correspondents, friends of friends passing through the city, a few sophisticated Egyptian women, a Belgian aristocrat studying Middle Kingdom hieroglyphics – but although his scruffy allure and desperate hunger for comfort purloined some hearts, he remained absent in every way.

'Wouldn't you know if I was married?'

'How can I know? In many months I do not see you. I know what I see, what I hear, no more than this.'

There was silence again. The sun's glare bullied Fin's eyes and his stomach whined for comfort.

'I lost it . . . the job, I mean.'

'Lost?' Farouk asked.

'I was fired. It's over, *khalas* journalist.'

The job had looked impressive enough on the business cards he had sent back to his friends in Dublin and, he would blush to admit, still flashed around self-importantly. At first, swathed in his linen suit, Fin had invested time and energy into researching stories that seemed important. He was a dreamer, that was true, but he wasn't completely detached from collective experience. Eventually he had come to understand that his passion and integrity were misplaced on a publication whose sole remit was to provide advertising notices to anglophone expats. From this point on work had become no more than a necessary inconvenience to the business of eating well and drinking late while Fin cast about for something else or somebody onto whom he could project his dreams.

'I don't care about the job, but somehow . . .' Fin shook his head. For a moment he was overtaken by a familiar conviction that things should be different. He dropped his head to his hands.

'Jobs are important,' Farouk offered, 'but they come and go like the pains of an old man. Today no work, tomorrow millionaire and the next day dead. How can we know? We cannot know. Think of Saïd.'

Fin frowned.

'Saïd, Skinhead Saïd. Of course you remember, on the roof of my house I told you. We were smoking hashish . . . No, it was a Friday and we were walking to the camel market to buy liver . . . I cannot remember, what is sure is that I have told you of him before, many times before.'

Fin shrugged. He had a vague memory that camels were slaughtered on a Friday.

'Only Allah sees the future. Sometimes, it is true, Mumbling Iqbal has a vision, but only the Almighty knows the truth, no one else. Not Saïd, that is sure. He was in his house, the house of his father and his grandfather. He was hungry because it was Ramadan – only the second week, it is a difficult time the second week. And he was sad because life was without love, without money and without respect. As he was thinking such things there was a great noise as the underground of his house fell into the earth.'

Fin looked up. 'I don't understand.'

'The underside of his house – *paff*. It fell into a hole, a space, an old space.'

'The house fell down?'

'No, the house was good, it was below the house, under.'

'The cellar?'

'Of course, as I say.'

'Where?'

'Here. Mena village. On the other side of the Great Pyramid. Mena lives above such things, tunnels open, tombs are revealed and treasure also. Ancient secrets, my friend. And at certain times – who knows when – these secrets reveal themselves. Sometimes there is gold, sometimes many things. A shepherd finds this, a foreigner finds that. Discoveries are made. And discoveries, English . . . discoveries change everything.'

A part of Fin, a part that he could not identify, reacted to these words. It was curiosity, but far beyond curiosity. As if he were a herd of grazing deer, and one of the herd, standing on the fringe, flicks up its ears at a noise it does not understand, and immediately every animal is alert and yearning.

'This Skinhead Saïd, did he find anything? Did he make a discovery?'

'Before the Great War,' Farouk replied, 'my grandmother found a sealed urn when the old bakery fell down. Two streets from this place.'

'What was in it?' Fin demanded

Farouk shrugged. 'Old papyrus. Exciting for scholars whose knowledge comes from papers, but worthless to men whose wisdom comes from their ancestors.'

'Farouk, that's amazing. But your friend Skinhead Saïd, what did he find?'

'Ten years before now, a new building in the tourist

complex fell into a tunnel and revealed the tomb of an ancient stone master who had been buried with more than two hundred types of coloured rock from across the known world.'

'And?' Fin demanded.

'A flask of wine and the bones of a dog.'

'How does this relate to Skinhead Saïd?'

'In no way,' Farouk replied solemnly. 'Discoveries are rare. When houses collapse and buildings fall, most times they are just dust and rocks, English. You have seen this yourself.'

Farouk fell silent, pinched out the cigarette he had been smoking and flicked it away, fixing his eyes upon the horizon.

Fin watched as the cigarette arced through the air, perfectly framing the pyramid for a moment, then landing in the sand with a delicate tap. A dung beetle abandoned its chores and went to investigate.

Silence.

The sun continued its ascent, lighting the needle-point tip of the pyramid, making it, and then everything, glow ... perhaps there was wisdom in this moment but Fin did not feel it. There might be a story here, but unless Farouk would tell it, he might as well head straight back to Khayam's and reclaim his breakfast. Perhaps he would order some fresh orange juice and see if they could find him those chargrilled chicken livers that came on little wooden skewers with a big bunch of parsley and half a lemon.

Fin felt anxiety rise like a guilty conscience. Things were too slow, already too slow. He was a sophisticated Westerner, he reminded himself. His life should be a pacy linear narrative with obvious and satisfying climaxes. Farouk was a village Egyptian, a Muslim raised in the shadow of the Great Pyramid. Fin examined the wall between his legs, poking and burrowing in the dry cracks with his thumbnail.

'Dust and rocks, that's great, Farouk. But what about Skinhead?'

'Who?' Farouk replied as if hearing his name for the first time.

'Skinhead Saïd . . . He isn't made up, is he?'

'Why do you say this? Skinhead Saïd is my friend, since we were children. Do you think I lie?'

'No, no, but it's a . . . well, it's a strange name.'

'Strange? What do you mean? It is an English name. It is not strange. Your Little John of the movies, the friend of the great English, Robin Hood, this is strange, because Little John is not little. But Skinhead is without hair – on his head not even one – skin and head then Saïd. It is not strange . . .'

'OK, I see. Skinhead. I'd like to know more about him – can we visit him?'

'You will visit my uncle. He is a good man. You are lucky. It is an honour for you.'

A cloud passed in front of the sun, shading the day, altering it entirely. Fin looked up. It was one cloud in deep blue sky, like a child's painting.

'At least tell me what he found.'

'What is there to tell?' Farouk sighed and shook his head.

'Come on, Farouk. "Discoveries change everything." Your friend's cellar collapses . . .'

'This is true,' Farouk took up the story, 'and perhaps he

was thanking merciful Allah for sparing him from injury, or cursing fate for cost of repairs to his house, I do not know, I was not there. But I will tell you this, *habibi*: I know the song he was whistling as he went to look under the house.'

'The song?'

'Yes, I swear on my mother, it was his favourite song, his only song. All the time he whistled it, again and again. It made his neighbours, his friends, everybody, crazy. He heard it when he was seven years old, from the tape recorder of an American hippie who had spent ten days eating hashish with his father.

'I tell you, my brother, none but Allah can know, but all is known. Only one month before Skinhead's cellar falls down, a tourist – dark-skinned like the people from Sudan but rich, I swear, like a Saudi or an American – this tourist he is visiting the Great Pyramid and he hears Skinhead Saïd whistling the song. He listens like a madman, like a Sufi, and then he runs to Skinhead. He asks him if he knows that the song he whistles is from a place called Jamaica and it is called "Carry Go Bring Come". Skinhead says yes to the man, but of course he does not know the name of the song nor even what Jamaica is. The dark-skinned man has tears in his eyes and tells Skinhead that he knows this music very well because his father, who was an orphan, had written this very song. The tourist weeps and Skinhead weeps. And Skinhead tells the tourist that he too is an orphan, and his father, who lives in the next village, he is an orphan also. The tourist is lost in happiness and clasps Skinhead's hairless head to his breast before giving him one hundred dollars.'

'How can Skinhead Saïd be an orphan when his father—'

Farouk interrupted him with a wave of his hand.

'You do not understand, *habibi*. The people of Mena village have lived with tourists for more than four thousand years. Understanding their desires, it is in our blood.'

Fin was hungry and hot, and if he was to sit in the sun waiting for Farouk's relations to wake up then he wanted to hear what this Skinhead Saïd had actually found. Of course, Fin realised, it was irrelevant to the story whether the man had been whistling an old Jamaican song, some other tune, or nothing at all. Farouk was not one to be led along linear narrative lines, or led at all. He would reveal details randomly, the way fragments of antiquity might appear over time, scattered over a vast area, tantalising generations of archaeologists. Fin was intrigued by the story, attracted to it in a way he did not understand, any more than a jackdaw understands the call of shining metal or a moth the fire.

'So, Farouk, was there anything under his house?'

'This is what I am telling you, in the stones and sand, Skinhead saw a space with blackness underneath. He crawled into this place without thought for safety and pushed his way through until it became a tunnel. At the end of the tunnel he discovered a great white slab of alabaster marked with hieroglyphs and the cartouche of a horned bird.'

'This is it. This is what I'm looking for. I want to meet him today – now. Can we visit?'

'Soon, my brother. He is sleeping. He is old, my uncle – strong also, like all my family.'

'No. Saïd! I want to meet Skinhead Saïd.'

Farouk looked down, shaking his head, perhaps even chuckling faintly. 'It is not possible.'

Irritated, Fin propelled himself off the wall and walked over to the shade of a palm, kneading his bruised thigh. Farouk had probably invented the story and now he did not want to admit it. Or he was hiding something, hiding the truth. Fin resolved to return to Khayam's, eat and go home, perhaps have a few drinks at the Continental, but this plan was disturbed by sounds of activity in the house.

'The Sheikh has risen. *Yallah*, let us go,' Farouk announced, heading briskly into the house.

5

Within the dusty taupe courtyard of the Sheikh's ancient house was an arched doorway with heavy narrow doors painted green by a previous generation. Faded yellow iron-work protected the panels in curving flourishes that might have been letters proclaiming the name of God. On either side the powdery lime walls were blotted with little hand-prints in ochre paint like old blood. These prints were the hands of children, protection against evil. Fin slipped off his shoes and stepped in.

The Old Sheikh stood in a corner of the cool dark room. In a white galabeya and finely crocheted skullcap, he was enormous. Fin had never before associated old age with tremendous height, but the Sheikh was a definitive lesson in both. More than a head taller than Fin but thin and wiry like the gaunt statues that paced through Fin's dreams, the Sheikh moved with such deliberation that each pro-gression of his giant limbs seemed significant. Farouk was deferential as he greeted the old man, smiling humbly as he refused the compliments that were being returned to him. Fin enjoyed the serious and elaborate introductions that characterise the Arab world. He found comfort in the courtesies of village greeting: exchanges of prayer and praise for parents, for one another, for future male children, *insha'allah* for wives, livestock, wishes, possessions and of course, 'My house is your house', *Ahlan wa sahlan*, a symbolic offer with literal intention.

'*Tishrab shay?*' the Old Sheikh asked.

Tea was being offered, but Fin did not want to linger. He was too hungry and too experienced to make the commitment to an 'official' cup of tea. He knew that even among the more cosmopolitan residents of Cairo accepting tea meant committing to a minimum of three cups and at least an hour's chat. But here in Mena village, where tradition seeped out of the venous cracks in the walls, well, it could be a matter of days. Fin declined the tea.

'Why do you not take tea with the Sheikh? He is a great and famous man,' Farouk hissed.

'I don't want tea,' Fin whispered. 'And, with respect, what's so great about him?'

'What do you know of respect? He has lived seventy years or more!'

'But what did he do?'

Farouk looked at Fin quizzically then called into the darkness of the next room. A chubby little boy, three or four years old, dressed like an American in jeans, a hooded sweatshirt and pristine running shoes, came barrelling towards Farouk and headbutted his thigh by way of a greeting. Farouk crouched down and affectionately pinched the boy's lips between his finger and thumb. The little boy struggled free and smiled, revealing a row of sugar-rotted teeth.

'Do you know nothing, English?' Farouk turned back to Fin. 'The old are special because they are old. Just as all children. Why? Because of their fat cheeks? Because of their smiles? No. It is enough that they are children.'

'*Tishrab shay?*' the Old Sheikh called again from the dark corner of the room.

If he were going to be a stranger anywhere, Fin had once concluded, there was no better place than the Arab world. Tea would be given; shelter, protection and the best food made available. This could take a long time in rural areas as it would begin with the slaughter of livestock. The only challenge was getting out before one was a great deal older. Fin was able to take a full and pure pleasure in this quality of hospitality because it was a quality inherent in him. But although Fin could not deny that he was intrigued by the Old Sheikh, even drawn to him, he wanted to get on with the day and find out more about Skinhead Saïd. He thanked the old Sheikh and again refused the tea.

Farouk grasped Fin's arm and whispered in his ear, 'Why do you say no? We will take tea with the Sheikh.'

Fin resigned himself to the situation. There was no point resisting. Farouk always knew exactly what he wanted to do and, if you were with him, you did that too.

'*Shay loh samaht*,' Fin replied, accepting the tea and settling himself on the cushioned bench that skirted the room.

Tea was served, and a vigorous conversation developed between Farouk and the Old Sheikh. Fin had not managed to advance his Arabic much beyond basic courtesy, swearing and food, so he had little idea of what they were saying to each other. He suspected they were talking about him as there was a great deal of pointing and head-shaking. He hoped that their criticisms were not too harsh.

Drinking tea with Arabs had been a small part of Fin's

childhood. Once, when he was six, on a trip to London his father had taken him to the rented house of a wealthy Saudi. Entering the house had been like stepping into the magical world of bedtime stories. The Georgian interior was like a tent, with luxurious fabrics draped from every wall, softening the hard surfaces. Men sat swathed in robes and servants crowded by, pouring strange-tasting tea from beautiful urns with curved spouts. Fin had sat as close as he could, full of pride and wonder that his father could venture into such enchanted, perhaps perilous, realms. Sipping the unfamiliar fluid given to him in a tiny cup, Fin had winced with revulsion but, worried that he might fail in some way, he closed his eyes and swallowed it with one brave gulp. To his horror, a servant had materialised from a sheeted wall and filled his cup and Fin had to again summon up his courage and finish the fluid back in two grimacing swallows. The servant must have been watching as he reappeared and again filled the cup to the brim, ignoring Fin's imploring eyes. Again and again it was filled, and the young Fin became frightened, somehow imagining that he was being poisoned or fattened up for food by these outlandish figures. After five cups his father had whispered to him that when he'd had enough tea, he should rock the cup from side to side. Fin did so and the servant whisked away the empty vessel.

Fin recalled the soft dry hand of his father, held too tightly as they walked down the street because he dared not request a bathroom in this strange and exotic house. His father told him that had he not rocked his teacup, his hosts would have filled it until their last breath, by which time their children would have grown up and they too would have kept on filling his cup until they had sold all their possessions or died of old age. This, he informed Fin, was 'hospitality', and only people of the desert could understand it properly. Fin had simply believed what his father had said, like he believed in Australia, God, school and flowers in summer.

Fin's musings were interrupted at cups three, five and six by Farouk, who refused to acknowledge that Fin did not speak Arabic, repeating phrases that he felt were particularly important.

'Did you hear that, English? The Sheikh's family has lived in this house for fourteen generations.'

More tea.

'What can you have learnt about life, living so far from Egypt?'

More tea.

'The Sheikh's first wife's cousin is a famous tailor in Glasgow. His name is Abdul Musawwir – you know him?'

More tea.

'The Sheikh has completed the hajj on many occasions and lived in Mecca for many months.'

At the seventh cup Farouk turned to Fin and said, 'For a small fee, the Sheikh will look inside your soul, where there is no future and no past.'

Fin looked at the Sheikh, at the teacup tiny in his great hand. It seemed like a good idea. He asked what Farouk meant by a 'small fee'.

'Oh, whatever you think, my brother. Whatever you feel. It is up to you. He is a great man, the Sheikh,' Farouk added. 'Very famous.'

Very famous and very big, Fin could see. He imagined he could pass a comfortable night in a tent made from the man's galabeya. There was a lot of the Sheikh, all of it old

44

and venerable. What if he was charging by weight? Fin sighed and hoped it would be a painless negotiation.

It took a few tense minutes to close the gap between what Fin 'thought' or 'felt' he should pay and the fee Farouk had already decided was appropriate. In the initial stages Farouk demanded a very large sum, which Fin refused, counter-offering the traditional tenth. Farouk said that such a sum would be an insult to the old man and refused to mention it to him. Indeed, he added unnecessarily, he would rather have his tongue pulled out, grilled on skewers and sold as food for wild desert pigs than mention such a derisory amount to his uncle, who, as he had already explained to Fin, was a great sheikh. Had Fin not heard that the old man had completed the *hajj* on three occasions? Fin confirmed that he had heard this, but wondered what difference it made. Farouk did not deem this flippant comment warranted an answer and lapsed into deep and stormy silence. Fin could bear no more than half a minute of this guilty hiatus and doubled his offer. It would be easier this way, he told himself. Farouk accepted the sum but eyed the larger bills in Fin's wallet with an expression which seemed to say, 'What finer destination could your wealth have than the pocket of an old and respected man who has passed months, almost a year, in the holy city of Mecca?'

The old man rose from the padded bench and called into the next room. His wife appeared with cushions and a brazier which she arranged on the floor. The Sheikh folded himself slowly onto one of the cushions, descending in purposeful stages like a wiry old camel. He tugged at the cushions and shifted his legs until he was comfortable, then beckoned Fin to sit opposite. When the two were face to face, he blew on the brazier and burnt beads of resinous frankincense that crackled and spat until they dissolved into smoke. He took Fin's head in his enormous hands and held him firmly. The Sheikh's thumbs pushed against Fin's eyes, holding them shut and filling his vision with a luminous nothingness that pulsed with each beat of his heart. It felt like an age since he had been touched, and as he surrendered the weight of his head to the old man's hands, Fin was engulfed by an exquisite sadness.

Fin did not cry. Tears would be a sort of incontinence, so he focused his attention to the immediate sense, the rich woody perfume lingering on the wrists of the old man. He breathed it in. It was a smell he had come to know well, a smell encountered in Khan el-Khalili bazaar in Cairo. He'd been ambling along the corridors of tightly packed stalls when something like an idea called to him in wonderful wordless thoughts. It was a scent. He'd searched and followed it through the perfume market asking this and that vendor until, after hours of chat and endless tea, he was shown a dark oily wood called *oud*. This was the source of the smell, he was told, and, if he understood the perfume seller's English correctly, it was produced only when a certain tree in Jordan was attacked by a parasitic fungus. Its price was five hundred dollars for one kilo.

Suspecting that he was being duped, Fin had left without the usual courtesies. A week later sometime before dawn in a bar that seemed to serve only gin, an Egyptian friend confirmed the truth of the perfume vendor's words. Rather than rushing off to work, Fin had sought out the merchant he had doubted and bought fifty grams of *oud* by way of an apology. He and the merchant passed the rest of the afternoon drinking tea, eating kif and agreeing that the history of all civilisation could be traced to the perfume bazaar of Khan el-Khalili.

Smoke from the brazier was curling into Fin's hair like the affectionate tails of monkeys. The Sheikh's fingers were palpating Fin's cheeks and scalp, as if communicating with his dreams in a language spoken only between hands and faces. The old man began to recite suras from the Koran, and, removing his hands, looked up to the ceiling, looked back to Fin and in broken English announced, 'You ... looking, looking ...'

Fin had hoped for more from the secrets of his soul, or at least something less obvious. Of course he was looking for something. Wasn't everyone? And anyway, he was a journalist. That's what journalists did. Farouk had probably mentioned it to the old man. So he was looking for something. It didn't seem like much to ask, it didn't have to be a burning bush of truth. ... A mere footprint in the desert would do, an impression of wise direction.

'Yes, Sheikh,' he responded. 'I am looking for something.'

The Sheikh nodded. He took Fin's hands and held them above the smoking brazier. His broad face filled Fin's vision. He was now as close as a lover and Fin could see himself in the brown-black of the old man's eyes, as if his soul had been drawn in for observation. He was held fast, mesmerised, and for a moment, he felt as if the stylus had been raised from the scratched record of his life and all around him was silence and space. He must never let this feeling go, he told himself. And then it was gone, and he found himself close enough to an old man's face that he could smell the mint leaves on his lips.

Fin tried to pull away, but the Sheikh gripped the back

of Fin's hands and slammed the palms down onto the vermilion coals of the brazier. Fin leapt across the room with a scream, balling his hands into his armpits. The Sheikh leant back on his cushion and smiled benevolently. When Fin opened his eyes he saw a date tree through the window, its fronds rippling nonchalantly in the hot wind as if nothing had happened. Fin looked into his balled fists. To his surprise, he felt no pain and there was nothing there, nothing except for the curved indents where his fingernails had dug into his palms.

Farouk, who had been looking on with calm disinterest, stood up.

'We go now,' he said with characteristic finality. 'The Sheikh is a busy man.'

6

Shuffling through the warm golden sand behind Farouk, Fin examined his palms in the sunlight and found nothing more than a mark on each the size and colour of a strawberry. Farouk showed no sign of wanting to talk about what had happened, or talk at all, as he hunched off ahead.

Fin caught up with him. What had the Sheikh been doing? Farouk shrugged. Didn't Farouk think there was something strange in the Sheikh's methods? Farouk shrugged again and walked off. Fin ran ahead of him and blocked his way.

'Come on, Farouk. This uncle of yours, is he really a holy man?'

Farouk looked at Fin incredulously.

'How dare you say this! Did you not see the Holy Koran at his right hand? Did you not hear him recite the sacred verses?'

'Just because he quotes the Koran doesn't make him a holy man or even a good Muslim,' Fin argued.

'It is the Holy Koran, the book of Allah! And the Sheikh is a holy man! Why do you talk of things you do not understand? Do I talk of your Bible?'

No, Fin thought, he didn't, except to say that its most worthwhile parts were to be found in the Koran. Fin found himself spoiling for a conflict. A conflict that he did not want, that would bring him nothing, so he stepped aside. As Farouk passed, Fin questioned him about their destination, but Farouk walked on, pretending not to hear as he turned off the path and up a narrow alleyway.

As Farouk's shadow disappeared, Fin experienced that peculiar sense of relief that being alone gave him. He often preferred the absence of people he cared for to the impermanence and unpredictability of their presence. His love affairs had always been at their most poignant when they broke up. And they always broke up, leaving him longing for his lover with a passion he had not been able to invest in her presence.

Fin kicked a stone towards a pile of something disgusting heaped in the dry gutter. It shuddered, startling Fin and disturbing a skein of glossy black flies that crowded an open sore. Seduced by the push and pull of disgust, Fin approached the mound, which was now faintly whimpering. Propinquity revealed it to be a dog. It opened an eye and pathetically pawed the air with its hind leg in a half-remembered scratch. Fin found himself saturated with a pity so intense that it cut through the stench of the decomposing animal. Forgetting Farouk and his quest, Fin turned and hurried back to a small shop. He purchased a bottle of water, a roll of flypaper and a pack of biscuits, and ran with them to where the dog lay. Fin shaded the animal with a side of cardboard and, crouching close, poured a few drops of water onto its cracked muzzle. A grey tongue appeared and weakly licked off the moisture. Fin continued until the animal seemed sated. With a few rocks and the plastic bag, he made a little pit for the water which he placed next to the dog along with a mound of broken biscuits.

A shout brought Fin up, wincing as he rose on his bad leg. Around the corner Farouk stood impatiently,

'Were you lost? Come, come, we must go.'

Fin did not answer, but as he put his hand in his pocket to touch his bruise, he found the soft cylinder of flypaper. He turned and ran back to the dog where he unwound the sticky brown strip and secured it to the cardboard of his lean-to. Fin's throat tightened as the dog tapped the sand with the tip of its furless tail.

'Merciful Allah, what are you doing?' Farouk cried as Fin turned the corner. 'Have I boiled your English brain in the sun?'

'Irish, Farouk. It's my Irish brain, and it was boiled long ago.'

But Farouk had not waited to hear his reply. He was marching off up the alleyway, leaving Fin to follow him to where the alleyway opened onto the tarmac road that led out of the village.

Fin caught up with Farouk as he stood alongside an immaculately clean but desert-battered Datsun, pointing out specks of dust to three urchins clutching rags. From the recess of a nearby doorway, a large man observed the scene, peering intently, his bulk bulging through his galabeya like a plastic bag stuffed with meat.

'Do you know that man?' asked Fin, gesturing to the doorway.

'They are boys, not men,' Farouk replied, tossing the children a pile of coins that sent them running off, whooping with delight.

Fin began to explain, but when he looked again, the doorway was empty.

'Whose car is this?' Fin asked.

'It is my car.'

Fin was surprised. 'You have a car?'

'You think Farouk is a car thief?' Farouk tugged open the door. 'Yesterday, I bought it.' He frowned through the window as the engine coughed to life.

Fin clambered into the passenger seat wondering why Farouk had not mentioned his new acquisition. The purchase of a car was an event in Mena village. High taxes and scarcity of money made cars difficult to acquire. Friends should have gathered at Farouk's house the previous evening to drink tea, congratulate him and speculate on the merits and cost of his purchase. The appearance of significant property was celebrated in the village like the birth of a child. Once they had danced for two days after Farouk's friend Tariq One Eye had bought a second-hand bicycle for his daughter.

'Farouk, it's great you have a car but why didn't you say anything about it?'

Farouk revved the engine till it screamed. 'Why, why, always why!' he shouted through the din. 'We do not speak for a year or more and now you must know of everything?'

'It wasn't a year, it was a month . . . or a few at the most.'

Perhaps he should have called Farouk earlier, Fin thought, returned his calls. But it had suited him to lose contact. Farouk had become exhausting company with his certainties and critique of everything Fin did. 'Why are you doing this? A man does not do this!' Fin needed no extra help when it came to self-criticism.

'Did people come to your house last night?'

'For the car? Some,' Farouk replied grudgingly. 'My wife's family, three sisters, my uncle of course, the cousins of my brother's wife and some others you do not know.'

'Not your friends?'

'Of course, they too,' he said. 'Salah, Mustapha, Tariq . . .'

'Tariq with one eye?' Fin recalled.

'Both Tariqs – Tariq One Eye and the other. You have not met him. Two Ahmeds also, Hassan, Barrak and others.'

'What happened? Did they like the car? Was it good?'

Farouk crunched the Datsun into gear and pulled away, glancing in the rear-view mirror.

'It was nothing. I did not enjoy,' he grunted.

'Why did you not enjoy it? Aren't you happy with the car?'

Farouk threw up his hands. 'Why, why, why! Are you a woman? Always why!'

Fin resolved to be more direct. 'You are angry with me, Farouk.'

Farouk swatted away this statement with the back of his hand. 'Why should I be angry with you? I am not angry with you.' He drove on looking ill at ease and gaunt.

They were obliged to wait at a corner while two men unloaded a truck piled high with wicker chicken coops. An old Mercedes pulled up close behind them, its windows blacked out. A woman selling vegetables rose up from the pavement and approached the car flaunting a bushel of mint. Seeing Farouk, she addressed him by name and pointed to the car, cooing in exaggerated admiration. Farouk answered her in the same grudging monosyllables he had used with Fin, pushing away the mint she had thrust through his window. She remonstrated with him in playful tones, caressing the car, but Farouk ignored her, beeped his horn and shouted at the truck to hurry. The woman turned away and went back to her shining piles of aubergines, onions and waxy French beans. Fin watched her settle comfortably onto the pavement and pick at the bushels of mint, the smell of which lingered in the car.

The truck pulled away and Farouk, with an anxious look in the mirror, followed then rashly pulled in front of the truck. On the side of the road a rheumy old man with a walking stick as thick as his arm waved a greeting at Farouk, but Farouk pretended not to see him.

'Where are we going?' Fin asked again.

'Some business. Cairo.'

Fin blew an angry stream of air through his lips. He'd had enough. He hadn't risen at dawn and braved Waled's purely intuitive driving only to put up with Farouk's sullen grunts for a day. He turned to Farouk. 'What's wrong with you? Why are you like this? Tell me what I've done. Was it your uncle? I'm sorry if I insulted him.'

At a crossroads the policeman waving traffic shouted a greeting to Farouk, kissing the air towards his car. Farouk managed a half smile and an unenthusiastic wave before driving on.

'It is not you,' he said, his eyes not even flickering towards Fin.

Fin looked out the window, looked at nothing, looked away. He did not believe Farouk. He would get out of the car as soon as they crossed the Giza Bridge. It had been a mistake to come here, he thought to himself. If anything had happened in Skinhead Saïd's cellar, it had happened years ago. The story was never going to be a newspaper article. Fin did not care about newspapers anyway. One moment they could topple governments, the next they wrapped the rubbish.

What had he wanted from Farouk? Would he still be here if it wasn't for the lure of this new story? It was difficult to work out now, sitting in the car with Farouk right there. It would be easier once he was back in town with the comforting ballast of a whisky and soda in his hand. He'd drop into the Odeon for a quick one on the way home and think about how to get his job back. That's what he would do.

Farouk turned off the road into a narrow street. Tired silver bunting from weddings long past hung motionless between deteriorating buildings. Plastic bags and greying paper littered the ground. Everything seemed to be either half built or half demolished: uneven piles of pressed mud-brown bricks, torn reed baskets filled with grey cement dust, rusting metal. Fin again sighed but kept his gaze away from Farouk.

They passed into a broader street thronged with a sea of schoolgirls in beige shirts, long black skirts and white headscarves. Gripping books and files, chatting in groups, walking arm in arm, hugging, laughing, they were pretending to ignore the archipelagos of boys smiling nervously beneath the proud beginnings of moustaches. There was no way for Farouk to progress and, after stabbing the horn a few times, he slowed the car to a grudging halt.

With the car stationary, looking resolutely out the window became awkward.

'Look, Farouk. I'm sorry if I didn't . . . Perhaps I should have got in contact earlier.'

'Do not apologise. There is no reason.' Farouk stared ahead. 'A man should do what he feels.'

Fin looked at the pale mustard-coloured wall of the school yard, its top crenulated with shards of broken glass. A cat gingerly picked its way along, going somewhere. Somewhere better, Fin hoped.

'If you won't talk to me, fine, I'll get out.' Fin attempted to open the passenger door, pinching impotently at the snapped-off lock release with sweating fingers.

Farouk turned off the engine.

'Everything that happens in this world is not because of you,' he said, pointing to a disappearing V of white spots in the strip of blue sky. 'Those geese flying towards Alexandria, they are not flying because of you. That ice cream you see lying in the street by the child who is crying, it did not fall because of you. It is nothing to do with you. And neither is my bad feeling.' He smoothed down a corner of torn vinyl on the dashboard and looked into the rear-view mirror, adjusting it imperceptibly.

Fin considered the possibility that what Farouk said was true. That he was not the source of Farouk's sullen mood. Whatever the truth, the process of self-examination transformed Fin's indignation into compassion.

'I'm sorry you're upset, Farouk,' Fin said quietly.

'I am not upset. A man is not upset!' Farouk shouted. 'And anyway, for what shall I tell you?' Farouk turned his palms upward. 'You ask questions and ask questions until you understand, and this you will not understand. So there will be only questions.'

'Of course, Farouk,' Fin agreed quietly. 'No more questions . . . but I'll just say this. Whatever is bothering you, it can't take away from the fact that you have a new car and it's a beauty. It's a great car, wonderful – anyone would love to own it.'

Farouk slapped the steering wheel with both hands. 'Exactly! You see?' he exclaimed. 'Why do you ask when you already know! They all want it. They want my car. Everyone is looking at my car and thinking evil. Where did Farouk get the money? Did he steal it from me? From his wife? How did he get this? This is what they are thinking. I can hear it, I can feel it, and it makes me ill. People desire my car, and from this desire has come evil. I have been feeling pain here and here since I bought the car.' Farouk pointed to his heart and belly. 'It is clear someone has put *el-ein* on my car.'

'*El-ein*?' Fin asked.

'*El-ein, el-hassoud*! The evil eye,' he answered, starting up the engine again, nosing the car through the shoals of schoolgirls and veering off into an empty street. A series of labyrinthine turns brought them to a narrow backstreet. Farouk braked in the middle of an alleyway, blocking it entirely, turned off the ignition and stomped away up the path.

Fin followed. They were now in a working-class residential area on the edge of Cairo. Mini tower blocks of dark grey untreated concrete were separated by an unpaved road no wider than a car. Each storey was unevenly stacked on top of the other, mortar swollen out between cracks, different shades of brick showing where concrete had crumbled off or never reached. Laundry spewed out of crooked glassless windows like lengths of sun-dried entrails.

Farouk stopped and scanned the highest floors of a block, searching for a particular window. He stooped, picked up a handful of stones and threw them, one by one, upwards towards the third floor. Most bounced back to the dusty road, and some found their mark, disappearing into a dark square where a window might have been.

A head appeared, answering the call of the stones and was soon discussing a price with Farouk.

'Fifty.' 'No.' 'Yes.' 'No.' Farouk feigned disgust. New price. 'Sixty.' Shock. 'You insult me.' Farouk walked in a small circle, anticlockwise. 'Sixty-three.' 'No.' Silence. Stillness. Agreement from the window.

The head withdrew into the blackness and Farouk stepped away from Fin, kicking non-existent sand from his shoes, reading a faded poster on the wall. Avoiding Fin's questions.

The head from the window arrived at street level, now a complete woman, clutching a live rabbit and a blue plastic washing-up bowl.

Ah, Fin thought, lunch.

The woman looked like an excellent person to make lunch, Fin thought. Luxuriantly ample, as big, soft and deliciously fat as a giant sweetmeat with heavy lines of kohl around her dark eyes. The rabbit, suspended by its brown ears, swung slowly, serenely with each of her heavy steps. She placed the blue bowl by Farouk's feet and began intoning a prayer. Farouk lit a cigarette and, except for the occasional congregational response, ignored her. She walked around the vehicle, muttering and singing and swinging the patient bunny over Farouk and his car.

This was not lunch, Fin realised.

The woman caught the rabbit's hindquarters under her arm and produced from the folds of her clothes a tiny kitchen knife with a broken blade and a fluorescent green handle. She stretched the little animal's head back and with as little ceremony as one might open a bag of rice slit its throat. People walked by paying only scant interest. A handcart piled high with old computer equipment could not pass them and waited patiently. The rabbit's back legs pumped in desperate shock and a jet of dark blood shot out over the vehicle. The woman swung the dying rabbit over the car spraying blood in slow looping arcs like an abstract painting. When there was no more blood in the little mammal she smeared symbols on the old Datsun's bonnet, working the rabbit like a dried-up old felt pen. She then skinned the animal as if pulling a child out of his pyjamas and plopped it into the bowl by Farouk's feet. Farouk flicked away his cigarette and, without making eye contact, picked up the plastic bowl and gave it back to the woman with a few banknotes.

He looked at Fin for the first time that day. 'It is done,' he said.

It was time to go.

SALAAT EL-DUHR

7

Fin and Farouk sat outside a café on the corner of a dusty street sipping cool melon juice. The car was in front of them, its fan belt still humming, its bodywork smeared with crude symbols in dried blood as if defaced by esoteric vandals. Farouk's mood had transformed. He was now expansive, calling greetings across the street, insisting on paying for the melon juice and surveying his suddenly beloved vehicle with the smile of a proud father.

Now that Farouk's petulant misery had lifted, Fin was unable to suppress a creeping resentment. Why, Fin thought, should Farouk get away with inflicting his bad mood on everyone and then, when it had changed, act like nothing had happened? It was he, Fin, who had the problems, who needed help, and all they had done was traipse about dealing with Farouk's imaginary difficulties.

'So what was all that about?' Fin asked, jerking his head towards the car.

'I have said,' Farouk replied. 'People were looking at my car in a bad way. There was bad feeling. The evil eye, *el-ein* was on the car. Now, through the grace of Allah the Bounteous, *khalas*, it is finished.'

'What's Allah got to do with it?' Fin asked, pugnacious.
Farouk looked at him with genuine surprise.

'Come on, Farouk,' Fin insisted. 'How do the mut-
terings of a mad old woman and the sacrifice of a rabbit
relate to your religion?'

'Allah is in all places ...' Farouk looked about him,
suddenly unwilling to have this discussion, as a distant
voice amplified through time-worn loudspeakers called
out the *Salaat el-duhr*, the noon prayer. 'You know nothing,'
he answered as another prayer began, almost drowning
out his quiet voice. 'It is not the rabbit. It means nothing.
The rabbit, it is life. I buy the rabbit from the woman
and give the most precious life to Allah and so the eye is
banished because nothing stands before Allah.'

The noon prayer was now echoing across the city, a
cascade of high and low voices, tinny piercing trebles,
distorted basses, crackling old speakers and state-of-the-
art audio devices with rich tones and colossal power. The
strength of a muezzin's voice once limited the height of
minarets, but now with electronic amplification no part of
Mena village, of Cairo, of the Muslim world, could resist
its intrusion. Every corner of space and time was filled
with prayer. To some, the thousands of different sounds at
slightly different times was a cacophony, but to Fin the
lack of homogeneity was proof of the faith's inde-
pendence – from government, from politics, from all the
things that bowed to the ticking clock. Although it was
not his God, Fin liked the *adhan*, the call to prayer. To him
it washed through every atom of the city like a spring rain.
But today, arguing with Farouk outside the café, he did not
even notice it, except to raise his voice so that he could be
heard.

'It's hocus-pocus. She gives the rabbit to you and then you give it back to her,' Fin said. 'It's like a magic trick.'

'Of course she gives it to me. You see with your eyes but are they not connected to your brain? She gives me the rabbit because I have bought it. You saw me give her money. It is the same in your country, no? When you buy your roast beef in your Coronation Street, do they not give you the meat?'

'Yes but . . .' Fin answered, baffled by the disappearing trails of logic. 'But we do not give it back.'

'Of course you do not,' Farouk replied triumphantly. 'Because you do not practise charity. But for we Muslims charity is one of the Five Pillars of our religion. So I give the rabbit to the woman and she will give it to the poor. The eye is banished, Farouk is happy and a family in Fustat will have a fine dish for their meal.'

Fin was undone by Farouk's arguments, but he felt as if he were being cheated. Cheated in a way that was somehow too obvious to be proved. Perhaps something had been lost in translation, but it was more likely that in this discussion, as in all arguments with Farouk, Fin was being bamboozled.

Fin jumped up and strode over to the car.

'Where will you find a mosque with this symbol, or this one?' Fin demanded, pointing to the blood-scrawled marks on the car door. 'I'm more heathen than Christian, but I'm not stupid, Farouk. I've read books and I have studied. God knows I was brought up a Christian and had the Bible stuffed down my throat by priests. "Faith, hope and charity, but the greatest of these is charity." Ever heard of that? Paul, one of the Christian saints – maybe the best. And do you know what? I know enough of your Koran to know that these scribbles have nothing to do with it.' At the sound of his own voice and the fluency of his expression, Fin felt his frustration become something less impotent. 'It's the same for Christians: we don't kill animals to appease an angry God either. It's the same in the Bible and in the Koran: your Ibrahim, our Abraham, thinks he must kill his son to show his obedience and love of God. This is true, yes? And then God, or Allah, sends his angel to tell him to stop with the sacrificing. Both books later say that if there is sacrificing to be done, it is yourself you should offer – sacrifice the self that keeps you from God. Outside the odd goat at Eid, there's no sacrificing in Islam, there's no fortune-telling, there's no rabbits, and there's no bloody evil *ein*. What you're talking about is superstition, not religion. You just include whatever you feel like and pretend it is done in the name of Allah, but it's not real, it's not true.'

With each word Fin felt better. He was proud of his education, his intelligence, the books he had read. He stood over Farouk, hands on his hips, waiting for the counter-attack.

Farouk sat with his heels hooked in the cross bar of the chair, cradling his melon juice and waiting for Fin to finish.

'Do you wish to do battle with me, Fin? Is it not enough that our great general Salah ad-Din defeated your people five hundred years ago? Must we begin again?' He shook his head in mock despair. 'Is this how I am punished for inviting the infidel into my company?'

Fin tried to suppress the smile creeping up from memory. In the past the crusades had been their running theme, raised at every available opportunity after they had discovered that each had been taught this history at the same time in their lives at schools a couple of thousand miles apart – Fin by a gaunt Jesuit with predatory hands and a greasy black suit, and Farouk by a blind cleric with a camel whip. For both men the summer of their ninth year seemed, at least in their memories, to focus entirely on this period of history: learning the stories, learning the dates and in Fin's case drawing the castles, knights and armour. There were so many similarities in this part of their lives – age, clerical teachers, likes and aversions, and, of course, the period of history they were studying. Yet, amidst all these similarities, there was one absurd concurrence that was determined, almost designed, to separate them. Both had been told that their side – the side of Truth, of God's people, of God himself – was triumphant.

Fin began to feel foolish standing with hands on hips. He rubbed his thigh as if to remind himself of his injury. 'Look, it has really nothing to do with the Crusades,' Fin said finally.

Farouk placed his glass on the pavement and leant into Fin. 'My friend, let us speak as men. With my heart I am sorry a thousand times, I am sorry to speak of your religion. We did not learn of your prophet Paul – peace be upon him – in our madrasa. But tell me, Fin, when you speak, who do you speak for?' Farouk asked. 'Do you speak for yourself? I do not think so. Do you speak for Allah? Our God may be different, or perhaps may not, but I swear we share the same Devil and it is for him that you speak – no?'

Fin interrupted. 'I'm not speaking for anyone; I'm just stating facts. There are books in Christianity like there are books in Islam, and they don't mention the things you say they do. I'm just saying what's true.'

Farouk put his juice on the pavement. 'The truth . . .
Yes, Fin, it is the truth. But who does your truth serve? You
should not give truth to the Devil, Fin. He should not be
given truth. He should be pelted with stones. I am not a
scholar but I know there is more to Allah than a book, and
I know that the Devil should be pelted with stones.'

A choice, like the two paths of the mythical pilgrim,
opened before Fin. He took the harder way because he
was as honest a man as he was able to be. This led to the
source of his anger: not concern for the orthodoxy of
Islam, nor entirely his impatience with Farouk's petulant
behaviour, but envy. Envy for the absolute certainty of
Farouk's world.

'I agree,' Fin said with a sigh. 'The Devil should be
pelted with stones.'

Farouk leant over to Fin and whispered in his ear. 'Now
you speak the truth, and I will open up my heart. I am not
a scholar. I am not a holy man. The Holy Koran was
revealed to the Prophet – peace be upon him – by the angel
Gabril only one and a half thousand years before today.
Egypt is a very old country, older than this, and Allah
knows our hearts and is merciful.'

Farouk leant back, balancing on the spindly back legs of
the chair, handing the melon juice to a ragged child who
had been staring at it longingly for the duration of their
discussion.

'Come, Fin, if you wish to know the laws go to the
mosque or the madrasa and the imam will tell you what
is true and what is not. I am a man, *habibi*, not a saint, a
simple man . . . Now, my brother, enough of this. It is my
wish to make you happy.'

'You want to make me happy?'

'It is all I seek.'

'Then tell me about Skinhead Saïd,' Fin said quickly. 'It is true, isn't it? The story.'

'True? He was my friend since we were children, since his head was covered in hair,' Farouk replied. 'First let us smoke a *shisha*. Take a table in the shade and I will return the happiness that has been stolen from your face.'

Farouk called to a waiter, who brought a tall glass *shisha* etched with curling patterns and crowned with a gleaming tower of beaten tin. He set it up at a table in the midst of the crowded outdoor café and, seeing that Farouk was with a foreigner, produced a light tobacco softened with rose petals, dried fruits and spices. Farouk all but spat on the ground and asked why they could not have the proper tobacco, loosing a volley of insults at the waiter's departing back.

He unwound the beaded pipe, elegantly twisted round the *shisha* like the neck of a sleeping swan, and cleaned the mouthpiece with his thumb before saying to Fin, 'You know, like you Skinhead was not married, but he too would sex with women.'

The waiter returned with a brass tray on which lay a shingle of smouldering coals and a wrapped brick of tobacco. Farouk tore open the cardboard and unleaved crackling cellophane to reveal a thick wet slab of tobacco. He took a wide pinch of the black-brown mulch, moulding it into shape and tamping it into the clay mouth of the *shisha* as the waiter hovered impatiently. Keen to attend to his other customers, the waiter leant over Farouk and dropped three or four burning shards on top of the wet tobacco as Farouk continued shaping and tamping. Farouk scowled but took up the mouthpiece and began to bubble air through the rose-scented water. The waiter bent down and blew on the charcoal, making it spit and crackle. Farouk looked on, sucking in long, increasingly angry draws as the rose petals bounced and spun in the water-bowl below. The waiter moved away, the tobacco still unlit. Farouk frowned.

After three more draws he put down the pipe and shouted and waved until the waiter returned. At his approach Farouk informed him of his shortcomings – not only as a lighter of the *shisha*s, he explained, translating for Fin, but as an Egyptian and a man. The waiter retorted something to the effect that he owned the café and had been lighting *shisha*s for twenty years or more, as had his father before him. He did not welcome any criticism of a technique that had been working for most of the good men of Cairo.

A vigorous discussion began. Farouk informed the waiter, translating every word for Fin, that his choice of charcoal was so haphazard it was either disrespectful or stupid. The waiter retorted that he had already made a selection of the best coals before approaching the table, and anyway, a smoker like Farouk, with the lungs of a dove, may well need to peer and examine each coal for its shape and heat, but a professor of the *shisha*, like himself, could recognise perfect coals with one sweep of his eyes. Had Farouk heard of the great warrior Schwarzenegger? Farouk shrugged and the waiter reached through the neck of his galabeya and pulled his T-shirt as far as he could through the neck, exposing the demonic grin of the weapon-toting movie star. This, he explained in English for Fin's benefit, was the warrior Schwarzenegger, the greatest movie star and strongest man in America, a man who could light a *shisha* with one draw of his mighty lungs. When he pulled out his guns to shoot people, he didn't ask them to wait quietly while he chose the prettiest bullets; he just pulled the trigger. This, the waiter concluded, was his way with the charcoal for the *shisha*.

Farouk looked at the Schwarzenegger T-shirt still held taut by the waiter, and told him that he and the warrior Schwarzenegger could suck his *zobra* as far as he was concerned, adding that if they did, they would enjoy a better smoke than at this café.

At this both parties began shouting directly into each other's faces, ignoring Fin, the *shisha* and all other customers.

A few years before Fin would have been unnerved by such apparent aggression, but now he was accustomed to the loud disputes that accompanied many aspects of Cairo life. Husbands and wives would shout between rooms; neighbours would shout across rooftops; friends would shout across neighbourhoods and children would run around shouting for the joy of shouting. Shouting was sometimes a matter of emphasis, sometimes a matter of anger, but rarely an expression of real hostility.

The coals cooled, and with a speed Fin still found remarkable, so did the dispute. Farouk lowered his voice, backing up his arguments with a gesture that implied the smoothing out of vertical strands of silk from an imagined loom in the sky. The waiter listened, shrugged and walked away, reappearing with a new brazier of coals, which he placed next to Farouk.

Farouk looked up at Fin.

'He is not a bad man, but he does not understand the *shisha*,' he explained, nudging the coals with his index finger. When he had coaxed life into the best pieces, he placed them carefully around the tobacco and took up the pipe. Within minutes the mound of charcoal was glowing red and sweet smoke was snaking out of the corners of Farouk's mouth and joining the communal fug.

'We were discussing marriage, no?' Farouk asked with a smile and a mouthful of smoke. 'Marriage would be good for you, English. Let me tell you, I have a niece, a good girl. Neema she is called. You will like her. Too thin of course, as if she had no food, but being English and a lover of boys, this is what you like, no? I will arrange a meeting.'

Fin refused to be provoked. 'We were discussing Skinhead. You said he had a girlfriend,' Fin reminded him.

'Yes, yes,' Farouk said. 'But no! She was no girl . . . she was a woman, *habibi*, a married woman.'

As the Cairo afternoon deepened, Farouk, with the instinctive understanding of shade common to the people of the desert, nudged his chair incrementally into the expanding triangle of shadow and made himself comfortable.

8

'There was a time when Skinhead was sexing with a woman who was married. It is, of course, wrong and forbidden under sharia law and the law of Egypt to have such contact with a married woman, but it is said that her husband was not able to satisfy her, and anyway' – Farouk lifted his hands so that his palms were above his head pointing up to the sky – 'he was not from our village.

'Skinhead did not love her, but he was unable to resist her for two reasons. The first was that Skinhead must sex many times in one day. It has always been true – even when he was a boy tending goats – but this you have already heard. The second was that the woman, who was known as the Sultana, was a great beauty. Fatter than a hippopotamus, with breasts like watermelons and a waterfall of hair as black and shiny as the oil that flows in the desert.

'In keeping with her size, the Sultana was a woman of great appetites. Of course it is the husband's responsibility to satisfy his wife, but perhaps this man was weak in the arts of love or cursed with a tiny *zobra*. Personally, I believe his wife was possessed with too great an appetite for one man to satisfy. If this were the truth, then her only path to happiness would have been to marry Skinhead Saïd because his desire always exceeded his satisfaction.

'The Sultana was a woman of two interests – sexing, as I have said, and eating. That her delicious fatness seemed to increase every month was not only a gift from heaven, it was the result of great quantities of food. It is well known that a man must bring some token to his lover each time he visits her, particularly when she is as fleshy and desirable as the Sultana, but she had no interest in such things as jewellery, boxes inlaid with mother of pearl, silk slippers, embroidered gowns, perfumes, French lipsticks or even the finest kohl from India. The only gift she would accept was food, which she would eat before her husband returned to the house. In this way, with so many lovers, she maintained her glorious size, eased the burden on the expenses of the house and avoided any bad words with her husband about love tokens found in her quarters.

'The Sultana had lovers each day except Friday, when she would visit the mosque. All of them knew it was expected that they bring different foods on different days. Thus Monday would be honeycombs or sweetmeats; Tuesday, butter or cream; Wednesday, poultry or roast meats, and so on. In this way she was able to keep to a healthy diet.'

'This story, is it about Saïd?' Fin interrupted. 'The one who found the tunnel?'

Farouk paused to expel the sweet smoke of the *shisha*.

'Of course, my friend. Open your ears or you will hear nothing . . . One afternoon Skinhead was visiting the beautiful Sultana. It was a Thursday, and Thursday, as all her lovers knew, was the day for fruit, so Skinhead, after much thought, bought her a kilo of finest Medjool dates. As he entered her chamber he saw to his dismay an Aswan sugar cane leaning by the doorway, as thick as a child's arm, more costly than the dates and as fresh as the morning. He was dismayed to see such a gift as it showed that he was not the first visitor of the day, and furthermore it was a more generous gift than his dates. At first his disappointment made his *zobra* weak, but as soon as he lost himself in the generous folds of the Sultana's flesh, all was forgotten but pleasure.'

Fin was consuming every word of the story, taking notes and glorying in the sensation that, finally, his needs were being met. So absorbed was he that he was only half aware that the waiter was translating and relaying the tale to the rest of the café.

'Sometime later, as Skinhead was kissing and slapping and tossing and turning with the shameless woman, the door flew open and the husband appeared, his eyes on fire and a police revolver in his hand. There was no reason for him to ask what was happening as the Sultana's feet were caressing the ears of Skinhead Saïd. The husband grasped Skinhead by the neck and threw him over the table. Then, pinning him down with one enormous arm, he, quiet and dangerous as a crocodile, looked to his wife. The Sultana was shaking with fear and without thinking reached for a date and slipped it in her mouth. The husband demanded to know who had provided such expensive dates, for it was not he. She nodded towards the terrified Saïd.

'"So you bring my wife gifts," he roared. "Well you shall have them back." And holding Skinhead down over the table, he pushed up his galabeya and thrust the dates into his *teez* one after another. After the tenth date the husband was astonished to see that Skinhead was weeping, not with fear and humiliation but with laughter. The husband demanded to know the cause of this humour. "I'm sorry," said Skinhead Saïd with tears in his eyes. "I'm just so happy I did not bring the sugar cane."'

When Farouk reached his punchline, a great roar of laughter swept through the café and hit Fin like a slap in the face. Men pounded their thighs, thumped the tables, wheezed, roared and stomped their feet. Farouk sat at the centre like a conductor, inciting laughter solos and choral guffaws with a wink here and crude gesture there.

Fin shrank into his chair and stole glances at the faces contorted around him. He made himself smile weakly, but it was unnecessary. He had become invisible. Fin rose stiffly and limped out to the street, where the laughter was just another noise and a low wall offered somewhere to sit. He gazed at the dry mud bricks of a cracked wall across the street, trying to make sense of his mood and his disappointment.

Farouk came out of the café dabbing the tears of laughter from his eyes. 'Come, *habibi*. What is wrong? Are you sick?'

'I had some problems, in Cairo . . . My leg was injured.' Fin caught his breath as he pushed deep into the bruise on his thigh with his thumb.

'Yes,' Farouk agreed. 'You are walking like a *khasi*.'

'*Khasi?*'

'You know, apricots cut off for the harem . . . You do not laugh, my friend. What is it?'

Fin arose. 'I don't want to talk about it, OK, Farouk? I didn't come here for advice, a wife or a joke. I came here to . . . I'm not sure why, but if you're not going to tell me what Skinhead Saïd found, just let me know and I'll go home.'

Farouk threw his hands up in a gesture which implied Fin's impatience would be more justly addressed to the Almighty.

'Skinhead? Skinhead? Stay here, *habibi*, and take one coffee and I will buy a beautiful vegetable at the market, an Egyptian vegetable, and you will be my guest in my house where it is cool, and on my life and the life of my mother I will tell you a thousand such stories . . . You have money? Small. Ten Egyptian.'

As Fin proffered his wallet, Farouk snapped out a twenty. He swung into his car and disappeared down the street beeping his horn while Fin resumed his place on the wall. His thoughts had not progressed when, a few minutes later, the car horn sounded. It was Farouk, shouting and goading Fin with an aubergine.

'So hungry is your English belly that you are hoping that a fine Egyptian fly will take pity on you and lay eggs in your open mouth?' Farouk shouted to him. 'Even a camel about to die from thirst has more life than you. Come, infidel! *Yallah*! We will make baba ganoush.'

Fin arose, particles of the wall sticking to the flap of his jacket where he had sat. He walked across the street and got in the car.

9

Farouk drove his car as if the brakes had not only failed but long ago been ripped from the vehicle and replaced with only a horn. His response to all oncoming obstacles – camels, schoolchildren, bicycles, donkey carts, the infirm hobbling across the road – was to accelerate towards them, honking and cursing, merciless in his impatience. But he would demonstrate monk-like tranquillity behind trucks blocking narrow streets or with leisurely workers smoking and slowly moving split-bamboo cages containing chickens or piles of bricks.

The greatest enemy of all was that many-headed monster the Other Driver, with his murderous incompetence, psychotic competitiveness and profound visual impairment. Such cars were passed with unceasing incantations. In cases of extreme provocation there was an escalating scale of response. Driving past and staring like a wrathful Hindu God was the least severe. Throwing both hands heavenward was the next level. The most serious and frequent reprisal was to wind down the window and articulate the anatomy of the offending driver's mother. It was always the absent mothers who took the punishment.

Fin wondered if, on some subtle level, they were actually responsible.

Finally they left the bustle of the city behind them, and Farouk turned the car off the main road, taking a series of right-angle turns along cart-width dirt streets. Farouk's aversion to deceleration generated an opaque cloud of dust around the car, but Fin knew that they must be near Mena village. Farouk braked suddenly, and as the dust settled Fin noted that they were in front of a small opening in a dusty blue wall. Of course, Fin thought to himself with a sigh that expressed both his relief at being stationary and his resigned appreciation of the destination, Benghazi, the whisky seller.

A boy tottered by on a donkey, balancing a bale of straw on the animal's neck, passing the car by a tiny margin. Farouk glared at him, ready to pounce if his car were brushed with even a stalk. A car moved slowly across the street ahead, loudspeakers, like black ear trumpets, mounted on its roof blaring a distorted message through the neighbourhood.

'Politics?' asked Fin.

'Death,' replied Farouk. 'A man died. They are calling people for the funeral. His heart finished. He was an old man. A good life, *el-hamde lillah*.'

'Why the loudspeakers?' Fin asked.

'The funeral, of course, to invite people. He died today; he must be buried today. You wish to go?'

'Did I meet him?'

'How can I know? But you will be welcome.'

Fin shook his head. 'It is better we talk.'

'You have money?'

Fin took out his wallet and brushed his thumb over the

soft edges of the bills. He grasped the creased corner of a twenty, but before he'd even pulled it out, Farouk closed his hand over Fin's.

'What is this twenty Egyptian?' he said, pushing the wallet away. 'This is nothing. *La', la'.*' He shook his head in disappointment.

Farouk had a sensitivity to money. He could sense the contents of Fin's wallet through layers of clothing and smell the balance of currency within. He was also expert at lightening Fin's wallet, able to keep a mental record of its precise contents for days. Fin would have remembered this had he thought about it, but instead pulled the wallet away from Farouk and offered him a fifty. Farouk again shook his head.

'Give me the hundred. We are buying whisky, Johnnie Walker, to celebrate. You have a note with a small tear. You had it this morning at my uncle's house. I saw you pull it out and thought, Allah be praised, he respects my family. But then you gave him only ten.'

As Fin was digesting this, Farouk removed the hundred Egyptian from the back of the slim wad, and congratulated himself with little grunts as if he had discovered something that Fin had lost. He held up the torn corner for Fin's inspection.

'You see, *habibi*, I help you in all things because you are my brother.' Smiling, he exited the car before Fin could object.

For once Fin did not want whisky. He wanted his story and he wanted food, and then perhaps whisky. His hunger had merged into his need for the story and become something insistent and jagged, like the edge of too much coffee. But if Farouk wanted whisky, Fin thought to himself, give him whisky. Whatever it would take to loosen his tongue.

Fin looked down at the double-knotted, blue and white striped plastic bag at his feet. The aubergines, swollen and promising, were still some hours from becoming baba ganoush, he realised, his mind slipping into half-formed dreams of eating. He gazed neutrally out through the windscreen, palpating his bruised leg the way a child worries a loose tooth, his mind creating and dissolving notions of absence, images of lack – food of course, affection, fulfilment.

Fin watched as Farouk approached the opening in the wall, and although he saw the two men following Farouk, they did not register on his thoughts until the larger of them, who was built heavily and unevenly like one of the cheap tower blocks in Heliopolis, lumbered into a run and, with the slow irresistible swing of a demolition ball, struck Farouk on the back of the head with a heavy lump of wood.

Fin scrambled out of the car and ran limping towards his friend, who now lay in the dirt. As Fin approached, the giant grabbed Farouk by his armpits and dragged him away, Farouk's heels digging parallel tracks in the dust, his mouth lolling open. Fin hobbled after them shouting. The giant pulled and dragged Farouk, Fin lurched forward closing in. As he neared, the giant halted and dropped Farouk in the dirt like a sack of rubbish. The smaller man sized Fin up with a glance, shook his head in sympathy and walked calmly away. The larger one, big enough for people to pay to see him, stood perfectly still, as a cliff waits for a lemming.

The man was fleshy but solid, like an enormous muscular baby. His head looked as if it had been impacted into his body with a piledriver, his neck and chin obliterated in rolls of heavy fat. He stood swaying, his torso thick and listing like poured concrete. Fin had seen him hours before. He was the man who had been standing in the doorway spying on Farouk's car.

Fin was unsure what to do now the chasing phase was over. According to what he'd seen in films, this was when the violence should begin – a swinging punch or an expert chop. But his meagre experience of fights was victim-based, and the man-mountain in front of him looked as though he could absorb any blow in the quivering lava of his flesh. The thug raised his arms. He made towards Fin, approaching with the resolute motion of an avalanche. Fin's deluge of outrage froze into terror. The creaseless horizontal face of the giant smiled sickly, leering. Fin glanced at Farouk, who was bleeding into the sand, and with a scream, threw his fingers into the tiny unfleshed space of the thug's nearer eye. Fin felt the ocular jelly flatten and dimple under the pressure of his fingertips. The thug screeched in pain and Fin kicked him as hard as he could in the shin. The thug collapsed to the ground with a yelp. Fin grabbed Farouk's clothes and tried to drag his friend back towards the car. He was unaware of the return of the second man until he felt a *swoosh* of air against the back of his head and a dull thud – too heavy for anything except a bad dream, as if someone had reversed a freight train into his skull, or his head were an egg cracked on the edge of a mixing bowl. Fin was aware only for a moment of the scale and unpleasantness of the experience before star-laden blackness enveloped him, consciousness spiralling away like filthy bathwater.

SALAAT EL-ASR

10

A bucketful of tepid water jerked Fin awake. With a nauseating lurch, he saw before him his assailant, swinging
the now empty aluminium vessel. The corpulent thug's
left eye was a bloody mess and he was no longer smiling.
Wherever they now were, it was hot and windowless. Fin
felt a sharp tug on the lapels of his linen suit and was pulled
to his feet. He grunted as a dull flash of pain exploded his
head and then gratefully slid towards blackness once more.
A crushing grip wrenched him back into excruciating consciousness as the thug gleefully squeezed his testicles like
a couple of pecan nuts.

A door was kicked open, and Fin was manhandled up
uneven stairs and bundled out into the hall of a large
prosperous-looking house. The walls and floor were clad
in a mucus-yellow onyx marble which made Fin sway
with nausea. He leant against the cold shining surface for
comfort. The back of the house was raw breeze block,
held together with uneven layers of grey-green cement.
An unfinished area of wall gaped onto a narrow alleyway
below.

Steadying himself against the cool wall, Fin noticed

that the extravagantly gilded mirror opposite him was mounted no higher than his waist and the two chairs on either side of it were Lilliputian. Squinting through screwed-up eyes, he saw that all the fittings – coat rack, table, door handles – were hung at child height. As he considered this affront to his perspective, the thug reached down to a doorknob mounted at the height of Fin's knee and propelled him into a spacious room with a dazzling scarlet carpet.

To complete the nightmare, a man no larger than a six-year-old child sat upon a garish yellow sofa that was encased in a protective plastic covering. Size was the man's only childlike quality. His face was covered in the thickest and most aggressive stubble Fin had ever seen, and in his right hand he gripped an unfeasibly large cut-glass tumbler the size of a fruit bowl. In it was a clear brown liquid which the bottle on the table confirmed was whisky. Whoever these people were, Fin thought, looking at the bottle and closing one eye in an attempt to arrest the swaying of the room, they were not religious fanatics.

In the corner Fin saw Farouk, grey with fear, his elbows and wrists bound behind his back with electrical wire. Farouk saw Fin and started to stammer.

'Fin, tell him . . .'

Fin flicked his eyes from Farouk to his diminutive captor still holding the heavy tumbler. It wasn't big, Fin realised, it just seemed so in the man's tiny hand. The guard, however, was huge and Fin wanted him as far away as possible. The smaller man interrupted Fin's thoughts, coughing and wheezing like a tramp before introducing himself in heavily accented English as Omar.

He did so with an incongruous courtesy which added a new layer to Fin's fear. 'Jalut,' he said, pointing at his thuggish colleague. He leant to one side of the sofa, and uprooted a filthy white hand towel that was jammed between the cushions. The towel seemed to resist, as if it sensed the fate that awaited it. Omar tugged with both hands, tumbling onto his side as it came free. He righted himself and scanned the eyes of the others in the room, daring anyone to show even a flicker of amusement. He coughed again and mopped at the extraordinary quantities of sweat which oozed like groundwater from his hirsute face.

Farouk broke in. 'Tell the man it was not me. Tell him I did not do this thing.' He was terrified. Fin had never seen Farouk afraid. It was unsettling, like seeing parents cry. Omar scowled at Farouk, loathing burning out of his eyes. Fin twitched as if to run but Jalut caught his eye and mimed an unpleasant crushing sign with his fists.

'You know this man?' Omar demanded gesturing at Farouk.

'Yes— I mean, not really,' answered Fin. 'His name is Fazouk or something.' Fin noticed that his friend's nose was plugged with dried blood. 'He's ... erm ... the worst guide I've ever had, and I'll tell you this much: I've had enough of his cousin's so-called antique shop and his uncle's bloody perfume outfit.' Fin felt himself gain momentum. 'Here's a word in your ear, Fallook, my boy. You can stick your antiquities up your arse, along with your so-called degree in Egyptology. And if there's still room, you can shove this Jalut monster up there too. No offence, Mr Omar, but my rocks are swelling and I've got a bastard of a headache.'

Fin was almost as surprised as Farouk by his performance. He flashed a look at Omar, who seemed neither offended nor interested.

'I'm an Irishman and a leading light in the Rotary Club of Castle-bloody-Townsend, County Cork and' – Fin tried to give Farouk a meaningful look – 'I think I should let you know that, grateful as I am for your hospitality, if I do not find myself back in that over-air-conditioned apology of a four-stars-my-arse hotel in, shall we say, twenty minutes, then I will be reporting you to the Irish Foreign Office, the Egyptian Tourist Board, my new friend Big Abdul on reception and, if it comes to it, the police, so help me God.'

Farouk looked on uncomprehending, but at the word 'police' Omar leapt off the sofa and charged towards Fin.

'NO! NO! NO! NO!' he shouted, jumping and waving his hands in front of Fin's face. 'YOU,' he shouted, stretching up his arm and poking Fin in the chest with a solid stubby finger, 'ARE MY FREN, MY VERY GOOD FREN. This man,' – he jerked his head towards Farouk with disgust – 'is *NOT* my fren. You say you do not know him. This is true?'

'No. I mean, yes . . . a bit . . . As I said, he's a crook, a con artist. He sidles up to me as I get out of the taxi down by the Pyramids and tells me he's an official guide with a degree in archaeology from the University of Alexandria. The truth is, he knows less than I do about ruins and he keeps taking me to buy crappy souvenirs and stupid bloody papyrus. Then . . . well, I can't remember what happened really. I've a headache and I think I should be getting back to the hotel and pouring myself a large Bushmills. Got a bottle in my room, you know. Can't trust this foreign muck – no offence intended.' Fin sidled towards the door but Jalut threw up an arm as thick as a girder and brandished the same fearsome lump of wood he had used on Farouk. Fin halted and spun back to Omar, whose grin was unaffected by Fin's weak attempt at escape.

'You are my fren! You are my fren! You are my fren,' Omar exclaimed, each time getting louder as if volume could make up for the bad start to their relationship. 'YOU ... ARE ... MY ... FREN!' he shouted, throwing open his arms in welcome. 'This man,' he said, pointing at Farouk, 'is not my fren.' Omar snapped his fingers and Jalut produced a plastic chair and placed it directly in front of Farouk. Omar climbed onto it so he was eye to eye with Farouk.

'YOU,' he screamed, spraying Farouk's face with spit and then slapping him with extraordinary force, 'ARE,' he slapped again, 'NOT,' slap, 'MY,' slap, 'FREN.' The last blow was delivered with such violence that Farouk was knocked to the ground. This seemed to satisfy Omar. He jumped down from the chair and made his way back towards Fin with streams of milky sweat pouring down his face.

'This man is bad man. Bad man,' he screeched, waving at Jalut, who dragged Farouk out of the room.

Omar's once-white galabeya was now translucent with sweat, revealing a torso covered in whorls of fur-thick hair. He shouted through the door to Jalut, who returned without Farouk but clasping a slim parcel neatly wrapped in brown paper. Omar snatched the parcel and tore it open, plunging his face into it and breathing in its aroma with a strangely innocent glee. He stood up and tossed the torn packet to Jalut, who carefully removed a miniature black galabeya bordered with thick gold braiding.

Omar turned away and shot his podgy hands straight up into the air. A prayer call commenced, the muezzin suffering from a throat complaint or an addiction to strong tobacco and the loudspeaker so close to their building that the shuttered windows rattled in the blast. Jalut approached Omar and pulled off the sodden galabeya with a quick and practised tug. Fin found himself confronted by a ridge of black hair running from Omar's neck down his back and disappearing like a weasel into tight white underpants emblazoned with a neat black playboy bunny on each buttock. Jalut guided the new galabeya over Omar's outstretched arms and pulled it down by the hem, primping and arranging with a care and absorption that was strangely intimate.

'I am good man,' Omar announced, running his podgy hands down his newly clothed body with satisfaction. 'A VERY GOOD MAN. Sit, sit. Bring this chair.' He pointed to a heavy armchair similarly protected with a thick translucent covering. 'You are welcome, my guest. You drink whisky? Come, sit.'

Fin dragged the armchair from the other side of the room, his sweating hands scrabbling for purchase on the plastic covering. The effort made him dizzy and he crumpled gratefully into the armchair. As he opened his eyes, Omar removed the bottle of Black Label from its box and poured a measure into the glasses on the table.

After sitting for a few moments the centrifugal nausea that was spinning within Fin seemed to calm. With its absence, however, came a sharpened awareness of the situation. He and Farouk had been assaulted and abducted by an unlikely and possibly insane person with a cavalier attitude to violence and a seething hatred of Farouk. That much was certain. Since Farouk was tied up, responsibility for action lay exclusively with Fin, who, enfeebled by a bruised leg and fear of further violence, had rarely felt more passive. A prayer call had just sounded – not dawn, not noon . . . it was still light, it must be the late-afternoon prayer, *Salaat el-asr*, so he'd been unconscious for an hour or two, no more.

Omar was nudging the whisky glass towards Fin, smiling insincerely, stroking and pushing the tumbler like a pimp procuring a very young girl. Fin thought perhaps the whisky might help him.

'Big mistake, you understand,' Omar was saying. 'You are good man, my fren. You like Omar? You happy? Drink with Omar.' Omar edged the glass forward again with a stab from his little fingers. His broad solid forehead was again wet with whitish beads of sweat, and his dense black stubble seemed to thicken before Fin's eyes.

'Why you not drink? You drink with Omar,' he demanded, his expression picking up sincerity as it flattened to a scowl.

Fin looked at the whisky in its heavy squat glass, a deeper gold than the braiding on Omar's galabeya but more attractive. It promised comfort, a familiar warmth and much-needed support. It was a cure-all, an insulator, an antidote to fear. But there was something deeply wrong with the situation. Fin looked at Omar. He was a hellhound, a miniature hellhound, but still terrifying. No, Fin decided, it was not the whisky he should fear, whisky never hurt anyone. But just for safety's sake, he pushed aside the glass he was being offered and drained Omar's in one long gulp.

Omar raised his millipede eyebrows in surprise and the scorched-earth sheen of his stubbly face cracked into a thousand lines of delight. He slapped his thighs with a wheezing laugh and pounded the cushions, coughing like a steam engine until tears flowed from his narrow eyes and joined the rivulets of sweat. He held up the glass he had been offering Fin and shouted, 'You think Omar poison you? Hahahaha. You think this?'

Omar tipped Fin's whisky down his throat and refilled the glasses, putting a splash into his own and another heavy slug into Fin's. Despite being kidnapped, Fin found himself embarrassed and, wanting to make a better impression, swallowed his second, even larger, glass of whisky in two gulps, wincing as it tore into his empty stomach.

Omar nodded, appeased. 'Good, good, this is good. You are my fren.'

'Food. Do you have food?' Fin asked through clenched teeth, his stomach lining fizzing in revolt. Food was always necessary, he told himself as Omar was issuing orders to Jalut. Fin slumped in the plastic-covered armchair, tears brimming in the corners of his eyes. Omar sat on the sofa, his legs straight out in front of him. They said nothing. Fin allowed Omar to refill his glass two, then three times, and slipped into the welcome anaesthesia of the alcohol until the warm aroma of grilled meat announced Jalut's return.

Fin watched fuzzily as a bulging parcel wrapped in a copy of *Al-Ahram* newspaper dropped in front of him. He opened the package and removed a number of organ-

warm plastic bags. Each contained a handful of chargrilled cubes of lamb, and at the bottom of the package, a folded wad of warm unleavened bread.

Fin looked in awe at the half-dozen lightly charcoaled cubes of meat before him. Each was plump with thick-grained gleaming juiciness. Fin tore off a palm-sized swatch of bread and wrapped it around the biggest chunk of meat. Hot, garlicky juices fired into his mouth as he bit into it, and he could taste that pink tender flesh in the middle give up its structure to a delicious mulch. As he chewed, eyes closed, almost swooning with aromatic delight, he discovered that one side of the meat was hiding toasted sesame seeds.

Chewing for Fin was an activity that absorbed all his attention. (His father had once revealed to him, as if passing on a great secret, that mastication was the only part of the digestive process that could be consciously affected.) The meat was extraordinary – spicy, luscious, tender and suffused with the flavour of thyme. One of the great kebabs of all time. And Fin kept a close tally of such things.

'This is good?' Omar asked.

'Not good,' Fin replied through a tiny space in his mouth. 'Perfect.'

He threw open his fists like two little stars and nodded. 'Of course, Omar Kebab very good. Best in Cairo. Why? Because you are my fren, my very good fren. We drink together, yes?'

Fin agreed with him, and when they clinked glasses felt a warm bloom of fraternity and a flush of pride at his own panache. Whatever Omar's social skills, he served an unforgettable lamb kebab and was free with his whisky. However, Fin noted, with an equivalent sensitivity to bottles of alcohol that Farouk had to money, despite the theatrical gulps Omar was drinking very little, while Fin had consumed more than a third of the bottle. A very good bottle it was too, despite being Scotch. Fin suppressed a belch as he finished his glass in three large gulps.

Omar refilled Fin's glass and issued a homeopathic splash into his own. Fin sank into a balmy contentment that engulfed him like a hot bath. As long as he could have a couple of drinks, he would always be able to make everyone feel good about themselves. He was clever, he thought with a soothing glow. He could get another mindless job, stop being so hard on himself and spend the next eighteen months floating around and enjoying life. Or find somewhere new and exciting where he could start again.

'My fren, we drink. Yes?' Omar held out the thick cut glass in his podgy little hand. Fin felt good. Unhappiness, tension, they were all symptoms of sobriety. It was time to act, to spread the love. He and Omar were friends now and friends talked, even about difficult things.

'Tell me, Omar, you are my friend, yes?' Fin took a reassuring sip.

'Very good fren,' Omar corrected.

'Why is the other man not your . . . fren?'

'Jalut? He works for me.'

'No. Not Jalut. He hates me.'

'All foreigners he hates. Especially English.'

'I'm not English,' Fin interrupted.

'It is the same.' Omar shrugged.

'I mean the other man. The one tied up. Why is he not your fren?'

Omar's already swarthy face darkened under its Vaseline lustre of sweat. He slammed down his glass and pointed towards the door.

'My daughter, Nira. Beautiful girl. Every day school, I pay. Best school for my daughter. She walk every day, no problem. Then this Farouk hit her. My beautiful girl. In his car. She is walking in the road and he hits her with his car! This man-whore, this prostitute ... No stop, no help. He drive away. Her leg broken. She cry, she scream. This man is bad man, very bad. So I pay. I find this car. And now we take him. He break my daughter. Now I break him.'

Omar's eyes brimmed with tears which concentrated the menace of his expression.

'Can't you call the police?' offered Fin lamely.

Omar snorted. 'In Cairo a man who buys a car can buy police. Everybody knows this. It is a matter of honour, and it must be finished with honour. As long as my daughter has suffered, this man will suffer – but seven thousand times more.'

Omar picked up the bottle of whisky. Fin smiled nervously and shook his head.

'You're too kind, Omar. Really, I've had enough.' Fin covered his glass with his hand.

'You will drink,' hissed Omar and sloshed the whisky through Fin's fingers until the bottle was empty and the glass brimmed with a liquid no longer benign.

'Drink!' Omar demanded.

The convivial atmosphere disappeared as if it had never existed, and Jalut stepped behind Fin with a long heavy screwdriver in his hand. Fin did not wish to know what he intended to do with the tool, which looked suspiciously large and too heavy for domestic use. He picked up the glass and swallowed in controlled gulps. The first was pleasant; the second produced a tightening in the stomach; the third, a spasm; the fourth and fifth returned to his throat with an unpleasant mixture of bile which he swallowed back with a grimace.

Fin put down the empty glass and exhaled. For a few moments the alcohol threatened to erupt back out of him, but it soon bowed to gravity and habit and things improved. Within minutes Fin felt good again, confident and relaxed, less attached to the myriad of concerns life, and in particular this situation, offered. When Jalut pulled him to his feet, a cloud darkened Fin's mind and a rebel song came to his voice. He felt an intense dislike for the ugly expanse of human violence who was pushing him around like a pile of rubble when he would rather be slumped in the armchair watching the lights swirl so nicely. Singing out the words from an old chorus, 'And loud and clear we'll raise the cheer, revenge for Skibereen!' he struck out with his fist in the direction of his oppressor, and feeling the great mass stumble, threw his arms in the air and cheered. Roaring with bravado, Fin dived towards the blur he had punched, but instead found the floor. His triumph ended as he found himself lifted into the air like a pantomime Peter Pan, slapped hard across the face and thrown against a wall. Before he could understand what was happening, Jalut was on him squeezing and twisting the contents of Fin's scrotum as if trying to tear an unripe fruit from a tree. Fin screamed, and before he knew what was happening, the sound transformed into the sour contents of his stomach retched over Jalut's smooth and wide face.

Fin passed out.

SALAAT EL-MAGHRIB

11

Fin flies. Not in dream, not in sleep. He moves through the air, friction-free, lifeless, relaxed, weightless, unimpeded by gravity's relentless drag. Fin is falling. Careless as an unborn baby. Flying, falling, it makes no difference until the ground. But Fin will not meet the ground. Fin will meet water. It is no more than fifty feet from the Nan Rhial railway bridge to the surface of the Nile, less than a second of the freedom Fin has been seeking. It will be short-lived, for the waters of the Nile are perilous and dirty and underneath its banks and deep within its muddy recesses lie dark and menacing shapes, monsters of infinite patience whose world is mud.

Wet and weightless, Fin sinks into the Nile, coming to consciousness with the fear that drunken incontinence has again washed over him. But on this occasion he has really let go and soaked the whole world. Fin takes a breath, and water scorches his throat and lungs. He screams through the viscous nightmare and scrambles for the surface. Disorientated, Fin swims down, lured by currents that feign buoyancy. He pulls himself through the liquid night until, close to passing out, he splutters out the last of his breath, which bubbles round his face and neck, urgently seeking the surface. A life-saving spark from his deepest self makes him invert his body and follow the path of his last breath. His hand breaks through the water and he hauls himself up, filling his lungs with the warm night air, gasping and roaring with shock.

Above him are lights, buildings, traffic, people. Powerful currents swirl and eddy as the sharp point of an island divides the river. Fin swims towards the land but the current saps all strength, sucking him away from the island and into the widest part of the river. Fin struggles, screaming in defiance, but his efforts are futile. At the point of surrender he recalls childhood summers on the rough Irish Sea, currents that could only be resisted in increments, and so he lets the force take him, edging gently across its face, closer and closer to the safety of the bank. When he is near enough to make out the shape of the bank he hears the sleek heavy splash of something large and streamlined entering the water behind him. Fin swims harder, imagining dark reptilian shapes swimming towards him with grim certainty. Behind him, underneath him, he senses forces waiting for the right moment to pull him below and twist off his limbs like chicken wings. His arms are exhausted and the muscles in his injured thigh seize and knot. He swims on, forcing his mind away from fear and into the skin of his hands. He imagines his shoulders as engines, pulling him through the water, conscious of every physical part of his body until he touches the slippery edge of land and pulls himself with a shout onto the filthy rubbish-strewn bank.

The ground is not solid. Fin knows that he must keep going. The ground is not safe. It oozes and rustles, it gives and slides under his shoeless feet. He must get to the city above him, where people are walking and driving, working and shouting, selling and building, where he can find sanctuary and salvation. Where he can find rest.

Fin stumbles ahead, slipping in the debris and waste; his feet crunch on something he is sure is alive and rotting, something he can feel with extraordinary acuity but cannot describe. A sickening thing. All around he is startled by the scuttling of creatures he disturbs. He is sick, wet and filthy. He longs for rest, for sleep, but more than this, he longs to live. He forces himself through the mud and waste, feeling the stench hungrily sucking at his feet, convinced that the shadowless tangles of oily decaying chaos will engulf and smother him. He reaches a frontier, a vertical limit of smooth concrete where the solid foundations of a bridge sink deep into the morass.

Fin tries to climb but there is nothing to grasp and each step slips or sinks down in the ooze which clutches at his feet with desperate gasps. Exhausted, Fin crumples into the filth, his head despairing against the rigid wall, his body yielding to the inevitability of descent. He hears the first notes of the *Salaat el-maghrib*, the prayer of sunset slicing through the roaring canopy of traffic, and Fin understands that it is only a few hours since he and Farouk were drinking tea and talking, and for every other person life is going on as it always has, and that somewhere on the horizon there is still a red glow because the *Salaat el-maghrib* must be called when there is light in the sky. This idea of light gives him strength. Fin rises and stretches up his arms, leaping against the wall until his fingers find an edge. He pulls himself out of the damp pit, drawing himself up, each movement taking him further from fear, each action fighting through the ache in his leg until he forces himself to the clean-cut flat of the bridge wall. He places his hands on the sun-warmed concrete and lies face down, tears of relief falling almost silently onto the hard flat stone.

Fin lay motionless but for the drops and rivulets of filthy water that slid down the gradients and parabolas where his body curved and hung, then dropped from stalactite hairs and stray fibres on the frayed edges of his suit. Time passed. Fin focused his eyes and recognised where he was – the bridge that linked Cairo to Giza. The Sharia 26 July Bridge. And although he could move, he did not.

Moving would bring the realisation that his clothes were wet and suffused in a Nile slime of decomposed rubbish, polluted mud and other frightening organic things. It would bring the realisation that Farouk was not only facing death or terrible injury but had knocked down a child and then left her in the road injured and screaming. It would bring the realisation that his life was still without direction, without even the story he had decided would save him.

Instead, Fin listened to the traffic clatter and rumble. He flexed his toes, then his feet, then his ankles, then his calves, then his knees. As he tensed his thigh, the dull throb of his leg injury returned, bounding through his body like a neglected dog. It had become familiar, almost welcome.

Fin pushed against the stone with his palms and rose unsteadily. He must get home, he thought. He must bathe and dress and call the authorities. That's what people did. Call the authorities. Cars and trucks were shooting past, the occupants looking at him and pointing. Fin glimpsed the white and black livery of a police car and waved. Of course, here was the answer – the police. Fin increased the tempo of his waving, scissoring the air wildly with his arms, casting wings of oleaginous water, making rainbows in the headlights of the passing cars.

The police car slowed. Fin composed himself, wondering how, with his almost exclusively gastronomic Arabic, he would explain himself, describe how he had been kidnapped and thrown into the Nile. The car came to a stop in front of him. Fin walked over to the passenger door, squelching with every step, straightening his jacket. Four policemen stared at him from within, smirking and sweating. Fin bent down towards the window but the car abruptly accelerated, the passenger door springing open and catching Fin on the side of the head. There was a roar of laughter as the car sped off, and one of the policemen in the back thrust his head out of the window and shouted, '*Zibbala!*'

Fin remained where he lay, stunned, dazed by the blow from the car door, by the word *zibbala* stamped into him where the door had struck. Fin knew what *zibbala* was. Everyone in Cairo knew *zibbala*. To live in Cairo was to live with *zibbala* – the nine thousand tons of rubbish produced by the city every day. Nine thousand tons of debris, refuse, garbage, waste.

Nine thousand tons of matter, of things beneath use.

Fin looked at his once-white trousers, now wet and foul, streaked with mud and plastered to his skinny legs. His jacket was no better, with the added indignity of one arm almost torn off like a wounded doll. He gazed ahead at the ramshackle junction of roads, overpasses, underpasses. In a car it would be at least thirty minutes' drive to his apartment. Too far to walk.

Fin stood, and pulled a broken whisky bottle out of his jacket pocket. How it had got there he had no idea, but he was lucky not to have been severely lacerated by it in his fall from the bridge. He patted his trousers, surprised to find his wallet still in his back pocket, his wad of Egyptian pounds untouched. Fin waved at taxis, and although a few drivers slowed down to take a look at him, some to shake their heads or spit in disgust, none stopped. Fin stood unsteadily on the bridge, the mud tightening as it dried, the skin on his face becoming taut.

Fin shut his eyes against the throbbing in his head. He longed for softness and dryness, for comfort and love. For the first time in years he found himself thinking of his mother and her warm arms and the unquestioning irreplaceable love that had disappeared with her death. So lost was he in this absence that he did not notice a cart draw up beside him until he was engulfed by its stench. As he looked up, two donkeys stood before him, gazing with the quietude of monks. Their driver sat, almost lay, behind the beasts, shoeless, sockless, shirtless and wearing a frayed grey and navy blue suit proudly done up with its one remaining button, a bony chest shining beneath. The wooden cart was painted with the luminescent heraldry of the *zibbaleen*-electric lime green, lemon-drop yellow, baby-doll pink, glittering chrome, the plastic colours of treasure that the *zibbaleen* recycled from Cairo's endless garbage. The man's black, gnarled feet rested on the wooden pommel of the cart; behind him a mountain of *zibbala*. A soft but steady pyramid of fruit skins, paper, headless dolls, chicken carcasses, broken *shishas*, plastic in all its magical forms, soiled and torn rags of cloth, metal crumpled and sharp, cigarette butts, candle wax, bundles of wire, ripped and sun-bleached magazines, dust from a thousand swept homes, defeated toys, razor-sharp cans and the shells of radios, all weighing down the fat pneumatic tyres of the cart, which bulged like the cheeks of an overfed baby.

The man addressed Fin, asking a question, but his Arabic was too fast and heavily accented. Fin began to explain that he did not understand, but at his first words the man sat up.

'*Ferenghi*?' he demanded wide-eyed.

Fin nodded. The man stared at Fin in astonishment, his arms open, palms out, as if cradling the image before him. Fin tried to explain with his few Arabic words and the language of his mud-caked hands that he had been thrown into the Nile. The man pointed towards the Nan Rhial railway bridge in the distance and to the Nile, his eyes widening in disbelief. Surely not, he seemed to be saying, surely not el-Nil? Fin nodded. The man stood up on his cart to look over the wall of the bridge at the black water below. Fin saw the man's shoulders heave up and down and his back shiver. The man sat back down and turned to Fin, exploding into whooping laughter as his gaze touched Fin's. Once he began to laugh, he could not stop, seesawing on his bench and slapping his skinny thighs. Soon he was gasping for air and tried to stop by wrapping his arms around his knees and staring resolutely at his toes. But after only a few breaths he could not resist peering again at Fin, and as soon as he did, erupted into laughter once more, rocking back and forth on the narrow bench of his cart until he almost fell off.

Fin waited, knowing that at some point laughter, like urine, must cease. But the man carried on laughing, each breath feeding his howls like the khamseen, the maddening wind of the desert, feeds fire in a thorn bush. Fin was confused. He did not know if he was angry, desperate or humiliated, so he turned and walked away. The cart driver shouted something. Over his shoulder Fin saw the man calling him back with one arm buried shoulder-deep in his mountain of rubbish, like a farmer calving a cow. The *zibbaleen* extracted his arm and produced a triangle of broken mirror which he wiped on his sleeve and offered to Fin. Fin took the shard and held it before him. The face that looked back was smeared with filth, his hair like the scribble of a madman, eyes burning red like Waled's. It had the look of something that lived under a rock in the filthiest silt of the river. With the faintest twitch of a smile Fin realised that the image in the broken glass was himself. All there was of him. Fin in all his glory. He chuckled, reigniting the cart driver's laughter, and the two men edged each other into hilarity until tears, indistinguishable from sorrow, ran down Fin's face, cutting benign cleansing scars through the drying filth of the river.

The driver eventually wiped his eyes with his suit jacket sleeve, shifted over on the narrow cart bench and patted the empty space. Fin pulled himself up next to the man and the donkeys trotted onto the highway. Cars and trucks zoomed past, provoked to screaming curses and blaring horns by the fragility and slow teetering movement of the cart. The cart driver was oblivious to the hostility, guiding his precious donkeys with a thick stick and singing soothing assurances at every noise or dangerous swerve. Fin leant back into the soft mound of rubbish and drowsed in the slow pace and gentle sway of the cart, while the *zibbaleen* pointed them north and whispered to his donkeys that they were beautiful Bedouin princesses and they would sleep in golden hay.

Fin sat up as he recognised the island of order, of boulevards and palm-gardened residences that was Zamalek, a place built by the colonial rulers on an island protected by the river, far away from the teeming entropy of Cairo's ancient heart. Moneyed Cairenes strolled down Parisian-style boulevards, cafés dispensed cappuccinos with neat pyramidal tonsures of chocolate powder and Cairo's most adored football team played before passionate crowds.

The cart clattered past diplomatic residences, discreet little boutiques and modern restaurants full of fashionably dressed professionals. They were places Fin had been on many occasions, people Fin would have known and drunk with. But he remained on the cart, safe in the comforting arms of the rubbish and the unquestioning kindness of the driver in his one-button suit.

The cart cut across the island and turned south journeying through an oasis of parks and the stone grottoes where the Fish Garden began – places that by day were a verdant refuge from the relentless bustle of the city, places where students would play truant and lovers hide and kiss. The sound of traffic faded to nothing alongside the pampered trees of the Gezira Sporting Club, but the idyll ended as they cut back across the island and the enormous concrete erection of the Cairo Tower loomed over them. Stretched out in the damp *zibbala*, Fin watched the tower's floodlit latticed concrete pass shakily through the sky. He remembered commenting on its ugliness to an Egyptian girlfriend. She had told him proudly that it was meant to be ugly, swearing that it had been financed with a bribe that the CIA had given to President Nasser. Nasser had taken their money but rather than give them the favours they sought, he built a concrete tower, a rude gesture, an erect middle finger, telling America where to go. Fin remembered that it was not so long ago that he too had tried to make a grand political gesture against an American.

Fin slumbered as the cart rattled back into the city across Tahrir Bridge, past the presidential palace and into historical Cairo, moving ever slower as the haul of waste grew taller. When the *zibbaleen* shook Fin awake, the streets had narrowed into lanes and the tarmac had become dirt. Where he was next going, he signed to Fin, was not a place for a *ferenghi*. But he would return if the *ferenghi* wished.

Fin yawned and looked around him. He did not know where he was. There were broken walls beside them and lights beyond. As always in Cairo, the rubble could have been a building site or an ancient ruin. Above them rose the black silhouette of a minaret. Fin slid off the cart and reached for his wallet, but the *zibbaleen* brushed his gesture away with a sharp wave. Fin took the *zibbaleen*'s right hand between his and thanked him. The man removed his hand, slid it under his jacket and pressed his heart. He touched his forehead, his left then right shoulder, kissed his fingers and whispered, '*Bissm al-saleeb*,' a phrase Fin had never heard before. Fin stood and watched as the *zibbaleen* pointed his donkeys towards a richly overflowing dustbin further down the street.

Fin headed towards light. It had always been his habit to walk in the middle of any street, particularly in the older parts of the city. In this way, he would tell himself with a shred of truth, he would avoid the open sewers, broken drains and the sudden deluges of dishwater from which the inhabitants' innate radar seemed to protect them. Now, as his beggarly condition attracted looks of disgust and antipathy from every passer-by, he moved to the edges, to the shadows of the crumbling walls.

From such a vantage point, he was able to observe the effect of his filth upon the eyes of the compulsively clean Cairenes. As he absorbed the fleeting looks of disgust, he realised the humiliating scorn his own gaze had so often contained. Shuffling damply in and out of the shadows, he came to understand that a part of his very deportment, even the physical position he would take on a path or in a room, had played out an unquestioned assumption of entitlement, and his protective layers of self-respect were no more than a costume.

Bright fluorescent lights and blaring Egyptian pop music announced a gleaming shopfront. Its doors and window were wedged open, wafting sickly snatches of mock-rose incense. Swatches of perfectly folded galabeyas arced across the display windows, the fan of colours dazzling amid the greys and browns of the darkened street. Fin ran a blackened hand through his mat of still-damp hair and dislodged a lank ribbon of river weed. He shuffled up to the shop door against which the proprietor leant gazing with pride and wonder at his mobile telephone. The man looked up as Fin neared and stared at him. Fin took this as permission to enter, but as he crossed the threshold, the man waved him away. Fin addressed him in English hoping to counteract the squalor he signified but the language of his appearance, and perhaps his smell as well, were too strong to be contradicted. The proprietor unleashed a tirade of insults, turning his head and flicking his hands away from him as if trying to rid them of something foul.

Fin pulled his wallet out of his jacket pocket and

unpeeled a damp bill from within. He waved it in front of the shopkeeper, repeating that all he wanted was to buy a galabeya. The shopkeeper ceased his threats for a moment and squinted at the note. Hesitantly, he reached his arm out through the door and took the sodden banknote between his forefinger and thumb. He placed it on an old copy of *Al-Ahram* and wiped his hands on a swatch of material which he then threw into the street with an oath. Flashing his eyes over Fin to establish his size, the shopkeeper turned and withdrew the pure white bar of a folded galabeya from a shelf above his head. He placed it in a brown paper bag which he folded and sealed with a square of yellowing Sellotape. He counted out a few crisp bills and shining coins from a cash till and, without crossing the threshold, placed the money on the ground in front of Fin. Fin picked it up and pointed to his bare feet.

'*Gazma*?'

The shopkeeper came back, threw a pair of old plastic sandals into the street and turned away, slamming the door behind him.

After pushing his feet into the shoes, Fin looked up to find a small knot of people had gathered to watch the goings-on. Ashamed he retreated into an alleyway and hurried away, his new galabeya tucked securely under his arm.

Fin soon found himself in a broader cleaner street, and paused to watch a woman in full burka, her eyes masked, hands gloved, unwrapping a lollipop for her wailing child. Pulling off the last corner of wrapping, she flicked it from her glove and let it fall to the ground while plugging the sugary treat into the open mouth of the toddler. Fin moved his eyes to the cellophane wrapper floating to the ground undisturbed by the slightest breeze. He wondered how long the clear plastic would remain there and whom, if anyone, would claim it. Perhaps it would be his new friend, the *zibbaleen*. It was possible.

As Fin's thoughts drifted, the woman became aware of him and, turning her back to protect her child from his intrusive gaze, cursed him. Fin did not begrudge her enmity. He felt that all his shady characteristics had seeped out of his skin, saturating his linen suit. Yet even if he now felt at home amid the dirt and the chaos, there was the violence he had met in the city to consider, violence on top of hollow disappointment – he would never feel at home with this. It was best perhaps to go, pack up his few things and take off, like an apple loosing from an upside-down tree. Break away and flee. He could get on a plane and leave it all behind. The shoddy empty world of the newspaper, the professional brutality of the American, the shallow promises of a dried-up city. He could leave Omar, leave Farouk and the other fifteen million people of Cairo to the feuds of their decaying overpopulated city.

Fin shuddered to think what might happen to Farouk if he left. Arms bound with wire, terrified, his frail anatomy receiving the full force of a small man's hate. Fin gripped his new galabeya crinkling in its flimsy packet. It had only been a few hours. Would Farouk be dead by now? Certainly he would be damaged – twisted and beaten until something broke, something worse than the fractured leg of the young girl. 'Seven thousand times worse,' Omar had promised. And could Farouk really have done such a thing? Driven into a child and left her screaming on the street? Fin thought of Farouk's fierce passions, his sense of honour, the ideas he would rant about with such force and abandon. Were they mere words, arid words from a thin man's whispering, with no more significance than the sound of the wind in the papyrus? Perhaps there was a certain justice in Omar's action, a natural justice that the police and courts could never attain. Fin shook his head in disgust. How many rabbits' lives, how much of their blood, did Farouk think it would take to wash away the screams of a young girl?

It was hard to believe Farouk had committed such a crime. One hundred thousand moments of his petty tyranny could not add up to this one act. It could not be so. Fin did not want to believe in a hollowness so total. The city was corrupt, swarming with bent police, unprincipled newspaper editors, American thugs and child-hurting hypocrites. If this was all there was, there was nothing to keep Fin. It was time to move on.

12

With his customary sense of indirection, Fin had walked in a large circle. Ahead rose the same minaret where the *zibbaleen* had left him half an hour before. He saw now that this was the minaret of Ibn Tulun, unmistakable with its spiralling staircase elegantly twisting round a square tower, itself melting into a curve. Fin loved this mosque, for its extraordinary shape and its antiquity, for the twenty thousand of the city faithful who had worshipped under its roof in the ninth century, for the legend of the lion with blue eyes kept by Ibn Tulun's son as he passed his days floating on a cork mattress in an artificial lake filled with mercury, for the great Ottoman emir who had ridden his horse up the spiral stairs and leapt off the summit into paradise. For Fin there was a truth in these stories more potent than history, a truth he could touch in each of the baked bricks of the great structure. Although he was not a Muslim, nor even a Cairene, Fin loved the mosque of Ibn Tulun, listing as it did against the blue-black sky.

He peered through the high rectangular doorway of the mosque and slipping off his shoes crept in like a beggar stealing into a palace. He kept to the walls, moving along the shadows under the ancient wood panels engraved with the entire text of the Koran. Farouk had assured him that the wood for these panels had been taken from Noah's Ark and was furious when Fin expressed a minute level of dissent by the merest raising of an eyebrow.

Fin hid in the darkness of a corner and, through an arch which seemed to be waiting for a giant key, he observed two men walking and quietly conversing. Beyond, Fin could see an open dimly lit room, with carpets laid upon carpets and motionless oil lanterns hanging from impossibly long ropes. Fin crept on, keeping close to the walls and avoiding the pools of light thrown by the flickering lamps. He hoped that if he skirted the vast courtyard he would discover the *fawarah*, the washing area common to all mosques, but after walking the entire perimeter, Fin could find no indication of where it might be.

Paths of whitened stone criss-crossed the immense square, radiating in from the corners and midpoints of each wall and meeting at a magnificent dome at the centre. Fin walked round again, grateful that the penultimate prayer for the day, the *Salaat el-maghrib*, had long since passed and the mosque was almost empty. At the end of his second circumnavigation, Fin sat down on the cool stone floor. He began pulling and picking at his clothes, trying to separate them from his skin, but succeeded only in permeating the air with the stink of the river and his own sweat.

The inside of his clothes was still damp and seamy, while the outside had set to a shell, as if sealing in the brutality of the last few hours. Fin longed to be clean, and now that he was within the mosque of Ibn Tulun, it was here he wanted to wash.

Fin peered through the arch before him, pointed like an Ottoman helmet, and beyond it, the curiously domed structure in the middle of the empty square, a perfect almost inexplicable meeting of plane and curve. He rose and set off towards the dome, his feet pitter-pattering across the deserted courtyard. Inside the dome was a vaulted chamber, empty and dark but for a silver shaft of moonlight beaming through a slit in the magnificent curved roof. Beneath it was a single modern tap mounted at waist height on the ancient stone.

Fin turned to the four corners of the courtyard to make sure he was alone, exulting in its profound spaciousness as if the vast emptiness enclosed by the walls concentrated empty space into peace. Fin removed his mud-stiffened jacket and still sodden shirt. The tap gave easily and gushed out cold clean water. Water – the medium of his defilement; it would be his salvation.

He let the water flow over his hands and head, upon his face, in his mouth, up and out of his nose. He washed his neck and arms, his torso. Fin longed for a part of him to disappear with the filth, to be washed away for ever.

Fin rose and, seeing no one in the brightening moonlight, stripped off his trousers, and after another look slipped off his shorts and stood naked. He crouched under the tap again and gasped under the freezing water flowing over him like a blessing. He scrubbed and rubbed, forcing himself to stay under until every part of him, every limb, crease and wrinkle, was washed. When he turned off the water a caesura of velvety silence enveloped him. As he rose, the familiar sounds of the city resumed and Fin stood naked and still, drops of water falling from him, striking the stone floor like strange music.

When he was dry he took the pure white galabeya from its packet and pulled the light cloth over his head. It floated down over his body like a state of grace.

Fin walked out of the mosque, no longer furtive, enjoying the moon shadows cutting softly across the stone floors, his suit a heavy bundle in his left hand. When he got home he would take it to the cleaner's at the bottom of El-Mahahdi Street. The indefatigable ancient who ran the shop was sure to have a relation who could mend its rents and tears.

As he turned out of a narrow street into a road alive with traffic he saw his friend the *zibbaleen*, his tower of refuse teetering behind the two straining donkeys.

'*Ya, besh! Ferenghi!*' the *zibbaleen* shouted, drawing up in front of Fin. The man nodded at the dirty bundle Fin was holding and pointed back to his rubbish cart with a smile. '*Zibbala lil-zibbaleen.*' Rubbish for the rubbish people.

Fin regarded his suit, once precious, now a sodden shapeless lump. He turned away from his new friend and secreted fifty Egyptian into the bundle before tossing it onto the cart. The *zibbaleen* raised his hand and the cart clattered off.

Fin paused to allow a car to pass. Its driver was simultaneously engaged in lighting a cigarette, talking on his mobile phone and shouting a benevolent insult to a passing acquaintance. As he crossed the road Fin thought again of Farouk and Omar's daughter, and although he could hold in his mind the motion of a car and could make himself hear the screams of a little girl, he could not place Farouk, the car and the girl all in the same place at the same time. Not with Farouk driving away. It was not possible. It did not fit. It was not the Farouk he knew, not the friend, not the man, not the Arab.

Fin stopped short at a realisation so obvious he knew immediately that it was true.

Farouk had only recently bought the car. When the girl was hit, it had not been his. The car had struck the girl, but the previous owner had been the driver. The previous owner was the guilty man. Not Farouk.

But even if Farouk were innocent, what could Fin do to help him? He didn't know who Omar was or where he lived. How could he find him among the fifteen million people in Cairo? What was he supposed to do? Put posters up? Put an advertisement in the paper – 'Desperately seeking dwarf'? And in any event, he pleaded with himself, if he did find him, what then? Fin would rather face a rabid dog than Omar's concentrated ferocity. Fin decided he would call Farouk's wife, tell her what he knew, then see when the next flight to Europe left.

Fin looked up and saw that he was beneath a wooden causeway, high above the street that joined two old houses. A man was shouting from a frail balcony no broader than a branch to a boy grilling cobs of bleached corn on a makeshift brazier. Fin walked on past another old mosque, fourteenth or fifteenth century, hardly old in this city of five thousand years. Perhaps it was the city's great age that made Fin love her. If it were antiquity that bewitched him, it was not just the reassurance of a past, it was something else. It was the chorus of deterioration. Rubble everywhere, modern dwellings leaning upon ancient monuments like card houses, tower blocks riddled with cracks or collapsed, listing minarets and mosque walls severed by vertical canyons of subsidence. Age stood whispering impermanence, calling to Fin that, flawed as he was, insignificant as he was, history was woven out of tiny threads of life like him but that he too would decay and crumble.

If he departed, Fin would miss Cairo. It was dirty and incessant, but good-natured and tolerant. Strewn with rubbish too, he thought, as he sidestepped a smashed-up sewing machine, wedged in the dirt as if it had been thrown from an aeroplane or had pushed its way through the dry ground like a sprouting seed. Cairo was an impossibly demanding mistress who at some point Fin had decided to love – beyond judgement, beyond exasperation and beyond understanding. Fin sat down at an outdoor table in front of an establishment he hoped was a café and ordered a tea from a boy he hoped was a waiter.

13

Many people, Fin had noticed, lost their appetite when under great pressure. Except when he was ill or on the lone occasion he'd passed a foodless week contemplating a quiet suicide, Fin was always hungry. So it was simple. Fin thought, he lost his appetite only when he was sick, and now, although he had a bruise on his leg that resembled a twilight sky, and had experienced more violence in the past few days than his entire life before, he was definitely not sick. In fact he felt good. With this in mind, and with a lack of choosiness that was uncharacteristic, indeed testament to the traumas of the past hours, he asked the waiter to bring him a lamb kebab, a glass of melon juice and – seeing as he had missed breakfast – a plate of *foul medames*.

It was dark in the heart of Cairo. Dark and warm. There was a point after sunset, Fin remembered, a moment when the temperature of the air was suddenly cooler than the ground temperature. It was at this point that a curious circumstance occurred, known as Evening Inversion. To the chemical weapons specialists, who were the first to explain it, the phenomenon represented a key moment for the effective delivery of their poison. At least that is what a homesick British major had told Fin as they had worked their way through colonial-strength gin and tonics in the not-so-Grand Bar of the Windsor Hotel. Whatever was in the air, the major had explained with an innocent excitement, would rise away from the warm earth just after the sun disappeared, only to come falling down within the hour on the rapidly cooling surface below.

To Fin, a troubled man slowly sipping a glass of pale-jade juice underneath a heavily blooming jasmine tree in the Islamic quarter of Cairo, evening inversion brought with it a deluge of perfume and a flash of happiness. So what if he didn't have a clue what to do with his life? So what if he spent so much energy on empty dreams and self-destruction that there was little left over to build anything? So what if he had been struck like an errant boy and the part of him that was man rather than human was still shaking. Here he was, an anonymous and irrelevant stranger watching this world, breathing in the jasmine and feeling his fingers around the once-cool glass.

People were driving, walking, shuffling home, fruit was being bought; lights were being lit; dogs were curring about; tea was being brewed, huge weeping sacks of rice unloaded and impossibly carried to and fro; cigarettes being hawked and sold in singles to serious-faced men with briefcases to be saved or smoked, children with sticky eyes were looking for a breast; shoes clip-clopping past, flip-flops, plastic loafers, leather bests, netlike slippers, bare horny feet. Cars were honking, neighbours greeting, husbands or children scolded; far off a donkey brayed and food sellers sung their wares. Everything here was part of life, but strange and unexpected and so mysterious, and in that mystery Fin glimpsed that only in his head did fears and torment thrive. Regardless of what happened to him the leaves would stay on the trees, babies would scream and lights would be lit and quenched.

'*Bil-hanah wil-shiffa.*' The waiter drove away all thoughts as he deposited the plate of kebab and pale beans in front of Fin.

Fin thanked the waiter's sweat-stained back and considered his words: '*Bil-hanah wil-shiffa*' – eat and be happy with good health.

Fin spooned up a mouthful of the beans. It was hard to destroy *foul medames*, but they had almost succeeded. The beans were overcooked, the tomatoes stewed and the poor dish drenched in stale garlic. Nevertheless, it was still acceptable. A little more salt and a thick pinch of cumin would improve matters. This was the sort of thing Fin understood automatically. Why could it not be the same with all other parts of his life?

Fin picked up the kebab, hoping for something delicious. He took a bite. The meat was tough and greasy – overcooked, underspiced lumps of an old ram that should have been allowed to see out its dotage in the rubbish dump it called home. Fin shook his head. Farouk had once told him not to expect poems of love from the arse of a goat. He smiled, thinking of Farouk's endless pronouncements, and pushed away the plastic plate. A nostalgia for all the great kebabs he had eaten lingered in his mouth, each remembered like an old friend. Abu El Sid's in Zamalek – an upmarket place with a svelte waitress he had tried to date. The kebab his friend Zaki had prepared in the City of the Dead. The new stands on King Faisal Road that he had written about with such passion. And of course Ismael Kebap's notorious 'chip-kebabwich' on Merrion Road, Dublin, could not easily be forgotten, although no one, to Fin's knowledge, had ever eaten one sober, and ... Fin sat up with a start as he remembered the kebab he had eaten with Omar.

That kebab – the perfect meat, sesame seeds and clouds of thyme enveloping each morsel – had been up there with the greats. Fin wondered whether the use of thyme was an innovation. He was sure he had not tasted it before, not on any of the countless kebabs he had eaten and he was always extending his food frontiers. A man 'seeking truth in things he could taste', that is what Farouk had said.

He would follow the kebab. If he could find the restaurant Jalut had gone to, he might find Farouk. No one travelled far to find a kebab. That was a truth of life. And the thug had been away for less than half an hour. If he could find the right kebab shop, he would have found the right neighbourhood, and then, at the very least, he would be on his way to finding his friend.

It was not the most impressive of plans, Fin thought, but it was a step. And he knew where to start. Where else but the King Faisal Road? Half a mile of new businesses and modern kebab shops. The new shrine on the kebab pilgrimage. A dish like the one he had eaten with Omar was surely good enough to be traceable. It had to be. Fin was uncertain about most things in life, had found disappointment in places where most people had found satisfaction – in family, in friends, in love, work and chiefly in himself – but food had never let him down.

He left money on the table and flagged down a passing taxi.

14

Fin leant back against the taxi's threadbare foam. He felt an indistinct sense of relief. Indistinct but palpable. This was a good sign. He would try at least. Farouk would do the same for him, he was certain. Fin mapped the bruise on his leg with his fingertips and pondered what he had done to precipitate the current mess. He was accustomed to being both perpetrator and victim of his own abuse. He tried to press away the throbbing in his temples and wondered if Omar's whisky was about to hit him with the dry claw of a hangover, or whether it was the aftershock of the blow to the back of his head. He closed his eyes and allowed his head to fall back. He did not want to think too much, especially about kebabs. Too close scrutiny of his plan might result in a complete, and possibly appropriate, loss of confidence. He would search the King Faisal Road, and should he, as was very likely, be unable to achieve a positive identification of the kebab in question, he would accept that he was beaten and hand over the matter to Farouk's wife. She would know people, have contacts or relations who might do something, although by then it would probably be a case of paying Farouk's hospital bills.

The King Faisal Road was busy, as it was twenty hours a day, slowing down only between eight in the morning and noon. Eighteen months before it had been little more than a dirt road, but now cars, trucks and the ubiquitous minibuses filled four lanes of staggering, honking traffic that moved slower than the old one-legged beggar doddering along the roadside with a discarded golf club for a crutch.

Fin strolled down King Faisal Road enjoying the breezy flap of his galabeya. The eddies of air that wafted about his body and in particular his sexual organs were delightful. Judging by the lack of attention, people did not seem to think it was remarkable that he should be wearing such apparel. In fact, no one seemed to notice him at all. It had taken him two years to follow the two-thousand-year-old example of the vast majority of the male population of Cairo. Fin now wondered if his Western clothes, particularly his soiled white suit, had served nothing but his desire to be special.

Now he felt liberated by his insignificance.

A strip of shops stretched a mile along each side of King Faisal Road no more than a storey high but with metal foundations reaching up like ugly ambitions, eager for the next level. Banks, butchers, television repair shops, mobile phone outlets and, as with all parts of Cairo, places to eat, open for business at all hours and full of people, as they would be throughout the warm night.

Global brands jostled for space on posters, flashing neon signs and hand-painted murals. Outside each building air-conditioning units hung like industrial ticks sucking out the warm air and excreting in the cold. On flat rooftops battalions of satellite dishes clustered like artificial sunflowers tropeing towards a metal sun. People everywhere thronged, chatting, buying, eating, gossiping, arguing, laughing, pulling carts, heaving shopping, talking on mobile phones and holding hands. It was not, Fin thought, an attractive road, but it was impossible to resist its vivacity, its joyful conviviality, its delight in progress, its promise of chaos and growth. And of course, Fin thought, scanning the road for the shops he'd reviewed, its kebabs.

Fin could no longer recognise which establishments he had visited for his article. Since then new buildings had sprouted, splashed with vibrant colours, signed with the curves, dots and swoops of Arabic script. Had Waled not smoked most of Fin's cherished newspaper article early that morning, Fin would have returned home and scanned it for clues of where to begin.

Fin forced himself towards the nearest shop, which was emblazoned with a cartoon of an obese Ali Baba. He crossed the threshold and ordered a shish, knowing before it arrived that it would not be the one. He could see that the cubes of meat were too small, eliminating any possibility of succulence and with that any possibility of it being the kebab he sought. He had to trust that the meat at Omar's had not been produced by serendipity, an accident from an otherwise mediocre kitchen. He must believe that it was part of a consistent standard of excellence achieved through passion and hard work, a virtuoso performance that could be re-enacted and so rediscovered.

Fin walked out of the shop and handed the untouched kebab to the one-legged beggar with the golf club, who was now sitting on the pavement. The man unwrapped the package and rolled the meat about, surveying it with a critical eye. He too seemed dissatisfied, perhaps with the quantity of meat or the shape and smell of the pickle. Grudgingly, after muttering complaints to himself and God, he began to eat. Fin coughed for his attention and asked him if he knew where the best kebab was to be found. The man looked at him in irritation. Couldn't Fin see he was eating? He waved Fin away.

Fin moved on to other shops, quickly devising an orderly system to his investigation. He would observe the premises, swing in, order a shish, smell, bite, chew and walk out. As far as tasks went it was one of the more enjoyable things he had done. But by now, six kebabs later and only half a mile down one side of the road, Fin had begun to wonder if his strategy was more the result of the whisky he'd been coerced into drinking than the functioning of his rational mind. The notion that he would be able to recognise Omar's kebab was becoming ridiculous. The most recent kebab had bedevilled Fin's search by being impressively tender and juicy but there had been no trace of the thyme that had distinguished the meat in Omar's little torture chamber. Fin asked the proprietor if he ever used the herb za'atar. The man seemed to understand, nodded enthusiastically and disappeared into a back room. He returned triumphantly with a can of Russian salad and a wilted cucumber.

Leaning against a dusty still-warm wall, feeling full and unsatisfied, Fin thought he should go home and call Farouk's wife. He didn't know what she could do, but at least it wouldn't all be down to him. Fin closed his eyes and sank into the warmth of the stone, the violence and dramas of the day and the food in his belly pulling him towards sleep.

As he flicked and sank into unconsciousness a delicious aroma wafted into Fin's nostrils and snaked its way into the antechamber of his dreams. A faint cloud of roast meat mingled with onions, sesame and fresh warm garlic. Fin opened his eyes to find a young man standing a few feet in front of him in a spotless white galabeya and skullcap, thoughtfully eating a kebab. Fin stepped closer and peered over his shoulder.

The man, feeling Fin's gaze, turned to catch him staring at his supper. The young man's face was kind and open with a broad forehead, wide smile-wrinkled eyes and the wispy ungroomed beard of a devout young Muslim. Fin could not take his eyes off the man's kebab; it looked so right. He wondered if there were sesame seeds, like even grains of oval sand, on the hidden side of the meat.

Fin pointed to the kebab. '*Kebab fayn?*' he asked.

The man pointed to the nearest kebab shop, the one Fin had just exited. Fin shook his head and gestured emphatically at the man's supper.

'*Kebab fayn*, where?'

The man was puzzled, but seeing Fin staring at his dinner, he tore his kebab in half, keeping the ragged part his mouth had touched, and wrapped the neat remainder in paper, which he presented to Fin. Fin shook his head and thanked the man with his hand on his heart.

'*Fayn? Fayn? Fayn?*' Fin repeated, pointing in all directions, emphasising each point with an exaggerated shrug of his shoulders.

The man nodded, gestured to the far end of the road and then hurried away in the opposite direction as if he had just remembered a pressing engagement. Fin could not tell whether the man thought he was crazed or had misunderstood the question, but headed off in the direction indicated.

Fin wove his way through thick clumps of people, crossing side streets and dodging bicycles, sidestepping piles of cement and half-covered building equipment. After a hundred-yard stretch entirely taken up by competing mobile-telephone suppliers, squeezed together as if this were the only thing people needed, Fin came across a kebab shop – dazzling orange, gleaming with care, medically clean. Fin stood outside for a moment, catching his breath before stepping in.

Behind a counter of polished chrome and invisible glass two cooks laboured with the practised grace of martial artists. Piles of clementines, melons, strawberries and mangoes were stacked in neat pyramids at one end of the counter. At the other was the *shwarma*, fat columns of layered lamb interleaved with garlic and herbs, turning lingeringly in front of three walls of heat. Cooking, then resting; cooking, then resting; being guided, Fin could see, towards an elusive goal of crispiness and succulence.

The *shwarma* cook toasted pitta bread, selected the freshest leaves of taut green lettuce, sliced green chillies and chubby gherkins, and with an accomplished sweep of his arm drizzled an ivory arabesque of *tahina* onto each serving. Despite this perpetual motion, a part of the cook's attention remained with the meat, his knife arcing through the air at sporadic intervals, slicing off perfect slivers that fell like ripe fruit onto the soft white carpet of the waiting bread.

Next to the *shwarma* was an ash-white furnace of

charcoal where the shish specialist stood. Before him a banquet of skewers were stacked to their tips with lamb, liver and what Fin suspected were the more exotic organs of familiar beasts. The cook's gaze was fixed in the space above the meat as he twisted the skewers in tiny increments, this way and that, as if tuning a complex musical instrument. Fin watched him, intrigued that there was no apparent schedule to the rotation. The cook never looked directly at the skewers, or even picked them up, except when, in an unbroken reflex, he selected a thick black arrow of glistening meat, and, placing a fork at the top of the skewer, drew it back like a Mameluke bowman, tumbling cubes of meat onto a waiting plate. This, thought Fin with a shiver of excitement, must be the place.

Fin pointed to one of the skewers of uncooked lamb interleaved with thick slices of onion.

'Shish kebab.'

Fin had once flushed with pride as he was told that when ordering food he spoke like a fifth-generation Cairene.

The cook nodded briskly and swivelled back to his grill and his nudging and shuffling of the meat. Fin surveyed the perfectly stacked piles of fruit glistening from a recent spray of water. Juice would be good, he thought to himself, inherently virtuous. Water of course was more virtuous, but juice was exciting, almost a cocktail.

'Asseer manga,' he ordered, glancing at the mangoes.

The cook spun back to him, a slight crease of discontent in his brow. Fin repeated his request and the cook shook his head. 'No juice,' he said, his whole body negating Fin's request and any relevance implied by the great piles of fruit.

Fin stared pointedly at the perfectly ripe mangoes, the metal juicer gleaming like a sergeant's badge and the three-foot-high pink flashing neon sign that he assumed proclaimed the word 'juice'. Fin considered the situation for a moment then turned away. Two years in Cairo and he had learnt not to pursue such cases. Pushing hard for an explanation in matters such as this, even if he could make himself understood, would produce at best only an echo of the question and, more often, something completely misleading. This Cairene paradox was, Fin had once extemporised to a honeymooning German couple in a bar in Alexandria, an example of Heisenberg's Uncertainty Principle. The more effort one expended to find out what something meant, the more one changed the results, and the further away one took oneself from any possibility of an accurate result. Any act of observation and enquiry changed the object observed and enquired after. In truth he was not sure that this was Heisenberg's Uncertainty Principle, but the Germans had looked nervous. At the time he had felt that it was good for morale to carry about a tool from quantum physics in his armoury, and now it was certainly better than losing himself in a needlessly juiceless world.

Fin sat down at a nearby table, absorbed in the cooks' precision. From a radio turned up beyond its capacity an Egyptian singer crackled into a mournful distorted song. By the second phrase he knew it could be none other than Umm Kulthum, the most beloved Egyptian woman since Nefertiti. As Fin wondered what he would do if his kebab search proved futile, a part of him gazed at his reflection in the gold-tinted mirror of the wall. His Nile baptism had made his hair billow into a thick bouffant like a Hindi action hero on a painted poster. Humming along to the mournful genius of the diva's song, he cast himself as a romantic lead, irresistible to the soft eyes of a conjured-up screen princess. She would be made entirely of love; he, a man of action ready to save the day by discovering the secrets of the kebab.

His dream evaporated as the music faded into news and he was left with the visible reality of his own puff-eyed reflection and the recognition that there was no way *Following the Kebab* was going to hold up, even in fiction. Fin looked around. The waiter was approaching with his clue on a shining white plate. Fin laughed at himself with familiar cruelty. He would look, taste, chew and then swallow his defeat and go home. Later, he would change back into Western clothes and perhaps ask one of the embassy boys at the Bar Odeon what he should do about Farouk.

The plate was placed in front of him and rotated a quarter turn so that its elements were in their proper position: a little pyramid of delicately charred kebabs and thick glistening slices of onion, a generous handful of bright green parsley and a bank of warm toasted pitta bread. There was no room for this dish and negative thoughts. He needed an answer. Fin bent over the meat breathing in its scents, his eyes closed in concentration. The waiter placed a bowl next to him piled high with *torshi* – thick slices of pickled turnip stained pink with vinegar.

Fin sat up, selected a thick round of the pickle and took a bite. It crunched and tasted of the earth as if it had been lifted from the ground only moments before. Fin loved *torshi*, the taste, the colour, the plastic five-gallon jars in which they were kept. He loved the way each home-made pickle would describe the household of its creation, in its own language of vinegar, colour and crunch. He loved the way women would lift the heavy jars from the high shelves where they were always stored, and the sound of the heavy red plastic lids as they twisted open like a duck's quack in reverse. He loved the treasures that would arise dripping from the vinegar: the chilli, the cucumber, the radish or best of all the turnip . . .

Fin shook his head and swore at himself. There was no point delaying. He picked up a soft cube of meat with his fingers and tossed it into his mouth. He rolled it around his tongue, feeling it tumble, savouring the film of flavour. He muddled it to the back of his mouth and held it gently between his teeth, letting it sit for a moment untouched, resisting the urge to bite until the tension became almost erotic. He knew already, but he wished to play it, enjoy his success before the acknow-ledgement of a fact that would require further action. He bit down and closed his eyes as the rich juices filled his mouth, the deep dimensionality of meat flooding down through his spine, garlic and cumin rising up to the roof of his mouth. He drew in his cheeks and tumbled the meat ninety degrees, squeezing his teeth down and exhaling . . . There it was, a breath of thyme.

He opened his eyes. This was the place, there was no doubt. This was the kebab he sought.

The outside world, however, was unaffected by his dis-covery. The chefs in front of him maintained their relaxed precision, pausing only to sip water from tiny chipped glasses.

Fin did not need to eat any more, but entertaining the

illusion that he was turning over the new possibilities of this lead, he continued to turn the meat over in his mouth, enjoying its perfection. When he had eaten every morsel, Fin rose and approached the cooks. Aware of his approach and accustomed to the effusive compliments that followed their efforts, they sliced, turned and seasoned their ingredients with extra flourish.

'Do you know Omar?' asked Fin.

The cooks stopped their work and turned to look at him. They said nothing.

'Omar. Small man. *Shwaya* – little,' Fin explained, pinching his fingers together. The cooks stared at him.

'Omar, tiny,' he insisted, indicating Omar's height with his hand.

'Mister Balesh?' The *shwarma* chef ventured uncertainly, reaching up and turning off the radio. He looked nervously at the door and then began wiping his hands on a cloth, then polishing the already immaculate countertops.

They knew Omar.

'Omar . . . Mister Balesh,' the kebab chef murmured. 'This, Mister Balesh shop. Look.' He pointed to the illuminated neon sign that Fin had assumed read 'juice'. '"Balesh Kebab" . . . You see?'

'Omar is Balesh, Balesh Kebab!' Fin exclaimed. '*Shwaya*. Omar. Small,' he said, emphasising his words with a gesture, 'You know him?' They nodded as if they wished they did not, their confidence and professional grace now vanished.

'Please give me his telephone number. He has a telephone?'

The men shook their heads and turned away. A

good day had soured and they wanted no more to do with Fin.

'*Shokran, shokran gazilan,*' Fin said, putting a generous tip on the counter.

15

Fin strolled along King Faisal Road, the injury on his thigh momentarily forgotten. It was pleasant to be outside after the heat and intensity of Omar's kebab shop. Following the trail of the kebab had been successful and rewarding. Not only had he discovered Omar's identity, but his business as well. Finding Farouk would be only a matter of time, he thought, as he stumbled over a man slumped asleep on a chair in the middle of the walkway.

'Excuse me,' Fin said automatically.

'*Malesh*,' the man grunted without opening his eyes, assuring Fin with one word that he was forgiven. People passed without the slightest sign of interest as if they accepted the logic of the man's choice of place for a rest.

Sensing that Fin was still standing over him, the man opened his eyes and held out his mobile telephone.

'Call, sahib? One Egyptian pound per minute, special price for you. Please, make a call. You are welcome. You are from . . .'

Fin had long ceased answering questions like this. The man was wearing a smart business suit, shirt and tie and Fin noticed a handwritten sign taped to the back of his chair. He could not translate the writing but there was no mistaking the Arabic numbers: '0.50'. Fin pointed to the sign and asked the man if the price was not fifty piastres. The man loosened his tie and yawned as if overwhelmed by ennui for a world in which so much explanation was required.

'Of course, sahib. Fifty piastres for the call and fifty piastres for my work. Total one Egyptian pound. Super-deluxe service for you. Five-star.' He wafted the phone at Fin.

Fin took the telephone and dialled Information. A few words with an English-speaking operator confirmed that there was no telephone listing for Omar Balesh.

Fin closed the telephone and placed it and a banknote in the top pocket of the recumbent entrepreneur, who grunted again and raised his hand a few inches in acknowledgement before sighing himself back into the arms of sleep.

As Fin walked off wondering how much baksheesh it might take to inveigle Omar's address from the terrified cooks, a piercing screech seized his attention. Amid the rubble, plastic sheeting and exposed iron supports of the building site next to him a tomcat the size of a small bear was tearing clumps of fur and flesh from a younger scrawny male. The overpopulation of semi-feral cats in Egypt was granted a tolerance not extended to other stray animals. Perhaps it was a memory of their pharaonic significance, or the influence of the Prophet Muhammad (pbuh), who, it was said, had once cut round his shawl rather than disturb a sleeping cat.

Fin watched the mauled stray scratch up a vertical surface in panicked escape. Suddenly he understood that, even if he found Omar's home address, it was not in itself an answer to the problems that lay before him. Fin was no hero, he knew that. He was a binge-drinking ex-journalist with too few friends and no contacts in the local police force. If he stormed into Omar's abode on his own he would not escape with only scratches and lost clumps of fur. All he could do was find out if Farouk was innocent and then convince Omar that his draconian punishments were misdirected.

He had mentioned the girl's name. Nira, Omar had said. Nira Balesh. Somewhere in a Cairo hospital there must be a little girl called Nira Balesh lying like a broken bird.

Fin saw a queue of taxis parked across the road. He threaded his way through the traffic as it jolted and stalled. Seeing in Fin a potential customer the taxi drivers began vying for his attention. All the drivers but one were hissing, clicking, blowing kisses and waving their hands. The exception was standing nonchalantly away from the group, resplendent, and Fin supposed very hot, in a long leather coat so luminously brown it was yellow. His hair was sculpted like that of the models on the posters outside old Italian barbers in Dublin. The man was so absorbed in preening and filing his fingernails that he seemed not to notice Fin until the very moment Fin's eyes were on him, then he met Fin's gaze, nodded as if confirming an agreement, and walked over to him.

Fin stepped away from the man and made towards the other taxis, but the driver anticipated him and blocked his escape with a graceful sidestep.

'"The transport authority of Cairo,"' the driver announced, taking Fin's arm and propelling him towards his car, '"requires all taxi drivers to conduct themselves with integrity and good manners using the quickest route and charging the appropriate fare."' The driver took a breath. 'This is the code of the Cairo Taxi Service 1938, as written by the great English. I live by this code, sir. It is like my family, my religion. Please, I beg you, allow me.'

The driver opened the door to his car with such an irresistibly insincere smile that his ears moved and a vein pulsated over one eye. Fin's resolve disintegrated and he climbed in. The driver closed the door firmly and slid into the front seat, his leather coat screeching on the plastic seat covers.

'I am Wafeeq, and you are . . .?' he asked, turning. Fin noticed that Wafeeq's eyes floated in dark shadows of exhaustion like the black spots of a peacock's tail. Did no one sleep in this city?

'I am a man in a hurry who wishes to visit certain hospitals,' Fin began. 'In fact all the hospitals of Cairo . . .' He trailed off, noticing that Wafeeq was not listening. The driver was absorbed in contemplation of his mobile phone, which lay open and inert like a dormant oracle.

'You are special.' Wafeeq turned back to Fin. 'I can see this, my friend, believe me. We Egyptians can see things, things you will never know. You are special and you are lucky, a lucky man. Why? I will tell you why. You are in my cab, the cab of Wafeeq al-Sabaj, and I am taking you to the Temple of the Sacred Baboons.' He turned back to the wheel.

Fin tapped him on his worn leather shoulder and reiterated his request to be taken to a hospital, but Wafeeq was not to be swayed.

'A tour yes? A grand tour. First the baboon temple, then the mosque of . . .'

'Listen, my friend. I'm not interested in going to the Temple of the Sacred Baboons or any other non-existent or permanently closed archaeological site on the other side of Cairo. If you wish to go to such a place, you must do so in your own time or with some other fool. But if you wish to keep me in your car then you must drive me to a hospital to find a young girl. Do you understand me?' Fin asked, opening the passenger door.

'The pasha asks if I understand,' Wafeeq replied, turning round again and observing Fin with his bloodhound eyes. 'Of course I understand. I speak English; I speak German; I speak Russian; I speak Chinese. Many languages I speak. But when I dream it is in the language of the heart . . . The pasha is seeking a woman?'

'No, I'm looking for a girl in a hospital. Just take me to a hospital.'

'If the pasha wishes to visit all the hospitals of this great nation to find a girl, a woman, a boy, it's the same to me; I will take him. But on my wife's honour I must tell the pasha that there are many hospitals in this great city and the girl the pasha seeks might be in any of them. There are too many: some for the head, some for the stomach, some for the baby, some even for the making of breasts – I swear it is true. Two, three days it would take to see them all, more if God wills. Cairo is a great city, very great. The pasha should visit a café of Internet and there he will choose hospitals to visit.'

Befuddled by Wafeeq's transition from annoying to helpful, Fin was unsure how to proceed. There was no doubt that Wafeeq's suggestion was more practical than his own ill-formed plan.

'OK, get me to an Internet café in fifteen minutes, no

temples, no excuses, and I'll pay double the fare.'

Wafeeq nodded solemnly. 'Café of Internet in fifteen minutes. I am your slave, pasha. Command me. Whatever you wish, I will do.' As he spoke the telephone burst into life, blasting out the latest Egyptian pop song. Wafeeq paused and allowed the cacophony to grow before picking up the telephone, singing along with the chorus, and then, with the air of one burdened by enormous responsibilities, he turned off the engine, settled back into his seat and answered the call.

Fin could hear a woman shouting on the end of the line. As her rant gathered momentum, Wafeeq held the telephone away from his ear and grinned at Fin. He said little until the voice had expended its fury then he sat up and retaliated, gesticulating as if addressing a crowd of thousands like a fascist despot. They bartered anger for a few minutes, oblivious to Fin, then Wafeeq roared a parting volley of expletives and snapped the phone shut. He looked at Fin through the rear-view mirror and shrugged.

'Marital problems?' Fin asked to fill the silence.

'What does the pasha mean?' the driver replied, frowning.

'Problems with your marriage,' Fin explained, wishing he had not said anything.

'Why should there be a problem? My marriage is good, what is my marriage to you?' There was a note of hostility in his voice.

'Nothing, it's nothing to me,' Fin faltered. 'It's just you were arguing, I mean. I didn't want to sit here and listen. I want to get moving, but you and your wife were shouting and—'

'Ah, hahahahahaha.' The driver laughed, shaking his head and pointing at Fin through the rear-view mirror. 'You are special man. I knew this. It was not my wife I was speaking to, it was my girlfriend. A man should not shout at his wife, it is not correct … Anyway my wife lives in Alexandria three hours from here.'

Fin took a five-pound note from his wallet and waved it between the front seats.

'Only six minutes left.'

'The pasha makes a joke, yes?' Wafeeq said, turning away from the money. 'Very funny, you are very funny man, but I do not laugh … Double the fare is twenty pounds.'

'Do you think I am mad?' Fin countered. 'Ten pounds and not a piastre more.'

'You eat my head!' the driver shouted. 'Why does the pasha eat my head?' he cried, managing to make it sound like a real question. 'My head is not a pork burger from America; it is the head of an Egyptian who will one day perform the hajj and cleanse all sins. Fifteen Egyptian and I will drive the pasha to an Internet café in six minutes or may ten thousand jinn feast upon my *zobra*.'

'Done, but you have only four and a half minutes—' said Fin, his words cut off as he was thrown across the cab in a screeching U-turn and then thrust between the two front seats as Wafeeq stopped dead on the opposite side of the road. Wafeeq turned off the engine and looked round at Fin with an expression of profound satisfaction.

'If the pasha looks to the left he will see Mahmud's Internet and Communications Palace, and if the pasha searches in his fat-as-a-virgin-in-paradise wallet, he will find fifteen pounds for his driver.'

Recognising that protest would serve only to extinguish the fading embers of his dignity, Fin passed three five-pound notes to the driver and exited the car as Wafeeq's telephone burst once more into its execrable song.

Mahmud's Palace was no more than two computers, a crudely constructed telephone booth and a desk behind which sat a young woman. She gazed at a toddling infant, one of whose tiny arms was encased in yellow plaster. The woman's eyes were large and dark, her eyebrows like black zips. Her nose broadened down her face, separating her plump cheeks as if holding them apart to expose her full and beautiful mouth.

Feeling Fin's gaze like a groping hand, she flicked her scarf around her face and rose. She moved to the nearest computer and with intricately hennaed hands typed away at the keyboard script until a connection was established and the language on the screen hospitably changed to English.

Fin sat down and placed his hands over the Arabic letters of the keyboard, his fingers moving automatically over the keys to unearth the Roman text as if the communication between his touch and the machine worked on a deeper level. Within thirty minutes he had gathered the names and telephone numbers of Cairo's main hospitals. The page printed, he went to the telephone booth, list in hand. The young woman observed him without expression, rocking the child to sleep with a slow heavy rhythm, her blue headscarf making a tight oval of her face. Fin looked at her as he picked up the phone. She nodded.

He dialled the first number on his list and waited. There was no answer. Unsure if he had dialled correctly he replaced the handset and tried again. He counted twenty rings, then another twenty, imagining a brisk and starchy nurse marching along an empty corridor, coming to answer his questions. He waited. There was nothing. He replaced the receiver and tried once more, slowly and methodically, speaking the digits aloud as he pressed each button. The phone was answered before the first ring, but hearing a foreign voice they cut him off. Cursing, Fin tried again, launching into a hurried mix of Arabic and English. His resources were soon exhausted and his efforts at communication dwindled into a demoralised repetition of the little girl's name until he was again cut off.

Frustrated, Fin put down the phone and walked towards the door, signalling to the woman with his fingers a millimetre apart the amount of time he'd be gone. A group of twenty or thirty young men and women was sauntering past, chatting and laughing. People in Cairo seemed to enjoy their crowds, Fin mused. He had a theory that this crowd comfort was the fruit of having many neighbours – not just the person who lived to the right or left, but the people above, below, in the same building or even street. Neighbours held special status. Like relations, they were people God had chosen for your life and so they were to be treated with particular care and respect. Fin sighed. He was probably romanticising the situation; perhaps it was just that they lived in the most densely populated city on earth. Perhaps the ease Fin perceived was no more than a survival mechanism, a necessary tolerance rather than a gregarious pleasure.

The crowd passed and Fin noted that Wafeeq was still outside, leaning against his cab, smoking a cigarette. Fin set off towards him, an idea developing as he neared. Wafeeq's telephone sounded and he flicked it open on the

third dreadful note, cooing seductively into the mouthpiece as the exchange developed into giggles and what
seemed, at least by the tone, to be whispered smut. Fin
became embarrassed and wanted to return to the café, but
each time he made to leave Wafeeq's eyebrows called him
back. After a few minutes and a variety of grotesque phallic
gestures Wafeeq closed the phone. He sighed theatrically.

'Your wife? In Alexandria?'

'Alexandria. Yes, you are right. But not my wife. Another
woman, a lover, beautiful ... huge, like the sea in Alexandria. You should visit Alexandria, the most beautiful
beaches in the world. I will take you there now. I know a
very good hotel.'

'I don't want to go to Alexandria,' Fin replied. 'I need
your help. An important job.'

'I am your servant,' Wafeeq replied.

'There's money in it,' Fin said, hoping to fix his
attention.

'Money is not important, pasha; serving you is all I
wish,' he replied, glancing at his phone.

'Thank you,' said Fin without conviction. He took a
deep breath. 'I'm looking for a girl. Her name is Nira, Nira
Balesh. She was hit by a car. I want to know which hospital
she is in, but I can't make myself understood on the phone.
Twenty Egyptian if you can find her.'

'Fifty,' Wafeeq replied, seemingly absorbed in depress-
ing the cuticles of his fingernails with his car key.

'For what?' Fin demanded.

'For whatever the pasha wishes,' Wafeeq replied,
looking up into Fin's eyes.

'I will pay you thirty-five Egyptian,' Fin replied automatically, no longer caring if Wafeeq agreed.

'I am the pasha's slave.' Wafeeq locked his car and followed Fin into the shop.

Wafeeq placed his hand on his chest and bowed with sentimental sincerity to the woman in the blue scarf. He greeted her as if he had been waiting to meet her all his life, and they immediately launched into an animated discussion. Fin assumed their conversation concerned his quest but when he saw the woman smiling and intermittently hiding and uncovering her face with her shawl he knew that he had been forgotten. He began to fidget and cough discreetly. Wafeeq and the woman ignored him and within a few minutes she was trying on Wafeeq's coat, laughing and admiring herself in a small brass mirror Wafeeq had quick-drawn from his pocket with the words 'six-shooter'. Two loud coughs failed to attract Wafeeq's attention so Fin took him by the arm and guided him towards the telephone booth.

'Please, Wafeeq, I don't have much time.' Fin pointed to the telephone.

'Ah, pasha, life is full of turns like the path of a rabbit,' Wafeeq replied by way of an explanation. 'This woman, Mrs Mahmud, she knows the sister of one girlfriend.'

'Another girl from Alexandria?' Fin asked, pushing the telephone handset towards him.

'No, no the pasha is confused. A different woman. The girlfriend I was talking to on my telephone, she is from Alex and my wife also, she is from Alex, but the girlfriend whose sister is the friend of this woman, she is from Giza. It is too difficult in English.' He put the telephone back in its cradle.

'Difficult in any language,' Fin remarked.

'Pasha?'

'You have so many girlfriends,' Fin explained.

'Yes, yes, this is true – and not just because of my beauty. Before I was in the taxi, I cut the hair of women. In this you must keep the mind open, all the time open. When a woman gives you the power to make her beautiful,' he confided, 'she gives you her secrets, and if you possess the secrets of women, they must give you their love. For many women I am the victim of their love.'

'Yes, well, congratulations. Now please call the hospital.'

'Life is hard, pasha,' Wafeeq insisted, shaking his head. 'And women, they are soft and beautiful. I will tell you a secret' – he placed his hand on Fin's shoulder – 'I am famous for my lovemaking.'

Fin cut him off. 'Please, Wafeeq, the girl!' He took Wafeeq's hand from his shoulder and folded his fingers around the telephone.

'There is no need,' Wafeeq replied, replacing the handset and flicking out his mobile phone. 'I have a telephone. Look, it has video.' He pressed a button and the tinny pop song resumed its torturous melody. Wafeeq held the postage-stamp-sized screen in front of Fin on which a woman the size of a large ant was gyrating in harem pants and a sequinned bra. Fin turned away, overcome with a hopeless exhaustion and the knowledge that the viral chorus of the man's mobile phone was already embedding itself in his brain. He slumped into the nearest chair.

'Do not be sad. I tell you, pasha, this girl, this Miss Balesh, if you know where she is, we will call her right now. We will use my personal telephone. But if you do not know where she is, we cannot use the telephone – mine or the one in this shop, it makes no difference. We must use el-Internet.'

Wafeeq crossed the room and placed himself in front of the computer. 'Believe me, it is better.' He cracked his knuckles with practised relish. 'I swear on my wife's honour.' Wafeeq began tapping at the computer, his fingers flying across the keyboard with impressive speed.

'You've done this before?' Fin asked.

'Of course. I have found many, many women on el-Internet. It is certain I will find one small girl.'

Fin remained in his seat and watched the cold blue reflection of the computer screen flash on the driver's face. He rested his head against the wall behind him and, lulled by the darkened room and light percussion of the plastic keys, he gradually deflated into sleep.

16

'Pasha, pasha.' Fin felt himself being gently shaken from a busy dream, his senses benevolently occupied by the fragrance of mint. He opened his eyes to find Wafeeq standing before him with a steaming glass of tea.

'Half an hour you sleep, pasha. Of course, you can sleep all the night and the day also for you have nothing else to do but thank Allah for your great riches. But what will Mahmud think if he returns and finds the pasha alone, sleeping in the same room as his beautiful young wife, eh?' The driver winked at Fin and then translated for the benefit of Mahmud's wife, who slapped him on the shoulder with an intimacy that surprised Fin. 'For me, I cannot wait here. I must go. There is a woman in Heliopolis . . .'

Fin rubbed his eyes. He stood up and patted his pockets. There was nothing where his wallet should have been. He frisked himself and, seeing Wafeeq and the woman smiling at each other, suspicion surged through him. He crouched on his hands and knees grunting that he'd had it when he went to sleep and looked noisily under the chair. Wafeeq tapped Fin on the shoulder and pointed to the table.

'It fell to the ground as you slept. The beautiful lady

picked it up and put it next to you. It is wet, pasha. A man's money should be dry.'

Fin picked up the wallet. It was still damp, but the money was there. Fin pushed it back in his pocket feeling guilty.

'Come, drink your tea. Let us go,' Wafeeq demanded.

Fin blew at the tea and sipped it as best he could. The woman insisted to him that he should take his time – there was no rush. But seeing Wafeeq's anxiety she took the tea and poured half of it into the saucer and then back into the glass. Not a drop was spilt, and when Fin touched his lips to the liquid he found that the temperature had reached that evanescent moment of perfection, like a perfect bath. He took a sip. It was sweet like Khayam's but hot, almost black, with a shoot of spearmint reaching out of the concentrated liquid like a seedling from rich soil.

Fin looked up from his tea and caught sight of the woman peering at Wafeeq.

'Did you do it – did you find Nira?' Fin asked, but Wafeeq had crossed to the door and was peering anxiously out onto the street.

'*Ba'dein*. Later we will talk, now we leave.' He was anxious, wiping his lips with a handkerchief, straightening his shirt.

Fin drained his tea until the last syrupy slush of sugar trickled into his mouth. Putting down his glass he asked the woman how much he owed her for the use of the Internet, but she shook her head and spoke a few quiet words.

'What is she saying?' Fin asked Wafeeq. 'Can she say it again slowly?'

'There is no time for slowly. Come, I will tell outside,'

Wafeeq insisted, hurrying Fin towards the door. 'I told her you are looking for a girl who is sick, a child, yes? She wishes Almighty Allah's blessing on you.' Fin turned to thank the woman, but she was smiling into the small brass mirror Wafeeq must have given her, tucking strands of hair back into her headscarf.

'Let us go, pasha. You have brought this woman enough good fortune.'

Wafeeq was clearly relieved to be back amid the bustle of King Faisal Road. He grinned and laughed, kicking a discarded bottle cap across the dusty pavement as he walked away from Mahmud's Internet Palace.

'Lila is very good.'

'Who?' Fin asked.

'The wife of Mahmud.' Wafeeq sighed.

Fin agreed: 'Yes, so kind of her to refuse money, very kind . . .'

The mention of money wakened Wafeeq from his reverie and he stopped dead, causing an old man to knock into him.

'*Ibn el-homar!*' the old man cursed. Fin smiled, knowing that Wafeeq was being called a son of a mule.

'*Inta sharmoot . . . gildak khishin awee,*' Wafeeq replied, walking on.

A number of passers-by sniggered and the old man flew into a rage, waving his stick and shouting.

'What did you call him?' Fin asked, catching up.

'I cannot say in English . . . A male prostitute with rough skin . . . and half price,' Wafeeq replied, before stopping and grasping Fin's wrist.

'Lila refuses your money, but I do not refuse money, pasha. You must pay me thirty-five Egyptian.'

'Thirty-five Egyptian was for finding the girl,' Fin replied.

'But I have found her! With the computer I found her. So many women I have found and kissed and made love to on el-Internet. Do you think I cannot find one small girl in a hospital, when the pasha even gives me her name? This girl Balesh, she is in the Mostashfa Boulaq el-Aam hospital. Her leg it is broken many times on the left side, but all will be well, *el-hamdelillah*.'

'Are you sure?'

'Of course. A nurse with a voice like the honey of bees told me her bones were healthy and, *el-hamdelillah*, the broken parts will become as one.'

'Are you sure of the hospital?' Fin insisted.

Wafeeq replied that if he were wrong may his skin rot away and his raw body be rubbed in a substance with which Fin was unfamiliar.

Fin took out two twenty-pound notes and handed them to the driver, who slid them into his wallet with immense satisfaction and a loving pat. He pulled out five pounds' change to give to Fin.

'Does the pasha know how to travel to Mostashfa Boulaq?'

Fin shook his head. 'I will take another taxi. You don't have time; you have to go to . . . Heliopolis, isn't it?'

'I go later to Heliopolis,' replied Wafeeq. 'Now I will take you to Boulaq, no charge, gratis,' he said, replacing the five-pound note in his wallet. 'Perhaps then merciful Allah will forgive me my many sins.'

17

The journey to the hospital was punctuated with a rash lane change into the path of an army truck, a provocatively slow donkey cart and the standard mortal challenge from a minibus – no more than the usual succession of near-death experiences for a drive across Cairo. During the last of these Fin suggested that Wafeeq dispense with 'pasha' and call him by his name. Wafeeq mumbled something and fell silent until they pulled up in front of the hospital. As Fin tugged at the loose metal lever of the car door, Wafeeq turned to Fin.

'This girl, Nira, she is a child, no?' he said.

Fin nodded.

'She is more than ten years?' Wafeeq stared at Fin, challenging him to meet his gaze.

Fin said he did not know but she was probably more than ten.

'Very young this girl, do you not think? And does the pasha know her family?'

Fin said that he had met the father but not the mother.

'Perhaps the pasha will telephone him?' Wafeeq

proffered his phone. 'Together you make a visit. It is better, no?'

Fin shrugged and said it was not better and anyway he did not have Omar's telephone number.

'I understand, of course,' Wafeeq muttered, shaking his head. He turned back, placing both palms on the cracked plastic delta in the middle of the steering wheel. 'It is not good for you ... from the West, to visit with young girls,' he said, picking at the faded leopard-print cover of the steering wheel. 'If you know her parents or you are neighbours or they are your family, there is no problem.' He was now looking straight at Fin through the rear-view mirror. 'But this girl, she is a child. I do not like it.'

Fin let go of the door lever and tried to describe to Wafeeq what he wanted from the girl. Only by speaking to her, he explained, could he discover the truth about her accident. Wafeeq considered Fin's words, chin on his chest, allowing one of the Arab silences that Fin was at last not only learning to accept, but inhabit.

Wafeeq suddenly gave the steering wheel a sharp slap.

'You wish me to believe your heart is white? I do, I believe your heart is white. But do you think that *they* will believe?' he exclaimed. 'No. To doctors, nurses, people of the hospital, your heart will be black and they will not allow this. To talk to the girl, you must visit with her father or you must be a doctor, otherwise ...' Wafeeq shut his eyes and rubbed them as if attempting to wipe away terrible pictures. 'You are not an Arab, pasha. People think you wish more than to talk with the girl – to take away her honour ... There are men who do this in your country – it is true, I swear it. I read this in the newspaper each week.

People will think you are a man like this and they will become angry.'

'It's not like that. I just want to talk to her,' Fin replied, opening the door.

'Of course, I believe you. Allah protect you, my brother. I cannot stay. If there is a problem, it is the Egyptian who will suffer – it is always this way. I go to Heliopolis. I have a woman, a friend, very beautiful . . .' He trailed off as Fin climbed out of the car.

It was a relief to be out, to feel the warmth of the night, but a few steps on and the air was thick with the rotting stink of the canals that crisscrossed the modern parts of the city. It was too dark to see the water, but Fin knew it was there, heavy with sludge, bloated dogs and stagnant mounds of rubbish. He hurried towards the dimly lit doors of the hospital, Wafeeq's warning repeating in his mind.

The hospital was large and bustling, noisy and chaotic, even now at the beginning of the night. Everything was white and shining, straight clean lines and a reassuring reek of disinfectant so strong Fin could feel it on his skin. Doctors hustled by in white coats and noisy shoes; mothers sat against walls holding children, looking as if they had been there for days and expected to be there for more. A thick crowd harangued three bored women behind a heavy desk. People jostled and pushed, sweated and clamoured to be heard. Fin sauntered past the desk and along the corridor. He attached himself to a noisy gang of young doctors, who fell silent as they squeezed themselves into a lift with an effortless compliance that implied routine. There was no room for Fin amid the solid mass of bodies, but seeing him stranded they gamely made space, inching one way and then another like bees in a hive. The lift lurched and rattled upwards, Fin's face cushioned in the soft white coat of a neighbour who smelled of frankincense and sweat.

Stuck to the other passengers like dates in a pack, Fin had no choice but to disembark when the doctors unfolded themselves out on the second floor. He trailed them down a busy corridor, wondering where to begin his search, noticing that all the doctors wore trousers under their white coats while he shuffled along in a cheap galabeya.

Fin dawdled, pretending to read a noticeboard, until the doctors charged through a scuffed brown door that was splintered at the base where hundreds of feet had kicked it open. Fin followed them up to the door, pausing to look in as it closed. It was a changing room. Fin paced back and forth along the corridor trying to look as if he was deliberately and rightfully where he should be, his hands clasped behind his back, head down, like a man pondering a vital decision.

The doctors soon emerged, resplendent in pleated slacks, brightly coloured shirts and clickety loafers. When the last of them had passed, Fin eased open the door of the changing room and hastened to a lavatory compartment. There was a finger-width gap between the door and the flimsy wall, the sort of space that would have unnerved him if he had wanted to use the facility but now it served his purpose. A few medics were chatting as they changed into or out of their white coats or surgical smocks. They disciplined their hair, applied creams, oils and combs. They stowed their clothes and accoutrements in noisy tin lockers, some folding, others favouring a quick bundle. The room was heavy with male scents, old towels, hair oil, tired bodies, clouds of deodorant. A den of animals in an antiseptic world.

Fin waited. A man entered, smiling, more African than Egyptian with a greying beard and gentle eyes. Most importantly he was Fin's size and build. The man moved to a locker and changed briskly from his white coat and trousers into surgical scrubs. Slipping off his watch and locking the cabinet, he exited the changing room without even a glance in the large mirror which so absorbed his colleagues.

When the changing room was empty, Fin crept out and snapped the flimsy padlock of the surgeon's locker with a twist of his pen. Two photographs gazed out as the thin metal door swung open. Smiling girls, twins perhaps, at a school graduation, beneath them an oval-faced Egyptian woman beaming with unbounded love in a 1970s print dress. Fin reached into the locker and unhooked the man's trousers from their blunt hook, pulling them on under his galabeya. They were warm, like the roads and walls outside, fleetingly remembering the surgeon's body. Fin tightened the man's belt a notch closer than its time-worn place and, as he thought of the bearded surgeon, darker and broader than he with smiling twins and a beloved wife, he felt a silent roar of emotion emanating from their difference and their similarity, filling the space between the two notches.

A wallet swung in the hip pocket, a pendulum of guilt that shifted as Fin moved. Fin pulled it out and placed it at eye level on the locker shelf. He looked behind him. There was no one, nothing except for damp towels and his own furtive discomfort. He took out a slip of paper, a receipt from the wallet and with his now cracked pen printed a note of apology. Fin propped the note on the wallet, reread it and slipped a few banknotes underneath. He reached for the surgeon's shirt but changed his mind, hoicking up his galabeya and tucking it into the trousers. The extra padding necessitated releasing the belt to the surgeon's preferred notch and this pleased Fin. It felt auspicious. He put on the white coat, smoothed down his hair and walked out of the changing room, enjoying the scent of the surgeon's aftershave, which clung like memory to the borrowed clothing.

As he walked along the corridor, empty but for a shaky young man in a pale grey galabeya leaning on the thin metal scaffold of his intravenous drip, Fin realised that there was something about hospitals he liked. The gleaming emptiness gave him space to think, the polished floor reflected the yellow and green doors like a murky but placid lake. He warmed to the fluorescent lights pooling for an unstable moment in the surface tension of the polished floor. He liked the *slap-slap* of his cheap plastic shoes, sounding the hard space. Hospitals were a haven of equanimity where being broken or flawed or misfiring was a condition of entry, a guarantee of unconditional care. It was an atmosphere that agreed with Fin.

He thought about the child Nira, a smashed leg no doubt adding to the handicap of her size. Would she be even smaller than her father? More importantly, where was she? He could look in intensive care, he reasoned, but then thought better of it. If she were in intensive care it was unlikely she would be able to talk to him. He would begin his search in the children's ward, in paediatrics. Fin approached a woman in a white doctor's coat and black headscarf. She was coiling a stethoscope into her pocket.

'Paediatric ward?' he asked.

The doctor stole a look at his unkempt hair and then pointed down the corridor. Fin nodded and followed her direction. Half a dozen signs in Arabic might have indicated different departments, but to Fin they communicated nothing. His instincts insisted that he take the corridor to the right, a route whose long uniformity was interrupted only by a missing fluorescent strip in its line of blue-white light. Fin turned left. When it came to direction his instinct was reliably wrong. He stopped and listened. Children were noisy, he reasoned, hearing only the sound of adults and footsteps. He walked on. Perhaps only healthy children made noise. He was about to turn back when he saw a blue rectangle of paper stuck to the glossy wall further along the corridor. It was a painting of a rainbow by 'Sulima, age 8'. Fin smiled. Children always painted rainbows, even here near the desert where rainbows were so rare. It was not just because they offered the opportunity to put every available colour close together in one sweeping arc, although this alone was a good enough reason, it was because rainbows were proof that something from the world of magic was demonstrably true.

Further down the corridor he found other pictures – lumpy stick-legged camels that might have been horses, palm trees with jubilant green fronds, horses that might have been camels, tanks that might have been camels, flowers, houses and triangular warplanes shooting red streaks of fire. Fin knew he was near, and when he found himself in front of a deep blue door, blue like the thickest part of a perfect sky, he knew he had found the children's ward.

Fin walked through the heavy doors into a large darkened ward with a row of beds along each wall and a starchy nurse sitting in a lone pool of light. Children occupied every bed, some bandaged, some sleeping. It was too late for rainbow-making, but a table in the middle of the room offered a quiver of coloured pens and a sheaf of paper. There was a quintessence of malady in the room, the irrepressible candour of children heightening the atmosphere of illness. Fin approached the nurse perched on her hard chair at the end of the ward. He exchanged the required greetings and asked for Nira Balesh in a tone that he hoped would communicate his medical authority. The nurse stood and led him back towards the blue doors, pointing to the bed opposite where a young girl lay, one plastered leg in traction. The nurse removed a clipboard from the end of the bed, handed it to Fin and marched back towards her chair.

Fin looked at the girl. It could not be she, a beautiful delicate creature, already a head taller than Omar.

'Nira Balesh?' he called to the departing nurse in a voice that echoed through the ward.

The nurse snapped round and scanned Fin from head to foot, her eyebrows stretching up her forehead as if making a break for freedom. She brought a ramrod finger to her lips, emitting a sound like air escaping from a tyre, before nodding in confirmation.

Nira was awake, listless and staring at the ceiling fan as it made slow uneven turns. Fin peered professionally over the clipboard and saw that the girl had the same large amber eyes as her father. Fortunately for her, this was the only noticeable feature she had inherited from him. Her skin was pale with the translucence that shock brings, and in her arms was a hug-worn stuffed bunny with large lop ears that fell across her throat. In his most soothing manner Fin told the little girl that he was a doctor and asked if she understood English.

'*Shwayya,*' a little, she said, her eyes alert for any medical unpleasantness.

Fin took her wrist in a gentle charade of examination. 'Your leg? It was eaten by a crocodile?' Fin asked, miming the jaws with a slight smile.

The little girl almost returned his smile but shook her head. 'Auto,' she murmured.

Fin watched as, with two slender fingers of her right hand, the little girl enacted herself walking across the starched white sheet of the bed and then, with her left hand balled into a fragile fist, she crashed hard into her vulnerable little fingers, leaving them crumpled and motionless on the sheet as the fist drove away and disappeared off the bed. Something in this pantomime explanation conveyed the injustice of the accident with greater force than her father's spectacular fury.

Fin looked away feeling moisture fill his eyes. He noticed that the nurse was staring at his feet, dirty and shod in the cheap plastic sandals. He turned back to Nira.

'Nira?'

She gazed at him without replying.

Fin moved both fists up and down in what he hoped was the universal sign language for driving. He pointed to himself.

'Who was driving the auto?'

She did not reply.

'Was it me?'

She shook her head.

'Was it a *"rahgel"* man or a *"sitt"* woman?'

'*Rahgel*,' she whispered.

Fin put his hand parallel to his head and let it sink down to pose the question of size.

She did not understand.

'Was he *shwayy*, small?'

She smiled wanly. 'Papa?' she whispered, sitting up a little.

Fin shook his head. 'No, no, papa is not coming. Not now, but soon – *bahdheine*.' He smiled weakly, attempting to conceal his untruth.

Fin put his hand in front of his belly, grimacing in cartoon obesity. The little girl blinked but offered no other reaction. He took a pillow from the empty bed next to him and pushed it under his doctor's coat, pretending to drive. Nira giggled, and as Fin drove through the hospital air, it seemed to him that she finally understood his question. No, she shook her head, the driver was not fat. Big nose? Fin pulled out an imaginary nose from his face. She did not know. Clothes? Fin picked at his white coat and pulled at his trousers. The child shrugged and suddenly tired of the game. She looked down at her plastered leg, moaned and shuffled up the bed as if trying to escape it. The nurse, who had been watching Fin's pantomime with growing suspicion, stood and smoothed down the stiff material of her uniform. Fin smiled urgently, imploring the child for patience. The nurse waved to attract his attention. Fin turned his back to her and scratched his head in concentration. Nira shouted excitedly, pointing to her own head.

'*Araa'*,' she called, patting her hair.

Nira was pointing at her hair and repeating the word.

Fin searched in the little girl's amber eyes for a meaning that he could not decipher, trying to ignore the bird-like squawks of the nurse, who now stood behind him, tugging at his sleeve. Nira repeated the word, her voice rising in excitement. *'Araa', araa'.'*

The nurse tapped Fin sharply on the shoulder. He spun round.

'Yallah imshi,' he barked as fiercely as he dared, hoping she would scurry off. But the nurse was undaunted, commanding him in hushed but vicious tones and stabbing her finger towards the door. Nira fell silent, cowed by the nurse's authority. Fin attempted charm, begging the nurse for a few more minutes, but she was beyond compromise, pulling at his coat and pointing at his dusty feet and ramshackle hair. Fin found himself being led and then almost dragged to the door. He shook off her hand and hissed, *'Teezak hamra,'* unsure of the precise meaning but remembering it was something rude.

Whatever its true meaning, it was too much for the nurse, who rushed out of the ward. Fin returned to Nira. Her eyes were wide with astonishment and she giggled behind her delicate hands.

'Araa'?' Fin repeated, pointing to himself. The little girl shook her head and once more drove her hand across the bedclothes. She pointed to her head chanting, *'Araa', araa'.'*

Perhaps the driver of the car had pulled her away by the hair? Was it possible that he had tried to abduct her? Nira called out and pointed over Fin's shoulder. The nurse was now accompanied by a security man who was peering through the windows of the double doors. Fin attempted a confident nod in their direction but the thickset guard pointed to Fin with a fierce stab of his finger, beckoning to him through the glass. Fin understood that they were trying to lure him out of the ward so the sleeping children would not be disturbed.

Fin walked slowly towards the doors, working out how best to prolong his visit. But as the gap between him and the nurse and security man closed, he could see from their expressions that at the very least he was about to be ejected from the hospital. Fin slowed to a shuffle and gave them a jaunty wave. The security guard poked his bald head through the door and whisper-shouted at Fin that he should come out immediately.

Fin shushed him with a flourish, letting his hand fall to the metal cot-guard on the side of an empty bed. He pulled at the guard and, feeling it scrape out of its holes, threw himself and it at the doors, sliding the metal gate between the two handles. Through the windows of the doors Fin saw shock register upon the faces of the nurse and security guard as they realised what Fin had done. They both threw themselves at the doors, making a terrifying racket. Fin could not resist turning and shushing them as he made his way back to Nira's bed.

All the other children in the ward were now awake – crying, laughing or shouting to each other. The little girl next to Nira slipped out of bed and scampered over to a metal cupboard behind the nurse's chair. She opened the cupboard and, standing on a chair, reached up and grasped a plastic bowl full of sweets which she sowed in glorious arcs to delighted children as she skipped about the ward. Outside, an angry mob was mustered and pushed in co-ordinated lunges at the blockaded doors.

Nira picked up a date-sized sweet, fallen upon her bed like manna. Fin watched her face undergo the ecstatic transfiguration brought on by sugar as he heard the boiled sweetness knock against her teeth. He looked around the ward. Gleeful chaos had replaced illness as the defining atmosphere. One little boy was hopping about in a T-shirt and nothing else, his bandaged foot held off the floor, shouting with the same commitment to joy that a toddler two beds away was dedicating to misery. A factory line of rainbows and abstract expressions was being created by an enthusiastic group of children in brightly coloured pyjamas. Taking advantage of the nurse's absence they were applying their creations directly to the table.

Fin looked towards the door now buckling with each charge. Nira called to him and pointed to the security guard, his bald head squashed against the window.

'*Araa*',' she exclaimed, striking her head.

'*Araa*'?'

Nira nodded. Fin rushed up to the table of crayons and swiped a rectangle of paper from the one child who was not defacing the furniture. He rushed back to Nira's bed and drew two stick figures, one with a curly squiggle of hair and one without, just a circle with arms and legs. He pointed to the bald stick man.

'*Araa*'?'

Nira squealed and clapped. '*Araa*'!' she confirmed with a smile.

Fin gave a triumphant laugh. *Araa*'. Bald. The driver who had hit Nira was bald.

There was a crash as the door handles finally gave way under the steady force of determined shoulders. Fin ran to the far end of the ward, towards a door with a red sign that suggested a fire exit. He barrelled through the door which cut off all light as it slammed behind him.

Desperately slapping the walls for a switch and finding only dank stone, he stepped blindly forward waving his arms in front of him. His hands found nothing but his feet stumbled over a step, launching him forearms first onto a staircase. He twisted to one side swearing as the cement edge of a stair caught his bruised thigh. Fin pulled himself to his feet and scrambled up the stairs as fast as he was able. The mob burst through the fire door behind him and as the fluorescent tubes flickered to life, Fin, ignoring his injury, sprinted up the stairs and launched himself through a door on the next landing.

The corridor was hushed, populated with elderly slow-moving patients. Except for an ancient woman inching along with a walking frame, no one noticed him, and she regarded him as no more than an unwelcome emanation from her dreams before resuming her incremental progress. Fin looked back to check for his pursuers and knocked into an elderly man who was catching his breath on his way back to his room. Fin apologised and, looking over his shoulder, guided the old man the last few steps, flicking the door of the room shut behind them. The man shook Fin's hands off and rearranged his keffiyeh head-scarf, before sitting down on the bed. Fin pulled out his wallet and asked in halting Arabic if the man would sell him the keffiyeh. The old man batted away Fin's offer with a curse and closed his eyes, sinking into himself with a sigh.

In the corridor Fin could hear his pursuers arguing. A thin finger jabbed into Fin's kidney and he turned to find the old man offering him the keffiyeh, folded into a neat triangle.

'*Hideya an*' – a gift – the old man rasped, his arms

trembling with age and effort. '*Khud!*' Take it.

Fin took the keffiyeh without a word and put his ear to the door. When all was silent outside he turned back to thank the old man but he was asleep, listing impossibly on the edge of the bed. Fin cracked open the door and stepped out. A young orderly standing at the end of the corridor saw him at once and raised the alarm. Fin sprinted away, his plastic shoes slap-slapping on the polished floor. His pursuers massed after him, shouting to each other. Fin turned another corner, his shoes slipping and cutting into his sweating feet. He dived through the first available door.

Panting, his back against the door, Fin could see that the room was empty. There was another door at the far end, a spotless metal trough with laminated diagrams offering instructions on hand-washing technique and white shelves stacked with surgical smocks. He heard his pursuers thundering by. Fin did not want to think what might happen to him if he were caught. He pulled the nearest smock over his head, slipped on surgical trousers and found a mask and cap in a box on the floor and a pile of shoe covers sealed in see-through plastic. He threw everything on and sprinted across the room to a short corridor of shining white tiles that led to another white door with a narrow window at eye level. Fin peered through. A group of surgeons crowded round an operating table. Snapping the mask over his mouth, Fin pushed through inside.

Air conditioning hit him like a bucket of dry water. In a few steps he was cool, cold even, and to his relief no one looked up as the door sucked shut like an airlock. The identically dressed figures were focused on a body on the table which was swathed in green. A frame held open the material at one end of the operating table. A seated attendant peered in at intervals, taking readings from a bank of machines, making notes and communicating with her colleagues in short precise phrases. As Fin moved the medic looked up at him, revealing a strong Coptic nose, her breath pushing and pulling at the grey-white gauze of her mask. Tiny spikes of fear prickled over Fin's body but she did not question him or raise the alarm. Fin watched her gloved hand reach within the covers and open one of the patient's eyes. She said something to her colleagues and they all looked up. Simultaneously Fin recognised that he was the only person in the room without surgical gloves. He clasped his hands behind his back and stepped behind the woman, catching sight of the patient's head. A blue corrugated tube was taped into the man's mouth and a pleated black balloon bloating and crumpling with an icy mechanical hiss.

Fin pulled at the waist of his surgical trousers. They were too tight and too short, the thin band of elastic crimped into his waist. He should have checked before entering the theatre. As if aware of his thoughts the chief surgeon suddenly backed away from the table and walked swiftly to the far corner of the room. Fin edged away, suddenly aware of the pungency of his fear.

The surgeon returned. He did not look at Fin but placed an empty compact disc case on a trolley. He peeled off his gloves and tossed them into a dustbin. As he pulled on a new pair with a well-practised snap, the first phrase of a Bach fugue bled out of invisible speakers. Fin had heard it before. It was one of Bach's last – slow, almost dour. Fin took a deep breath and relaxed his shoulders. The surgeons were not concerned with him, he realised as the phrases of the harpsichord answered each other. There was only one point of focus in the room and it was not him, it was the exposed flesh on the operating table which the surgeon's assistant was now painting with a nicotine-ochre wash.

Fin edged closer as the surgeon cut down along a thick pen mark in the middle of the patient's torso. A line of vivid red trailed the surgeon's hand, welling up with blood until an assistant sucked out the fluid with a noisy transparent tube. The music filled the room in glorious but incongruous cascades, arrhythmically counterpointed by the relentless hiss and suck of the oxygen bag.

A high-pitched whine cut through all other sound and jolted Fin's attention back to the chief surgeon. He stood with an electric saw, the fan-shaped blade motionless over the pink split of flesh and wheat-yellow fat. He murmured a question to his assistant. The assistant produced a clipboard, consulted it and gave the necessary response. The surgeon nodded, and with a whine that geared from high to low as the blade bit into bone, cut through the patient's chest. The surgeon passed the saw, white-flecked and bloody, to his assistant, who exchanged it for a shining metal clamp which the surgeon fitted to either side of the incision. Fin's knees weakened as the surgeon ratcheted open the implement and the ribcage separated, revealing a fist-sized lump, strangely milky in colour, throbbing with relentless intensity. The heart.

The doors of the theatre smashed open as three security guards burst in. Fin kept his eyes on the opaque pink translucence of the heart. The surgeon berated the intruders. He heard the men apologise and they backed out of the theatre.

The surgeon returned to the operation, pinched at the heart's membranous casing and snipped it open with long alloy scissors. The heart itself appeared like a flower opening, red and powerful, twisting and expanding with exhausting force. So here it was, Fin thought: the truth. The music flowed and eddied, themes inverted, broke away and rejoined. It was clear, cerebral, an experience of divinity, thought more than felt, as clean and intangible as prayer.

Fin saw in front of him the visceral physicality that pumped beneath everything. Whatever triumphs or catastrophes, love, disappointment or terrors he fantasised were important, his heart would beat, never despairing as he did, keeping up this vital kinesis, and when it stopped everything would cease. This was fact. Everything else was merely an idea.

Fin decided it was time to leave the theatre. The washroom was empty, the doctor's trousers on a chair, rolled into a loose cylinder just as Fin had left them. He started to remove his surgical clothes but then changed his mind, picking up the trousers he had borrowed and walking out into the corridor. The bald security guard stood guard in front of the lifts with two fidgeting orderlies. Halfway along the corridor a post-operative patient lay unconscious on a trolley. Fin knew he could not turn back so he kept walking, his breath quickening through the surgical mask. When he reached the trolley, he made a show of checking the drip before taking hold of the metal handrail beneath the patient's head and giving it a decisive push. It glided easily across the polished floor and Fin signalled for the guard to hold open the lift while Fin backed in and pulled the trolley in after him. Fin watched in horror as the security guard and the two orderlies squeezed in behind. He gazed down at the patient, aghast. He could hear the men's conversation and the word *ferenghi*. A heavy drop of sweat fell from Fin's forehead onto the face beneath him. Fin watched it roll down, cutting a glistening path across the patient's sallow cheek.

'Doctor, *kayf haalak*.'

The bald security guard was speaking to Fin.

Fin ignored him.

'*DOCTOR, KAYF HAALAK*?' He signalled for Fin to remove his mask. The orderlies looked on, suspicious and a little afraid. Only the length of the trolley separated them. Fin pulled down his mask as the lift halted with an innocent *ding* and the door behind him concertinaed open.

Fin exploded out, sprinting for the main exit. He passed the front desk, pushing and dodging through the crowd, but the guard and the orderlies were catching up and the crowd was dense ahead. Fin took the loose cylinder of rolled-up trousers and tossed it into the air.

'*Allahu akbar!*' he screamed as he ran.

People scattered, recognising in this affirmation of their beloved God the overture to acts of horrific fanatical violence. A woman screamed and dived over her children. Others caught her panic and leapt away from the windows and heavy glass doors or spread themselves flat on the polished floor, allowing Fin an unhindered path to the exit.

Fin darted along the hospital road, his pursuers nearing with every step. A car ahead came to life and reversed to a skidding halt in front of Fin.

'The pasha needs a taxi?'

Fin dived through the back window of the taxi as it roared off, leaving an angry crowd shaking fists and batons.

Wafeeq turned and grinned again as Fin struggled to sit upright.

'The pasha's plan was good? AHHHAAHAHA!' He slapped his knee. 'You are lucky today, pasha. Lucky or cursed, who can say?'

Fin leant back into the familiar softness of Wafeeq's back seat.

'Take me home, Wafeeq.'

SALAAT EL-ISHA

18

The noise and bustle of El-Mahahdi Street greeted Fin like a favourite uncle. Fatty Abnedi sat outside his barber shop, thighs straining against the shining fabric of his trousers, smile stretched across his face.

'*Masaa' el-khayr*,' he shouted across the crowded street. Fin nodded and almost laughed to himself. Evening of goodness was so far from his evening.

'*Masaa' el-noor*,' Fin replied, touching his heart. Evening of light. It was pitch dark. Of course it was dark; people only wished each other what was absent. Fin ducked into the doorway of his apartment building and climbed the uneven stairs, his body automatically compensating for the fourth and sixteenth steps, which had long since fallen away.

Fin inserted the key, pulled the door to him, twisted the key halfway and, as he completed the key's turn, barged forward with his shoulder. Other than knocking the door off its hinges, there was no other way of gaining entry to his apartment, and the technique had taken many frustrating hours to discover.

Inside all was still, just as he had left it early that

morning. He looked at the hammer leaning by the door. He inspected the framed map and scattered tacks on the floor, untouched for ... how long? Weeks? Months? Fin did not know what else he had expected, but there was something poignant about the lack of change, like finding a much-worn but forgotten item of clothing. Signs of a previous Fin. He snatched up the hammer and a tack from the floor and banged the tack into the wall with two hard blows. He pulled on the nail, expecting it to crumble away with a piece of wall, but it held fast. He picked up the framed map from the floor and turned it over. 'Arabia' it proclaimed in Imperial Copperplate. A colonial promise. Like Ireland, a promise broken. Fin held the map flush against the wall and edged it down, gently, slowly, until he felt the picture wire snag on the tack. It balanced and hung.

'"I am soft sift in an hour glass,"' Fin muttered to himself, snatching the remains of a poem from the archaeological site of his education, '"but mined with a motion adrift."'

Fin stepped back and regarded with satisfaction the way the map transformed the wall around it. He herded the remaining tacks together with his foot, gathering them up in pinches of two and three until they were all cupped in his hand.

He pushed open the door to his study. Books strewn exactly as he had left them, an ashtray, rubbish, a sock, shoes, an empty bottle of gin, a line of ants marching to and from a dirty plate, glasses with moulding slips of lemon, an earthenware bowl with calcified crust of *fouls medames* – so dry that even the ants disdained it. Fin pulled open a drawer in his desk brimful of papers, sticking tape, pens, pamphlets, notebooks, coins, wires, bits of string. At a certain point miscellaneous objects had reached a critical mass and entropy had taken over. Fin forced a crevice between the jumble of paper and dropped the tacks into it.

All was chaotic and stale. He pulled the shutters and barged open the windows, wedging one side with a phone directory. There was still no breeze, but the noise of the evening seemed to move the air around. What was left of Fin's newspaper article lay on the desk. Waled had used only as much paper as he needed for his joint, and in place of headline and photograph was a neat rectangle of negative space. A few lines caught Fin's attention: 'The combination of good ingredients, flawlessly executed preparation and experience will always produce food that is inspirational – be it the greatest restaurant in Paris or a kebab shop on King Faisal Road.'

Fin sat at his desk and stared at the article. It was satisfying to see one's work in print. There it was, real, in the world. He marvelled at the neat black letters. Tiny marks, twenty-six in all, three less than Arabic, meaningless in themselves but when ordered tens of thousands of blocks of meaning could be described and assembled into infinite significance. Just as a painter made volume and distance with marks and edges, these linear borders conjured creation. And yet there was something hopeless about them, like wishing for an evening of light, an impulse wedded to heroic failure. The ancient Egyptians knew this: for them there was no sense of art. Their depictions were not an image, they were the thing itself, pale and paltry next to the work of the divine from which they were taken, but an act of magic nevertheless, a creation.

Fin's eyes hung on the word 'inspirational' as his mind whirled. It was a word his boss had insisted he change. It was inappropriate, she had claimed, but Fin had argued, defending it with a passion that had surprised them both. She said in the end that she did not really care and left the room to speak to the advertising people. Fin had felt both victorious and deflated.

It was amazing the job had lasted so long. Not even amazing, he remembered it was because he was cheap. How pathetic. Fin laughed. It had not occurred to him to ask for a rise; he earned enough to meet his needs and twenty times more than most people in the city. Had he been able to drink his salary – and he had often tried – he might have asked for more. But he never could. Even when the money ran out there were always other drinkers prepared to buy drinks to keep him from breaking up the dream.

Fin's confidence, unstable and vaporous, leaked out of him and he crumpled. It was not much of a newspaper, he knew, but it still ached to be sacked from it. He couldn't even say he was a journalist now. At least he used to be something – a pedestrian hack on a worthless paper – yet it was better than . . . better than what? What was he now? If he left Cairo at least then he could hold his head up and call himself an 'ex-journalist'. Now he was . . . nothing. Merely a man looking for a friend he couldn't find and a story he couldn't fathom.

Fin stood up, impaling the most tender part of his bruise on the sharp corner of the desk. The pain jolted through him and with it the memory of Farouk. Sitting in his apartment pondering his insignificance was not going to help anyone. Farouk was innocent, he knew this now. Someone else had knocked over the little girl, Nira had made that clear. He had to find Omar. He must go to the kebab shop, demand to see Omar and convince him of the truth without being thrown off any more bridges.

The brutal image of Jalut and his gourmet relish for violence pitched through Fin's mind: soundless thuds, hefty fists swinging like demolition balls. Fin crossed his arms and exhaled through pursed lips. The chances of being dragged out of the kebab shop and crushed like a ripe mango were unacceptably high. Pain, violence, even the idea of them, tightened wires of fear around Fin's throat.

He recalled the moment of immobilising terror when the American had attacked him. He'd known what he was doing, Fin now realised, telling Fin that he planned to shatter his jaw, swinging back that telescopic cosh with deliberate slowness, and as Fin threw up his hands to protect his face, smashing the cosh expertly into the top of his thigh. It had been a purposely ignoble injury but the pain . . . the pain had been remarkable, exploding throughout his body, becoming everything until Fin had found himself rolling on the ground, screaming and pounding the cracked cement with his fists.

Sitting in bars, lazing in bed, coming out of a film, he had sometimes imagined such situations, always granting himself martial skill or at the very least the heroic stoicism of a journalist defending the truth. But the truth was he had been no more than a whimpering little boy, gasping for breath and prepared to do anything not to be hurt again.

Fin winced at the memory and sat down again rubbing

his thigh. He wondered which was worse: the American's cool brutality or Jalut, who leered and drooled with an almost erotic delight at the pain he inflicted. The American was a professional, doing a job, telling Fin in a language that would penetrate his drunken bravado that it was foolish and dangerous to make comments about his supposed work in a bar 'crowded with goddam terrorists, for all we know'. Should Fin ever again insinuate that the American was anything other than what he said he was, a communications consultant, he swore he would find Fin and ensure he never spoke again.

Fin had detested the man at first meeting; cold eyes, thick neck, narrow mind, big words – a noisy show-off who talked a lot about listening. As the night wore on in the crowded bar, vivid with girls and strong drinks, Fin had convinced himself that he had a heroic duty to out the muscle-bound bore as the undercover intelligence operative that Fin suspected him to be, to expose his thin-lipped, high-protein smile for the arrogant colonial sneer that Fin was sure lay beneath.

It had been stupid of Fin. He saw this with the benefit of sobriety. His puerile comments had helped no one, engendered by his own impotent rage against the injustices of the world or just his own failures. Fin thought of Omar. He and his thug were probably laughing about the hapless Irishman they had tossed into the river. They must assume he was dead, and if they saw him again they would surely want to finish the job.

A muezzin, or more likely a tape recorder, began a late call for the final prayer of the day, the *Salaat el-isha*. The ultimate prayer could be made at any point after the last red glow of the day had disappeared and before dawn, so it was slightly later every day as the season approached the equinox. Fin did not know when people slept in Cairo. It certainly didn't seem to be at night, unless there was a sort of tacit shift agreement and some slept while others milled about in the streets.

The call to prayer filled the room, occupying every space so that even Fin's fear of violence was momentarily over-powered by a sense of something else. He thought of himself during the *Salaat el-maghrib* only a few hours before, lying on the cement wall of the bridge sobbing with relief. He wondered where he would be when dawn brought the first prayer of morning. He thought of the millions of people bowing down at that very moment, and in an unfamiliar gesture that somehow came naturally as breath he closed his eyes and made his own prayer, hoping that it would commingle with the entreaties of the faithful.

In the exquisite silence that followed the *Salaat el-isha* Fin opened his eyes and rested them on a postcard received a few months before from three Russian babushkas he had befriended in the Valley of the Kings. It showed Perseus and Medusa, the hero holding up his shield to turn the gorgon's stony gaze back on herself. Fin smiled, remembering the women and their litres of home-made vodka carried in freight-container handbags. He laughed aloud as he recalled how the women, all three of them, sisters, had shared two sets of false teeth, passing them like secret notes under the restaurant table. Before the end of the trip, and with a certain degree of repulsion, Fin had fixed the third set of teeth with superglue. He had not deciphered the Cyrillic script the sisters had written on the back of the card nor even questioned the significance of the picture, but now it gave him an idea.

He pulled the heavy telephone directory from the window and flicked through the dry almost transparent pages: electrician ... elevator ... embroidery ... employment, he turned back a page ... embassy. That was it. He discovered the number of the United States embassy and jotted it down on the back of what remained of his kebab article. He would leave a message for his American, and just to ensure it received the proper attention, he would call from a public telephone nearby ... Afghanistan, Cuba, Korea, Iran. The Iranian embassy was perfect and not too far from his house.

Fin's eyes rested on a wood-wormed cupboard door in his bureau held closed with a yellowing wad of paper. He opened the door and pulled out a bulging envelope of photographs he had eagerly taken during his first year in Cairo. He flicked through pictures of souks, camels, artfully piled fruit, old men in extravagant turbans, a lover smiling beneath a battered straw hat. As he leafed through the photographs, a part of his mind mingled with the musty smell of the opened bureau, invoking a memory of the hot and forbidden attic of childhood summers. Fin pressed his forehead against the warm wood and wondered where his life had gone.

A picture of him and Farouk, arm in arm, smiling drunkenly at a village party, brought Fin back into the moment. He placed the rest of the pictures back into the envelope and jammed the cupboard closed, sliding the photograph of him and Farouk into his pocket.

Fin considered changing out of the cheap white galabeya, but he had enjoyed its simplicity and anonymity so he kept it on. He stuffed the remainder of his money into its deep triangular pockets along with what was left of his newspaper article and limped back out into the night.

19

Omar's kebab shop gleamed with neurotic perfection. Chrome was burnished till fingers must have bled; the orange plastic panelling was speckless and mirror-like, the floor dust-free. It was immaculate, crime-scene clean. Fin entered, enunciating a greeting with a confidence he did not feel.

'*Masaa' el-khayr.*'

Neither cook replied nor looked up. Instead they plunged themselves into cutting and paring, seasoning and grilling, with feverish intensity, hoping Fin would vanish in the same unexpected way he had appeared. When he remained they met his gaze in telepathic unison. The squat kebab cook turned away immediately, leaving Fin and the willowy *shwarma* specialist in a strangely intimate moment of contact. Fin's attention was distracted by a plump apprentice who was now manning the juicer. Delighted with his position, he sliced and crushed fruit, wiping and re-wiping his work surface and knives, looking to the cooks for approval as he proudly completed each task. An old man with wisps of grey hair and a heavy grey galabeya perched like an ageing vulture on a rickety stool next to the juice station, in front of him a cash register.

The restaurant was full and every table but one was taken, peopled with the cross-section of humanity that Fin knew to expect in great eating establishments. Single men joined tables of twos and threes, eyes focused on their food, making contact only in greeting and departure. Matched pairs of young women, students or professionals, concentrated on one another's words and dispatched four or five different dishes without a break in the conversation. A besuited patriarch gleefully attacked a meal he might have been dreaming of through interminable business dinners at fancier restaurants while his wife, manicured, trimmed and tucked in a stylish Western outfit, ploughed a minute twig of carrot through a plate of hummus. One of their overstuffed children was playing a pocket video game, the other sat disgruntled with arms crossed; both wished that they were eating bright sugary burgers at their local fast-food outlet. Two waiters – perhaps a father and son, certainly related – wove in and out of the tables, balancing impossible numbers of plates and taking orders from all directions. A man rose from a table of men, salesmen from the same company – something that caused them to have identical briefcases. He approached the older of the two waiters, who was carrying five dishes teetering in one hand and a tray with two teas and a glass of warm milk with a sachet of Nescafé in the other. The salesman kissed the waiter three times on each cheek and they exchanged news. For a moment they were lost in the pleasure of seeing each other, transported to a shared past far from the restaurant, until the patriarch shouted for his chicken livers and the two men parted, the spell broken.

Fin made for the single empty table. The younger waiter

breezed round and cut him off, attempting to corral him to an unoccupied place with the group of salesmen. Fin made a feint towards the proffered seat, then sidestepped the waiter's lunge and sat down at a large and empty table. The waiter asked him to move: 'Family table,' he explained. Fin shook his head, grasped the waiter's arm and enunciated two words: 'Omar Balesh.'

The waiter held Fin's gaze for a moment then hurried away to fetch the cashier. Fin removed the newspaper article and the photograph from his pocket and smoothed them out on the spotless Formica. In seconds the cashier stood glaring in front of Fin, requesting to know what business he had with 'Mister Balesh'. Fin ignored his question and demanded a pen. The cashier obediently complied. Fin circled his name on the newspaper article from the *Cairo Herald* and, taking the photograph of him and Farouk standing arm in arm, carefully folded it and tore it down the middle with a sharp rip. Fin surveyed himself in the torn picture. He was smiling euphorically, his eyes almost closed, looking away from the camera. One arm, a shoulder and part of his body were now cut off at the jagged edge like a ruined arch cleaving to empty space, longing for completion. Fin returned the pen to the cashier, along with the torn photograph and his newspaper article.

'For Mister Balesh,' Fin ordered.

The cashier snatched the items muttering incantations against the evil eye.

Fans cooled the eating area but Fin was damp with sweat. The other half of the picture looked up at him from the table. Farouk had stared hard into the camera, as single-minded about having his photograph taken as he was about every other thing in his life. Fin thought about his journey to the restaurant and wondered if his impulsive plan had been a mistake. He had told the taxi driver to take him to the Iranian embassy, although almost any Islamic embassy would have suited his purposes.

Fin had instructed the driver to circle the embassy until they came to a public telephone. The driver had offered Fin his mobile phone but Fin had refused. He wanted a public telephone, he explained, the nearest public telephone to the embassy. He had heard that the Americans tapped all the phones around hostile embassies on the grounds that embassy staff assumed that their own lines were tapped and so used public telephones to make unorthodox calls. When they discovered a working payphone, Fin called the US embassy and in a cartoon Middle Eastern accent asked for the American. The Communications Liaison Office was closed, the receptionist informed him, but he could leave a message. Fin had told her that he had important information for the 'communications officer', gave the address of the kebab shop, and hung up.

Fin shook his head and turned the picture of Farouk face down. If the receptionist had any sense she would assume the call was as bogus as it sounded, but Fin was relying on the Islamophobia that seemed to be the defining feature of US foreign policy. The only thing he could do now was order some food and wait.

The older waiter appeared and nodded approvingly as Fin ordered the green-flecked falafel known as *taa'miyah*, a plate of rocket, a salad of tomato, parsley and green chilli, and *roz bi samnah*, the local rice dish.

'Drink?' the old man asked in English.

'*Asseer manga,*' requested Fin for the second time that day.

'*Lahma, aiz lahma?*' Meat, what about meat? the old man demanded.

'*La', la',*' Fin said, shaking his head.

Fin should have some meat, the waiter insisted; Fin was, after all, a man. Fin refused and the waiter made a phallic gesture with his forearm. *Lahma* was good for men, didn't Fin know this? He walked away before Fin could answer.

A dozen perfect stems of rocket soon arrived, each pointing like a green arrow on the small white plate. Fin picked up a leaf and folded it into his mouth. It was crisp and pungent, hot as horseradish. The other dishes arrived soon after: the *roz*, the *taa'miyah* and a wooden bowl of finely chopped salad. Fin scooped up the parsley, tomato and green chilli with a bent spoon. He was not hungry, but the food was so fresh and vibrant it made its own space in his stomach.

A faint cough announced the old waiter's return. Fin looked up. The waiter was grinning with pride, a steaming bowl on his tray. Fin shook his head: he had not ordered anything more. The waiter winked and placed it in front of Fin as if it were a sacrament, shifting each of the other dishes like planets around the sun. It was a meat dish, probably mutton, swimming in aromatic gravy and dotted with an exotic constellation of tiny bright green peas.

'For the *zobra*,' the old waiter said, delighted with himself, patting Fin on the back.

Fin sampled the unordered dish; it was delectable. For a moment the sheer accomplishment of the food suspended all worries, and Fin pulled, ripped, dunked and chewed with such absorption he was the last person in the kebab shop to notice the arrival of its owner and his outsized colleague.

Omar Balesh and Jalut made for Fin's table, the hench-man clearing a path for his boss with the natural menace of his bulk. Omar marched behind, looking like a miniature dignitary in a closely cut black galabeya buttoned to the neck with a grey roll-neck pullover showing underneath. On his head was a white keffiyeh with a traditional black braided cord holding it in place. His head was huge upon his miniature body; his brutal face was thick with a scorched forest of black stubble slick with sweat. One of Jalut's eyes, Fin noticed with fear-tinged pride, was teary and bloodshot, the other a black hole into which the remnants of Fin's courage disappeared.

Jalut stacked four chairs on top of one another for his employer. Omar hoisted himself onto the tower, pushing away the thug's proffered arm with a curse. Omar rocked from side to side, unsticking his galabeya from his thighs and then his armpits, letting his fingers linger beneath his nostrils in unembarrassed appreciation of his own odour. When he was settled he looked up at Fin and erupted into fury.

'You lie! You are not tourist. You live *Al-Kahira*,' he shouted. 'YOU,' he screamed, shooting a stubby finger between Fin's eyes, 'are not my FREN!'

The hostility of a man prepared to kill him hit Fin with the force of a jet engine, but he did his best to appear nonchalant, making a show of chasing the last pea round the mutton bone before answering.

'Who would want to be your friend? Not to put too fine a point on it, your hospitality is shit,' Fin replied with as much insouciance as he could muster.

'Why do you say this? I make a mistake to take you, but my whisky is good, no? Top quality. Fifty US, one month salary for Jalut. Hahaha. I tell him this – you drink two, three weeks' worth of his money.' Omar chortled, pleased with himself.

Fin countered that he had no problem with the whisky; it was being thrown into the river he objected to.

'El-Nil?' asked Omar, looking genuinely surprised.

'Yes, el-Nil!' Fin confirmed.

Omar was silent then barked a question at the thug who stared at the ground and looked almost bashful. Omar repeated the question more forcefully, and Jalut reluctantly answered, keeping his eyes downcast. Omar fell silent for an instant and then burst into wheezing laughter.

'I swear on my daughter's life that I did not ask this,' he said, recovering himself. 'This was big accident. It was Jalut. Hahaha. He threw you in el-Nil.' Omar laughed again, wheezing symphonically. 'Jalut says he does not like you. And now I do not like you also.' Omar coughed and snorted until the swamp matter in his chest was coaxed up to his mouth. He waved the old waiter over to him, snatched the pristine cloth from his hand and spat into it, tossing it onto the table, where it fell like a sack of offal.

'Why do you send me this?' Omar demanded, taking the article and picture Fin had sent him.

Fin took the torn photograph and joined it with the half he had kept.

'I admit I lied. I know he's not a guide. He is a friend. But you've got the wrong man. You must let him go.' Fin searched Omar's face to see the effect of his words.

'No!' Omar slammed his fist onto the table.

The restaurant fell silent. Fin smelled the cheap and pungent cologne of Jalut as he moved behind his chair. He pressed his hands together to stop them shaking.

'Perhaps Jalut can give you more whisky?' Omar asked, regaining his composure and raising one thick caterpillar eyebrow.

'No whisky,' Fin replied. He picked up the newspaper article. 'This is the *Cairo Herald*.' He held it in front of Omar. 'This is my name.' Fin pointed to his byline. 'A few months ago, before I met you, I wrote an article about kebab shops. I said that the new kebab shops on King Faisal Road were good, excellent even.'

'Not all shops!' Omar corrected him. 'Balesh Kebab is number one, the best in all of Cairo.'

'It's very good, Mister Balesh,' Fin agreed.

'Omar good, everything,' agreed Omar. 'I work like three men. My father say this: "You are small, so you work like three men." He is dead three months and five days.'

'I'm sorry, may he rest in peace,' Fin replied.

'*Shokran*,' Omar said, wiping sweat from the corner of his eye.

Fin peered at Omar's face and thought of the little girl. Their eyes were the same.

Fin again pointed to his article.

'My friend is innocent, Mister Balesh. He did not hurt your daughter, and if you harm him I will write a story and tell all of Cairo that the man who owns this restaurant is a criminal, a kidnapper and a gangster. The judges and politicians will read it and know that you tried to kill a *ferenghi*, and even with your friends in the police you, Mister Balesh, will go to prison.'

Fin had played his high card. He pushed the torn article over to Omar, who put his tiny damp hand on it and slid it onto the floor.

'Again you lie,' Omar said, staring into Fin's chest. 'Many people saw this car. I pay twenty-five people to look for this car. They find it and tell me, and I send Jalut and his cousin, and they see you with this whore. In and out of the car, half the day. Now I have him and I keep him healthy so he may know when I break him ... And if I break you also? It is no problem for me, and Jalut, he will be very happy.'

'I am a journalist, a foreign journalist. You cannot touch me. There will be big trouble.'

Omar raised his hands in front of his face. 'Touch you? I will not touch you. I have a family, a business. Jalut, he is from a village; he has nothing. He will touch you.' Asthmatic laughter overcame him again.

'The car hit your daughter, yes, but Farouk was not driving it,' Fin pleaded desperately. 'The man who hit your daughter sold the car after the accident. Farouk bought the car because it was so cheap. If he had known that he was buying the car that hurt your child, any child, he would not have bought it, he would not have accepted it as a gift – even if it was filled with pearls.'

Omar thought about this for a moment. 'Of course, I understand. You do not wish Jalut to break your friend. More than your honour you wish this, so you lie.'

Omar's sweat now resumed as if wrung through his pores by his hatred for the man who had hurt his daughter.

Fin persisted. 'One day you will find out that I am telling the truth, and the man who hurt your daughter will be free, happy and rich, perhaps laughing with his friends about your daughter's pain. You will pass your life knowing that you hurt the wrong man.'

Omar was silent. Fin picked up the photograph of Farouk and passed it to Omar.

'Show this picture to your daughter. Ask her if this is the man who was driving the car. She will tell you. She will tell you, "No". Take it to the people you hired, to the people who saw the crash, and ask them if this is the driver, and they will say, "No". I swear on my life, Mister Balesh. Another man crashed into your daughter and then sold the car to Farouk. Ask her, ask anybody. This is the truth.'

'The truth, from you who have lied to me. Why should I believe you? Swear on the head of al-Hussein.'

'I am not a Muslim,' Fin replied.

'Swear on your martyrs, on your god.'

'I swear!'

'Which martyrs? Which god? Of course you lie, you have no god,' Omar said contemptuously.

'Show your daughter the picture,' Fin begged. 'She will tell you it was not him. Many people know this Farouk. He lives in Mena village, the last house looking over the desert. But if you hurt him, I will write in the newspaper and you will be famous Mister Balesh, but not for your kebab.'

Omar leant back in his chair and rummaged in his nose with a stubby finger. After a while he removed a thick fillet of mucus which he wiped on the table.

'I will not be famous. I will do nothing. I will sit in my restaurant where all can see me. You also will do nothing because Jalut will take you now. He wants to take you. He begged me. He does not like you. He wants to break you, perhaps also to use you like a woman, who can say? It is his business.'

Fin looked around at the emptying restaurant. 'You cannot just drag me out of the restaurant. I'll scream; people will see.'

Omar shrugged. 'We people of Cairo live so close by our brothers and sisters, we see only what we wish to see.' He nodded to Jalut, who placed his hands on Fin's shoulders like two concrete epaulettes.

'I wrote the article before I came here,' Fin blurted out, fervently wishing he had. 'I gave it to somebody . . . If I do not speak to them in one hour the article will be published tomorrow.'

Omar nodded as if he had been expecting this. 'Of course, only a fool enters the house of his enemies without his weapons.'

He nodded to Jalut who swung a heavy arm round Fin's neck and dragged him off his seat. Omar shook his head angrily and shouted at Jalut, who sighed and dropped Fin back into his seat. Omar stabbed numbers into a telephone and barked a series of instructions. Finishing the call, he conferred in whispers with Jalut, whose murderous expression changed to delight as he lumbered off to the kitchen. Moments later shouts of protest could be heard from the cook followed by a yelp of pain. Omar chuckled at the noise.

'It is done. Your fren is free. I will take this photo picture of him. I will show it to my daughter, to my people, and if you lie, I will find you and I will find your fren . . .' He held up the pictures. 'And I will break you all.' Omar closed his fist around the pictures. 'And the newspaper?'

'The article will disappear, I swear it.'

'Yes, yes, you swear, but perhaps tomorrow, walking around with your fren, happy, happy, your oath will vanish like food in a house of rats. Perhaps Omar will wake up with the police at his house, looking at his business. I have much business.'

Fin shook his head vehemently.

Omar shrugged. 'What can I do? You lie one time, maybe you lie again. You are not an Arab. No, I bring you something from my kitchen. Jalut is making you something very . . . especial.' He kissed the air and folded his hands in his lap.

After a few uncomfortable minutes Jalut came out of the kitchen holding a small bowl in both hands. The waiters peered out of the kitchen door, watching, shaking their heads, as the dish was placed in front of Fin.

Fin looked at the blue patterned bowl sealed with an upturned plate. He did not care what was in it; he was not hungry and he pushed it away. Jalut stood directly behind Fin, enveloping him in the horribly perfumed fat of his belly.

'You eat this or Jalut will be very unhappy,' Omar said, grinning. Fin lifted the edge of the plate and a sweet waft of garlic escaped, trailed by spices, and then something terribly wrong.

'He make it, especial for you.' Omar laughed. 'Jalut, help our fren.'

Jalut dropped next to Fin like gravel from a truck. As his protean body massed against Fin's thigh, the sweet nauseating stench of rotten meat tightened in Fin's throat.

'It is dog,' Omar guffawed, slapping his thighs. 'We *think* it is dog. It is dead in the street many days and cooked for you, my fren. After you eat this, you stay at home, very sick, front and back.' He translated this for Jalut, who laughed wetly onto Fin. With medicine, two maybe three weeks sick ... too busy for newspapers. No problems for me.' Fin tried to sweep the bowl from the table but Jalut caught his wrist and twisted it until he could feel the bone bending.

'Eat or Jalut will break you,' Omar said calmly.

Jalut picked up the fork and speared a lump of the putrefying meat, at the same time increasing the torque on Fin's wrist. Fin yelped, and Jalut brought the meat to Fin's gaping mouth. Retching as the meat neared him, Fin ducked the fork and sank his teeth deep into Jalut's fleshy hand, biting down until he felt the skin break and his mouth fill with the metallic tang of Jalut's blood. The thug snatched his hand away and picked Fin up by the hair, prepared to smash his head against the wall.

'*La*', *la*',' Omar shouted, jumping onto his chair and throwing his glass of water into the thug's face. Jalut paused and nodded as Omar spoke to him. A wad of money was offered and Jalut dropped Fin and pushed the bills into the pocket of his galabeya.

'You make a bad mistake. It is true what the wise ones say: "Fear makes a donkey fight a lion." It was better for you to eat and suffer,' Omar said with resignation. 'Now I must promise Jalut a little time with you, just you and Jalut. But not here. It is bad for business.'

Just then the American burst through the door, glowing with confidence and muscle. All eyes turned to him as he scanned the restaurant. Spotting Fin, the American came straight over, his eyebrows raised in surprise.

'What the fuck are you doing here?' he barked at Fin. 'And who are your friends? What is this, carney night in

Cairo?' The American gestured with his chiselled head towards Omar and Jalut.

Despite his civilian clothes, pressed blue jeans and zipped jacket, there was no mistaking the American's military attitude. Buzz-cut hair, solid chest – everything about him was hard and trained. Jalut lumbered towards him, six or seven inches taller and half again as heavy.

'Sit the fuck down and we'll have a talk,' the American ordered calmly, unzipping his jacket to reveal the dull butt of a handgun. 'Now, which one of you ayatollahs wanted to speak to me so bad?' he demanded, his eyes darting back and forth between the two men.

'It's not what you think: they aren't from Iran,' Fin answered. 'This is Omar Balesh, the owner of the restaurant. We were having dinner.' Fin covered the fetid dish with its plate. 'But now dinner is finished and they are leaving.' Fin looked meaningfully at Omar.

'No one's going anywhere till I find out what's going on. Which of these guys called me?' the American hissed.

'They didn't call you; I did,' Fin replied. 'Don't you see? It was me. From the payphone outside the Iranian embassy. These two have no idea what's going on. It was me who called. I wanted to talk.'

The American's eyes widened. He looked at Omar and Jalut and calculated that they were unlikely to be of interest to him. He gestured to the door with his head. 'Leave,' he commanded.

Omar jumped off his tower of chairs and hurried away to the kitchen, the photograph of Farouk still in his hand. Jalut followed, clutching his bleeding hand.

The American sat down opposite Fin and settled his

cold eyes upon him. 'This better be good, or you are in a world of shit.'

Fin slurred his words. 'Look, I'd had a few drinks and was strolling over here and I thought of you, so I called you on the payphone. I just wanted to apologise about my behaviour the other night.'

The American leant forward over the table. 'You're fuckin' kidding, right? I'm out eighteen hours straight and get a call from the MPs about some "Iranian intel" and it's you. Drunk fuckin' limey.'

Fin held up his hands. 'I know, I know but . . . well, it was important to me. I behaved appallingly the other night. I mean, we're on the same side. I simply wanted to say sorry, no hard feelings and . . .'

'And what?' the American demanded.

'And, strictly speaking,' Fin continued, 'the Irish are not "limeys". The word you're looking for is—'

'Shut the fuck up.' The American shook his head in disbelief and uncovered the dish that stood between them. He shovelled a heaped spoonful into his mouth and grimaced. 'Disgusting foreign shit.'

He swallowed it back with a swig of water and then leant back. 'You're in a world of shit, limey. I warned you outside the bar, but you didn't listen and now you and I are going to leave and go someplace quiet where I can help you understand what a world of shit means.'

'Look, I simply wanted to offer to buy you dinner or a drink. You know, to show you that I harbour no ill feeling towards you or your great nation.'

The American's face, taut with menace, began a slow, twisted contortion into something else entirely. Fin looked at the exit; there was no way he could outrun him.

200

'Ah, well, then allow me to get the bill and we'll just slip out and have a chat, find a nice bar.' Fin tried to look unconcerned and waved for the bill. The old waiter approached nervously and informed Fin that it was on the house and that he and his friend could leave as soon as they liked. Fin insisted that he be allowed to pay, but the old waiter shook his head and hurried away. At that, the American stood with a look of quizzical wonder and immediately a cascade of vomit exploded from his mouth. He stumbled towards the bathroom, retching through his fingers, leaving a path of overturned chairs in his wake.

Fin sat for a moment and then ran to the door.

He sprinted down King Faisal Road, fear transforming to hope with every step. He stopped and looked nervously over his shoulder. There was no sign of anyone pursuing him, not the American, not Jalut. He turned to look more closely, scanning the shapes and faces of the numerous pedestrians. No one. Fin felt a surge of elation rise from his chest. He was stepping into the road to hail a taxi when a minibus pulled out from its lane and accelerated towards him with murderous speed. Fin tried to jump out of the way but tripped on the hem of his galabeya and fell hard onto the newly tarmacked road. The minibus skidded to a halt. Fin could smell the oil of its engine as the waft of burning rubber washed over him like a rebuke.

Fin was still outstretched on the road when the driver leapt out of the crowded bus and began berating him for his pedestrian incompetence. Three, then four, then ten people materialised, eager to participate in the drama. They helped Fin to his feet, brushed him down, patted him on the back and, recognising immediately that he was unlikely to mount any sort of entertaining defence, began arguing on his behalf with the minibus driver.

The passengers of the minibus, noting that their driver was now outnumbered, unpacked themselves from their vehicle in impossible numbers and entered the melee. Shaken but unharmed, Fin attempted to resume his escape but the crowd prevented him, insisting that he wait until justice was done. A self-appointed champion berated the minibus driver for his dangerous driving, exhibiting Fin's pitiful state as proof of the man's misdemeanour. As with all Cairene disputes, everyone who felt the need to vent tension on a variety of topics joined in.

When everybody except Fin had been heard a peace treaty was declared which obliged the minibus driver to issue an audible, albeit insincere, 'Ma'alesh' in Fin's direction. Fin pulled out a crowd-stealing finish by extending his hand towards the driver, which was shaken limply. Satisfied, the gathering dispersed and the minibus started up with a growl. Fin scanned the area again; there was still no sign of the American. He crossed in front of the minibus, which burst into gear and lunged towards him. Fin leapt onto the kerb. The remaining onlookers roared with laughter at the joke. The minibus accelerated away, its back window emblazoned with Arabic script picked out with flashing lights. Fin looked down at the black smudges where his galabeya had met the tarmac, wondering what the bus was called or if the words had a meaning – a religious invocation perhaps?

'It says, "Shehta abu sri",' a familiar voice beside him said. 'It is, how would you say it, my brother, "Daddy of speed"?'

Fin looked up. Farouk was standing next to him, rubbing his wrists.

'Farouk?' Fin said in astonishment.

'We must go,' Farouk replied, summoning a taxi with a quick hiss.

'Mena village ... yes?' Fin looked to Farouk for confirmation.

'Mena village!' Farouk agreed.

20

They said nothing as the taxi crossed the Cairo suburbs. Fin stared out of the window, shaking with shock or excitement, he did not know which. Farouk rubbed his wrists and arms as if he could erase the horror of the past few hours.

When the taxi crossed the Gezira Bridge Farouk finally spoke. 'I do not understand what happened but I know what you have done, *habibi*. I will give you anything, anything you wish – my house, money, my car. Say it, *habibi*. I swear on my mother, I will give it to you.'

Fin opened the cab window and inhaled the exhaust-tinged air.

'Tell me, *habibi*. It is yours. On my life.'

'I don't want anything,' replied Fin as if from a great distance. 'Well . . . you know what I want.' Farouk tried to persuade Fin to accept something of greater value like the statue of Anubis he had found when he was a child or his grandfather's dagger inlaid with pearls from the Arabian Gulf.

'At least let me take you to Sharm el-Sheikh or to Alexandria,' Farouk begged.

Fin shook his head. 'I want to hear the story about Saïd, Farouk, that's all.'

Farouk said no more, except to direct the taxi to Benghazi's liquor shop. The prized Datsun was as they had left it – the passenger door open, keys in the ignition, aubergines stretching at their white and blue plastic bag, one spilled out as if making a break for freedom.

'Lucky the car wasn't stolen,' Fin said.

'It is not luck,' Farouk answered, leaning in, gathering up the bag of aubergines and removing the keys.

'Aren't we driving?' Fin asked.

Farouk shook his head. He didn't want to be in the car. He had a bad feeling about it. 'Perhaps tomorrow, *insha'allah*.'

Farouk walked over to Benghazi's and banged on the closed shutters until a small boy appeared gnawing at a chicken wing. He purchased a bottle of whisky, paying for it with the torn bill he had taken from Fin earlier that day. The boy watched them walk away together in silence before throwing the chicken bone into the street and pulling down the metal shutter. Fin stopped and took off his shoes, wanting to savour the dry scratch of sand on the soles of his feet.

Farouk's house was on the outer edge of the village looking over the desert, but the entrance was in the narrow street behind. Had there been light Fin would have seen the colour of the walls, but he remembered them: washed green up to waist height and then the rich gold that people who have not seen the desert dream is the colour of its sands.

The actual sand was grey-white, and in the alleyway behind the house it had been packed down by the hooves of countless horses, goats, people and the occasional car. The thick fabric of awnings that hung over the balconies to keep out the heat of the day were rolled up in a way that promised tomorrow would come. A metal chair with a torn padded seat, its four legs stuck deep and uneven like pins in the cushion of the sand, stood next to the door. A bare bulb above the doorway made the chair the centre of its light, as if awaiting an actor to come onstage and deliver a soliloquy that would explain everything, bring it into focus.

Farouk tugged the sleeves of his sweater over his wrists and banged on the door, slapping at the noisy metal with the palm of his hand. The door was pulled open by a woman, who, when she stepped into the light, exposed wide striking eyes and a face thick with twisted skin like an unfinished sculpture. Fin shrank back stifling a gasp, at the same time remembering Farouk's servant. He clumsily covered his revulsion with a respectful greeting. Too late. The woman quickly pulled her scarf over her disfigured face as if drawing curtains on a terrible scene and stepped back into the kitchen.

Rana had been Farouk's maid for many years. Her body was a mass of atrocious burns received as a baby when the police had blockaded the door of her parents' house and burnt it to the ground in punishment for some minor crime. Fin called out another greeting but Rana had already withdrawn into the shadows with her strong eyes.

Farouk followed her into the kitchen, instructing Fin to use the house as his own, and dispatched him to the roof. As Fin plodded up the stairs, he cursed himself for shrinking away from Rana. The bruise on his thigh awoke like an echo but subsided as he stepped onto the wide flat roof, where a vast awning of stars absorbed his conflicts and quietened his thoughts.

He looked out towards the ceaseless bustle of Mena village, the borders of which now touched the suburbs of Cairo's fifteen million people. As always there was noise: ducks quacking on rooftops, nameless metal things being dragged over rocks and beaten with hammers, men talking, women shouting, men yelling, horses galloping, not one or two but it seemed like forty, cats were screaming like babies, babies screaming like cats, wooden thuds of old country doors, trucks roaring, ululating women at a wedding, families clapping, televisions turned to maximum, *dhikrs* sung out by drunken friends, pop music blaring out from duelling hi-fis: it was a nocturnal orchestra but not a symphony, not to Fin, who was separate from everything, everything but his memories and his yearning.

He thought of Omar. How would he be contributing to the noise of the night? Would he be whispering to his daughter, shouting at his thug, weeping into a sweat-damp towel?

And the American? Perhaps he was even now lying on the floor of his bathroom, racked by the flash floods of his bodily fluids. Fin smiled at the thought and hoped he would never see these people again.

He gazed across the rooftops at the lights of the city, stretching without end. Every moment cars were being crashed, limbs were being broken, babies were being born; fathers, grandmothers and children were dying or being saved; people were crying and laughing, looking for food, for love, for shelter, for meaning. Fifteen million people, each with their own peculiar story that was truth – fifteen million lives, each looking from a different I, until life ceased with the same breathless finality.

Fin turned towards the Great Desert, eighteen hundred miles of nothing, of west, of sand and silent space. Farouk's roof was the axis, between the city – the noise in Fin's head, the desperate urgency to find or do something – and the desert, empty, vast and still. Sand everywhere, from the panorama before him to the flaking stone of the roof, cracked and layered with tiny grains of loose rubble. Even the solid rock was made of the sand, no more than that. Sand, which by natural alchemy had consented to be formed for a time into stone, and then fashioned into buildings and cities by men, before losing its enchantment, its magical gregariousness, and, like any magic or idea, disintegrating, reverting to its chaotic nature in the desert.

Fin turned again and saw a boy a few roofs away climbing up a ladder to a rickety bamboo perch. The boy picked up a long black flag and cut it through the air in fluttering sweeps until a flock of delicate pigeons materialised out of the darkness and landed one by one: specks of white life, cooing softly.

Fin heard his name called out and leant over the edge of the house. It was Farouk, his head stretched out from the kitchen window like an upended tortoise, demanding that Fin join him. Fin wanted to tell him that he was not hungry, that he had all he needed on the flat roof, but Farouk had not waited for an answer and where his head had been there was now nothing.

Fin had assumed that Farouk's idea for the preparation of baba ganoush would be to hand the aubergines to Rana and open the whisky. But no. As with the camel liver, which Fin now recalled eating with charred onions and fierce green chillies, it was a dish that Farouk wished to make himself. 'For you I will make baba. Rana, she cannot make it properly,' he said. Fin doubted this, as Rana was a gifted cook. 'Come, help me, English. We will do this together.'

Usually Fin felt an easy calm in the kitchen; he knew how food worked and felt a value and uncomplicated clarity in preparing meals. But at this moment he did not wish to cook. He wanted the story that he had worked so hard for, suffered for. Farouk was behaving as if nothing had happened, polishing the vegetables and lining up the ingredients with an attention to detail that was affected and extremely irritating. Fin resisted articulating his frustration and instead immersed himself in chopping the garlic, squeezing a lemon and toasting cumin seeds. Fin peeled and chopped, and the focused activity engendered a sense of peace which grew with the pile of finely diced cloves under his knife.

Farouk left the kitchen and returned with a handful of sticks for the fire. Olive wood, he explained, dropping the wood so close to Fin that particles of bark and dust billowed onto his neatly piled mound of garlic, was essential for the smoky flavour that was the heart of baba ganoush. Any other wood, he insisted, and you might as well give up.

'What about oak?' Fin asked, wiping his board clean. 'Oak is a good wood.'

'Oak is useless,' Farouk replied. 'How many oaks do you see in the desert? If baba was to be made with oak would not Allah have put oaks in the desert?'

Fin replied that this was a question for an imam, or perhaps they should ask the Old Sheikh if Allah the Creator was thinking about baba ganoush when he selected the vegetation for the Western Desert. Farouk did not respond, so Fin carried on: 'Why use wood at all, Farouk? Why not just stick the aubergines in the oven? In that way we might eat before dawn and there will be less for Rana to clear up.'

Like the inked lines of a barograph in a storm, the contours of Farouk's forehead rucked and clustered. He turned away and snapped each stick in two with particular care.

'Look, Farouk, I really don't need to eat. It's been an appalling day. I should be getting back to the city. But before I go, tell me what happened. Did Skinhead get past the wall? Did he find anything?'

Farouk silenced him with his hand. 'Later, later . . . One question, English. Why are you not married?'

'Must we talk of marriage?' Fin asked. 'Can't you just get on with the story?'

'You should be married.'

'Why the hell should I be married?' Fin retorted, surprising himself with his vehemence. 'You used to complain that marriage is like a besieged fort – those who are on the outside desire to get in, and those on the inside desire to get out. I've heard it a hundred times.'

Farouk nodded, delighted to hear his own words repeated back to him.

'Of course, but I was talking of desire, not marriage. Many desire to be in marriage, *habibi*; many desire to be out of marriage. We desire many things, but only what we do not have. You must not have to desire, *habibi*; where else would desire flower?'

Farouk moved closer to Fin. 'What I said was true – always I speak the truth, I swear on my mother – but now

I tell you something else, and you should listen. A wife is good. A man should have a wife. The shadow of a woman is much better than the shadow of a wall. Don't wait so long, *habibi*.' Farouk gripped Fin's shoulder. 'Women do not want an old and useless husband with hair like a camel's hindquarters.' He smiled, pleased with his description, and then added, 'Unless he is rich of course. And although in my village you may think you are rich' – he paused and patted Fin's forearm – 'you are not rich.'

'I accept I'm not rich,' Fin replied, 'and I accept that women do not want a man with hair like a camel's arse, but what I wanted to ask you—'

Farouk interrupted him. 'Marriage brings happiness, *habibi*.'

Farouk was on his second wife but Fin did not know if either marriage had been happy. Perhaps each had been half happy, and this added up to one decent marriage. He understood that he would not achieve anything by talking to Farouk about his relationships – or lack of them. Everything was so cut and dried to this man. 'I want this. She wants that. We will do this.' Fin lacked this clarity. He did not even wish to think about his relationships, he knew the routine so well. He would love a woman or be loved, and then she would change into someone he didn't love or someone who didn't love him. Then he would leave and be resented, or be abandoned and resent. He had longed for his relationships to work, believed that they might have been the answer he was searching for, but they inevitably resulted in suffering – his, the woman's, everyone's. And at some unacknowledged point he had concluded that it was just a question of how long it took to recognise this truth, or how long he could live with it.

'You are right, Farouk. Thank you for your wisdom. I will listen to your advice and get married, perhaps next week. You are a great and wise man who knows many things, but this particular secret is not what I seek.'

Farouk raised his eyes. 'Secrets, of course there are many secrets ... Do you know the secret of a happy marriage, do you know this?'

'No, I don't. And I don't really care.'

'I'll tell you what it is, *habibi*, the secret to a happy marriage ... It's still a secret.' Farouk laughed. 'But don't worry; you are my brother. Like my brother, I mean. I have no brother. I will find you a wife, *habibi*. Many Egyptian girls would like to marry a foreigner. What about Neema? She is good girl, the daughter of my cousin Yusuf. You will like her. Too thin for an Egyptian man of course, but this is good for you, no?'

'I didn't come here to find a wife, Farouk.' Fin rose and stepped away from the table. 'I want to know about Skinhead Saïd.'

Farouk nodded as though they had always been in agreement. 'Skinhead! Why do you wish to talk of this? This is nothing, it is past. *Ellei faat maat.* Let us talk of women, *habibi.*'

'I want to hear about Skinhead, Farouk,' Fin demanded.

'More than you want a woman?' Farouk raised his eyebrows. 'I think it is woman you need. Tell me, you have no girlfriend, English? You have had *sharmoota*?'

'Look, Farouk, the only reason I rescued—' Fin stopped himself and looked at Farouk, who was grinning encouragingly. He sighed. 'Oh God. OK. Of course I've had girlfriends, but nothing serious ...'

'You are sexing with them, eh?' Farouk stretched out his

arms as if grasping motorbike handlebars and pumped his hips with unfettered delight.

Fin sighed again. 'Of course there's sex ... sometimes. But it's nothing special.'

Farouk was shocked. 'Not special? You take a woman and it is not special? Something is wrong, *habibi*. Perhaps your *zobra* is weak. My *zobra* is strong as the date palm.'

'No. My *zobra* is good ... Look, I don't want to talk about my *zobra*, I want to talk about Skinhead.'

'Skinhead? Skinhead Saïd? Why do you want to talk of this one thing?'

'I don't know what I have to do to get through to you,' said Fin in a low voice trying to contain his frustration. 'There is just one thing I want. Not food, not your niece, not any woman, just one thing: Saïd. That's all I want: Skinhead Saïd.'

Farouk paused a fraction before answering gravely. 'Listen, my brother. I do not judge, it is only for Allah to judge. And it is true, they say, Skinhead fucked a dog one time ... but not a man, never a man. Anyway it is not possible.'

'I DON'T WANT HIM!' Fin shouted, slamming his hands onto the table and standing up. 'I want his story! I want to find out what he discovered under his house!'

Farouk stared at Fin, motionless – perhaps the corner of one eye was twitching in amusement. Fin could not tell. Farouk turned away without comment and set about constructing a smoky fire out of the olive wood. The black-purple aubergines were placed over this and he hovered about the fire, incrementally turning the bulbous fruits while keeping his back to Fin. He said nothing until the heat blistered the skins and smoke from the olive wood filled the room, stinging their eyes.

'You wish to hear of Skinhead?'

Fin nodded.

'I tell you the truth,' Farouk began. 'Skinhead Saïd is my friend and my brother . . . but I swear he is less intelligent than Abdul al-Hakim's mare.'

Fin exhaled and sat down, placing his hands on the table.

21

'The most important thing for Skinhead Saïd was to make sure that no one, but no one, would hear about his dis-covery. He swept away the dust. He closed the door to the cellar and he stayed inside his house, dreaming of riches. As soon as the *Salaat el-maghrib* was called he could sit no longer and he walked to Khayam's tea house so that he might not tell anyone about his discovery.

'On entering the tea house, Skinhead spoke his salaams, took his normal place and snapped his fingers at Khayam, ordering tea with extra mint – "Good mint," he shouted, "not the goat-chewed stalks you use." Khayam was a good man who understood that money is sometimes hard to find but tea is always necessary. He had been generous with Skinhead over the years, so Skinhead's manner showed no respect, especially as his words had been heard by many men in the tea house. After a few minutes Skinhead created anger in a number of other people with comments like this, so it was natural that they began to make jokes about him.

'Nasser, whose uncle owned the third-largest perfume shop, began the attack. He was angered because when he arrived at the tea shop he had asked Skinhead for a friendly puff of his *shisha*. Skinhead shook his head, pointed to his family area and suggested that Nasser puff on his *zobra*. This was unjust because Nasser was always the one to share with Skinhead the sticky molasses tobacco to which he was so addicted.

'Nasser waited until people were quiet, then shouted across the tea house to Skinhead, asking if his proud mood was the result of recent sexual conquests. And if this was true, would he tell everyone where his new lover might be, because Nasser's family dog had been missing for a few days and the children were worried about it? All old friends have subjects about which they are teased, and for Skinhead Saïd it was his childhood union with a dog.'

Fin could not help interrupting. 'Did Skinhead Saïd truly have sex with a dog?'

'I cannot swear to it. In all fairness it could have been a goat.

'Others, all friends, now joined in the teasing of Skinhead, as is the custom, but instead of fighting, begging for mercy or laughing at himself, Skinhead moved to a table of his own. After a few minutes of silence he stood up.

'"Very soon," he called out, "I am going to be richer than all of you . . . and you will tell your grandchildren that you once knew the great Saïd al-Jabari bin Ishaq."

'One of the men, it might have been Magdi, congratulated Skinhead on finding himself a rich dog. Another quipped that Skinhead's new lover must be the president of the USA since he was the richest dog in the world. When someone else shouted that at least Egypt was fucking America for a change, everybody was laughing. Everybody but Skinhead Saïd.

'Skinhead sat and nodded as if he understood, but he did not understand. He turned his back to his old friends and puffed away on his water pipe like a locomotive leaving Al-Ackran station in the heat of the afternoon.

'All civilised men know that teasing is not to be used like the heaviest root of the olive tree might be used to strike a robber or an enemy, but as a feather to tickle and delight, a mirror to throw sun onto shadows. As soon as the old friends in Khayam's understood that Skinhead was unhappy, they tried to change his mood. I went to Skinhead's table and begged him to return to the company of his friends, tables where we have sat, drunk tea and smoked ten thousand *shisha*s together. Skinhead turned his back, said we were mules and he a magnificent stallion. As I walked away Skinhead said, "Why should I care? Before long I will be so rich that my new friends in the Mena House Country Club will look down on me if I spend time with the *zibbaleen* of my youth. It would be unseemly." When I asked the source of his great wealth Skinhead looked heavenward, shut his eyes and waved both hands in front of him.

'"You may pile up all the stones in the desert," he said, "onto my bald head till it crushes like the eggshell of a hen that has not been given enough grit in its feed – and I will never tell my secret."

'Skinhead had a great love for poultry,' Farouk explained to Fin with great solemnity.

'Of course, before Skinhead Saïd had finished his second glass of tea, before even his nose, which was large and bony like the vulture that eats eggs and rotten fruit, before this great nose had found the mint at the bottom of the tea, Skinhead Saïd had spoken of his great discovery. He spoke of the thunder as the basement fell, he spoke of the hole that was revealed and the tunnel. He spoke of the alabaster and its markings and how after this it was clear to him that behind the cartouche of the horned bird was sure to be unimaginable treasure. After swearing on his ancestors that he would tell no more, I offered him a third cup of tea. He accepted, and even before it arrived, he revealed his plan, a plan, he boasted, worthy of Salah ad-Din. He would rent a road drill the size of a camel's leg from Salim the builder's eldest brother in Cairo, and drill through the great slab of white stone to riches, two or three wives and an enormous flock of beautiful Fayoumis chickens with willow-green legs.

'Now tell me,' Farouk asked Fin. 'Do you know of Salah ad-Din?' Fin nodded but Farouk shook his head. This was not the answer he was seeking. 'You think you know, but you know nothing. Do you know why he chose Muqattam for the great citadel of Cairo, why he chose this place when there are so many?'

Fin shook his head. This, he conceded, he did not know.

Farouk was pleased. 'Salah ad-Din, the greatest of all generals,' he recounted, 'had his men kill fifty goats of the same age and hang the meat on every hill within the city walls. I mean no disrespect but your people were living in caves and eating the dung of animals at this time . . .'

Fin thought to retaliate but Farouk silenced him with his hand.

'After two days the mighty ruler rode through the city, and all the meat was spoiled except that on the Muqqatam hill, which because of the cool breezes remained fresh. So there he built the citadel, the greatest citadel in the world . . . you see, English, you say you know of the great Salah ad-Din but you know nothing.'

'And how is this connected to Skinhead Saïd?'

Farouk sighed. He was merely demonstrating that Skinhead Saïd's plan was not, as had been suggested, worthy of the great Salah ad-Din; indeed, it was not worthy of a beetle.

At first Farouk had been only mildly concerned by the information Skinhead revealed to him, but when Skinhead divulged the particulars, he became deeply troubled. Farouk, by his own admission, was a man of limited education but, also by his own admission, was unusually intelligent and capable, confident that he could apprehend all the problems of the world through the power of his mind. And, as he explained to Fin, he did not need to turn up the power very far to recognise that Skinhead Saïd's new plan lacked . . . How could he put it gently to his old friend? It lacked . . . *henka*.

'*Henka*?' Fin asked.

'Like the *samra*. You know this . . . the small dog of the desert.'

'Fox?' Fin suggested.

'Of course. *Henka* like the fox.'

'Subtlety?' Fin offered, suddenly forgetting what it was that foxes were meant to be, but Farouk was not listening.

Grave robbing was a very serious crime, he had told Skinhead. Everybody in Mena village knew about the severity of the law when it came to grave robbing – at least for Egyptians. *Ferenghi* had been lifting whatever caught their eye for thousands of years, but the government had come to recognise the immense value, not just of the artefacts, but of the international aid that could be raised for massive and carefully planned archaeological digs. These of course never happened, but the actual money was warmly welcomed and ploughed into valuable schemes like building (the mayor's new summer house) or education (for the minister's sons in England).

There were terrible penalties for anyone threatening to upset this annual deluge of money. Furthermore, Farouk went on, he had tried to explain to an increasingly fidgety Skinhead that renting a great road drill from Cairo was hardly the most subtle plan – it wasn't the sort of tool one could discreetly disguise under a galabeya and stroll unnoticed into one's courtyard with.

Finally, Farouk had explained to a by now scowling Skinhead Saïd, the loudest noise in the village was Abdul al-Hakim's television – yes, he of the unintelligent mare. What did Skinhead plan to say if the police were called to investigate the great noise coming from his cellar? 'I am sorry, officer, I have eaten too many *foul medames* and I am generating the wind of As Amen Ra from my back door.'

Farouk paused and looked expectantly at Fin with the presumption of all people telling a story they believe to be funny. Fin did not react.

'This was a comment of great wit,' Farouk explained to Fin, shaking his head in disappointment. 'Had I spoken out such words to my other friends in the café, who, *el hamdelillah*, are men who understand life, they would have laughed and admired me greatly. But I did not share this with them. I spoke only to Skinhead Saïd knowing that his moods were as unsteady as a tray of milk.

'As Amen Ra is a god of the pharaohs. Some people of the village – not me of course – they say As Amen Ra is the *khamseen*, the wind of the desert. Had I not been so generous with the feelings of Skinhead Saïd everybody would have laughed at the joining of this ancient god with the terrible music of Saïd's digestion. But there is no one to thank me for my kindness, and only Allah sees my virtue. Anyway, it made no difference. What followed was fate or the workings of a passing jinn.'

Salim Ali Rassul, not the builder, Salim, but the Salim who worked in the papyrus shop opposite the Sphinx – Farouk assured Fin that he had met him two or three times – this Salim roared with laughter from the other side of the café at some crumb of scandal, some small piece of conversation *zibbala*. In doing so, he upset his tea over his galabeya and a tiny bush of mint leaves stuck to him like the triangle of hair that sits over a woman's *cus*. The sight of this mint-leaf pubis created a great storm of laughter which spread throughout the tea house.

Skinhead, who like a child believed creation circled around him, suspected that people were mocking him and that Farouk, jealous of his discovery of the riches that were soon to be his, was the source of this mockery. Furious, he left the tea house and stood outside puffing away at the costly American cigarettes he had purchased as proof of his impending wealth.

After perhaps four American cigarettes (as many as Skinhead Saïd could afford in a week) he returned to Farouk's table confident that he had prepared a response worthy of Mullah Nasruddin himself.

'You know of Mullah Nasruddin, of course?' Farouk asked.

Fin nodded.

'Of his adventures on the Syrian border?'

Fin shrugged.

Farouk had introduced him to the tales of Mullah Nasruddin and had initially insisted that Nasruddin was a historical figure. Fin had been as credulous as a child at the time, eager to believe any story that would cast Egypt as a place where fantasy and reality met. Fin had soon discovered that the stories of Nasruddin were as numerous as the people who spoke them, and his treasure chest of tales had grown almost daily, as taxi drivers, waiters, shopkeepers, government officials and people at the newspaper added their versions to the legend. Each story was different, but as to the mullah's characteristics, it was agreed that he was either foolish or cunning or both, depending on the requirements of the tale.

Fin told Farouk that he could not be certain if he had heard the story, but was sure he did not wish to hear it – unless it had something to do with Skinhead Saïd.

Farouk brushed his hand in front of his face as if shooing away a fly. 'Of course. Are not all things connected?

'Every week Mullah Nasruddin would ride a caravan of horses across the border to Syria, each horse loaded with panniers stuffed with straw. When the border guards asked him the nature of his business, Nasruddin would answer, "Smuggling," and the guards would often search him, sometimes emptying out the panniers and combing every strand of straw. Nevertheless, the mullah kept crossing the border, becoming richer and fatter each week. After some years Nasruddin retired a wealthy man and moved far away to Alexandria or beyond. One day in a café he met the chief of the border guards, who had also retired and moved nearby.

'"Tell me, please, Mullah Nasruddin," the retired chief

begged. "We were never able to catch you. What was it you were smuggling?"

'"Horses," the Mullah replied.' Farouk slapped the table in delight and looked to Fin. 'Horses!' he repeated.

Fin forced a smile. 'I fail to see the connection.'

'A story without a horse is like a camel without a *tafir*.'

'*Tafir*?'

'On its back,' Farouk insisted.

'A rider?'

'No, no, a small hill . . . a lump.'

'A hump.'

'Exactly,' Farouk said, satisfied.

Fin could not see the connection, Farouk explained, because he did not listen properly. The mullah's plan was wise and crafty, but the plan of Skinhead Saïd was the plan of a goose.

Fin nodded and Farouk resumed his story.

'"You, Farouk al-Mabsoud bin Faisal," Skinhead had said striding back into the café, "are like an impotent cockerel puffing himself up and scratching in the sand to attract the hens." Skinhead had surveyed the room to make sure he had an audience. "Yes, they will cluck, yes, they will coo and cluster round you until they realise that beneath your feet – what is there? Grains of corn or plump worms?"

'Skinhead was now drunk with madness, a madness hidden for years like wine from the pyramids, but his intoxication was derived not from fermented dates and honey but from broken dreams and his own weakness. His voice was high and strangled like a hen's and all the customers of the tea house listened in, gripped by Skinhead's wild and, to them, meaningless, speech.

'"No, not grains of corn and plump delicious worms,

but rat droppings and dust!" At this point rage had stormed the citadels of Skinhead's reason and he ran to the open door of the tea shop, where he paused and gathered what he felt were his wits before delivering a final and, he believed mortal, blow. "And they all" – he gestured towards the tea house regulars, who were the imaginary hens of his speech – "will admire the great prize cock Saïd al-Jabari bin Ishaq and realise for ever more that as I scratch in the sand there is, and will be, an abundant paradise of fruit and strange meats!"'

While announcing this passionate and confusing speech, Skinhead puffed out his chest and clawed and scratched at the wooden floor with his sandalled feet. Some people, particularly Farouk, had made heroic attempts to listen in a respectful manner, but the sight of an angry six-foot man-chicken was too great a provocation and soon everyone, even Farouk, tumbled into the arms of laughter. This final betrayal was too much for Skinhead, who turned as red as the combs of his beloved Fayoumis chickens and, throwing his head back, stormed out of Khayam's.

'This was the last occasion I was able to speak to him in any proper way. On a good day Skinhead would just turn away but usually he would stare at me and cluck quietly, his eyes full of hate.'

Fin, who had been riveted to the story, turned his attention to his friend's face and could not identify if it was a flicker of regret or amusement he caught in his expression. Rana entered the kitchen, coughing and reciting holy verses to protect herself from evil spirits. She scolded Farouk for the smoke, which had become inappropriately thick for a modern kitchen. Farouk replied by raising his arm as if he intended to beat her. Rana laughed and continued to admonish him. Farouk gestured to the kitchen window. He'd already opened it; what else did she expect him to do? Rana shook her head, and as her voice descended an arpeggio of requests to local saints and passing angels, she pushed open the front door to the house, creating a draught which cleared the smoke in moments.

'We are more comfortable now,' Farouk said as if the door had been his idea. 'I do not know why she did not do this sooner.'

Fin nodded and kept his mouth closed to allow silence – the soil from which stories grow.

Skinhead Saïd was raising debts like a man with no family and no future. Most people in the village had seen him parading up and down in new clothes, smoking American cigarettes and, it was rumoured, planning a massive chicken coop in the style of the Great Pyramid. A few in the village were impressed by him and some irritated but no one except Farouk knew of his foolish plans until the afternoon a truck from Cairo thundered through the village and stopped outside his house.

In a place like Mena news is so precious that when it arrives people are not content to merely enjoy it, they must flock to its source. This was why, when the enormous road drill arrived, Skinhead Saïd found his house besieged by everybody he had ever known in his life, a crowd no greater or fewer than the population of Mena village.

Khayam's nephew, a boy whose dream was to earn enough money to get to the beaches of Sharm el-Sheikh to see for himself the foreign women without clothing, hastily set up a tea stall by Skinhead's door. People crowded, sipping tea, speculating and basking in the delight of an undeniable happening. Normal levels of chatter were reduced to a respectful hum punctuated with occasional ooohs as parts of the exciting tool were unloaded. Although they could clearly see the equipment being heaved out of the garishly painted truck and although they were witness to Skinhead signing over something as a deposit, people did not know, nor even speculate what the tool might be for. That it was there was enough for the people of Mena.

No one slept that night in Mena, not because of excitement or gossip or indigestion, but because much of the village was shaking with the roar and vibration of the enormous, and as became evident, clumsily managed drill.

The following morning at sunrise Skinhead emerged from the basement to find a large crowd in front of his house. He was coated in fine white dust and missing part of a toe from his left foot. The drill was designed to be used vertically rather than horizontally, and although Skinhead Saïd had managed to reduce his smallest toe by a quarter, the only thing he had done to the alabaster, it was later discovered, was to obliterate its ancient hieroglyphics.

Since the village was already assembled outside Skinhead's house, he was able to receive swift medical assistance from Malik the local barber, who was not only the appointed circumciser but in time-honoured tradition the local surgeon.

Pale and bandaged, Skinhead had borrowed a cart to leave the drill at his brother's house, and when the police arrived two hours later to investigate the excitement they found only Mumbling Iqbal, who, despite giving them a surprisingly accurate description of events, was not believed on account of his position as the village idiot.

For the next few days Skinhead Saïd kept to his house, perhaps mourning the deformed toe, perhaps hiding from his expanding circle of creditors, the questions of the police or just the sniggering of the village. But when he did appear again it was not as a penitent but with new and exciting news. Skinhead Saïd would have a party. Everyone was invited and all the greatest horses from Abu Sir to Bapha would dance. There would be mutton and the finest mint tea for all, and, of course, the famous Zar musicians would be summoned from the south. It would be, he promised, the greatest party since the wedding of the drunken bastard police captain Wahib al-Sabbah three years before.

On the Friday after Skinhead's announcement Farouk was chatting with Salim the builder as they made their way back from the mosque after prayers. There was bright clear sunshine but they still wore their thick scarves against the bite of the *khamseen*. They discovered Skinhead Saïd buying rose water from the stall that sold perfumed waters for cologne and puddings. Since Skinhead was angry with him, Farouk whispered to Salim that he should ask Skinhead Saïd about his party while Farouk went ahead to Khayam's.

Salim caught up with Farouk before he reached Khayam's and related that, after offering greetings and the usual courtesies, he had demanded of Saïd the purpose of his celebration. Saïd had replied, 'To celebrate the new Saïd,' before turning his back and purchasing enough rose water for several hundred puddings.

Was that all? Farouk had wanted to know. Had Skinhead Saïd said nothing else, given no clues? Salim shrugged. Perhaps there had been something in Saïd's normally dull eyes – a flash, a glint – but that was as much as anyone could know.

'Although no one was actually paid, Skinhead Saïd immersed himself in the careful ordering of all the supplies for the party: mutton to be rubbed with cinnamon and stuffed with apricots, chicken marinated in cumin then filled with raisins and pine nuts, aubergines, chick peas with preserved lemons and spinach, rice, potatoes stuffed with ground beef, *kahk bil-laoaz* the delicious sweet almond bracelets of the desert – and of course rose petals for the *mihalabeyah* pudding – not to mention the piles of coloured bunting, the bushels of mint, the firewood, the musicians and the hay for the dancing horses. Everything Skinhead bought on credit.

'Of course, some people concluded that Skinhead had already discovered the treasure and the purpose of the party was to attract a wife, but the majority believed in the "new Saïd", a term that had become almost as common in the village as "New York" in America. Saïd had troubled the village with his schemes and madness for thirty years and now everyone hoped that he would mend his ways, that he would *amr bil-ma'rouf* – "make himself one with good works", and *nahiy an al-munkar* – "turn away from evil". This was not just the view of strict religious people. How a person behaves is important to everyone in the village just as a pain in the belly or a thorn even in the heel of one foot is important to the whole body. This was not about who went to the mosque, who kissed which man or woman or who broke or bent the laws of Egypt. It was about the life of the community: people greeting one another as respected friends and sharing their luxuries, and caring for the sick, simple and poor. How a person behaves as a Muslim is about him or her and Allah, but also it is about the *umma*, the community of Muslim people, not just in Mena village but every Muslim in the world. In the village it was not so much about praying as praying together, and if Skinhead was changing his behaviour, well, what better reason for a party? And so what if he had some other secret purpose? As the old desert proverb goes, "Must a man understand the secrets of a chicken to enjoy its eggs?"'

Fin interrupted: 'You talk so much of God and prayer and I've never seen or heard of you so much as visit the mosque, not even on Fridays . . . and you drink.'

Farouk rose abruptly from the table, saying that he loved God, he respected his parents, he gave to the poor and one day, *insha'allah*, he would make the hajj and receive forgiveness for his sins. Then he would return to the mosque – not each Friday but five times every day. If he was a bad Muslim, this did not make Islam bad and it certainly did not give a *ferenghi* blown in on the back of Satan's digestive wind the right to criticise his religion. Farouk turned away and glared out of the window.

Worried that part of the story would abscond from his memory, Fin scribbled disordered notes on a scrap of paper until distracted by the barking of a dog padding past the window. For a moment Fin allowed himself to believe that it was the dog he had tried to save earlier in the day, but it was the wrong colour and size, although just as scrawny – as if it had borrowed a larger dog's ribcage. Fin went back to his notes, experiencing the familiar sense of falling that life outside stories always seemed to bring.

'Let's go and see him,' Fin declared.

'Who?' Farouk looked up from the fire.

'Skinhead Saïd.'

'Impossible.'

'Why?'

'Why? Because it is written.' Farouk peered into the flames, blowing and shifting the embers of the olive wood.

'What do you mean, "it is written"? Is this some religious thing again? You're telling me that it is Allah's will that we cannot go and—'

Farouk spun round. 'Why would the great and only God, Allah, decree or even consider that an insignificant servant like me should, or should not, speak to his oldest and most stupid friend? What is your view of Allah? That he is some kind of Father Christmas singing your Beatles, playing for Manchester United and sending a list detailing which of your friends you can talk to by Her Majesty's Royal Mail service? Allah is truth. He is pure love and wisdom. He is beyond man and his worries.' Farouk shook his head. 'It is the law of Egypt that I cannot talk to Skinhead,' he concluded, as if this brought clarity to the situation. He moved back to the grey cloud where the aubergines lay thick, soft and rumpled like children asleep in quilts and turned them gently over.

Fin had risen. He could no longer bear the smell of smoke, he announced; he was going up to the roof for some air.

22

Fin stretched out on the desert side of Farouk's roof, looking out towards the floodlit wedge of the Great Pyramid. He rubbed his hands gently across the wall, his exhaustion and anxiety succumbing to the heat that still leaked out of the stone's depths like oblivion returning to the night. Fin wished he could do the same. He pictured miles of golden-crested sand dunes, though he knew as he fell towards sleep that the sand was grey and stony. As he dropped into unconsciousness he felt his living cells melting into themselves, falling into the space between stone; stone becoming sand; sand becoming sleep . . . until a thundering report exploded around him.

Fin leapt to his feet as another boom resonated across the desert, then another, speeding up into a slow roll like the heavy drums of an old-fashioned Hollywood epic. As he shouted down the stairs for Farouk there was a crashing orchestral chord at stadium volume: 'GU AI JIIIII . . .!'

A voice echoed across the emptiness with demonic intensity: 'WEN MING DE XING YU SHUAI!'

Farouk arrived on the roof. He was unconcerned by the drama and more intent on pushing crumpled cigarette boxes and other bits of rooftop detritus to the edge of the wall with one lazy foot.

'BU XIU DE SI FEN KE SI XIANG QUAN YI QIN YAN MU DU!'

The voice filled every space, ten times louder than the muezzin's call, interspersed with histrionic chords that shook the whole village. Farouk stretched, looking up as the Sphinx was soused in candy-pink light. 'China.' He yawned. 'So many Chinese now. Very serious people, but they buy nothing.' He rubbed his wrists adding, 'Perhaps they know that the antiquities we try to sell them are made in their own country.' Farouk was pleased with his observation and raised an eyebrow towards Fin to see if he too was taken by it, but Fin was still acclimatising to the drama below.

'ZHE JIU SHI HU FU ZHI MU, QI TU YU SI SHEN DUI KANG!'

'I thought it would be finished by this time of night,' Fin said, the script of the son et lumière coming back to him: 'This is the tomb of Cheops, built to defend himself against death,' words that he had heard so often he had ceased to notice them.

'The Chinese come at night,' Farouk replied. 'They have a special deal. It was the same with the Russians ten years before, but now the Russians are before the French, and the Americans, they don't even come.'

There was another histrionic crash of sound as the Great Pyramid was saturated in golden light which flicked from yellow to green as the Nile was inundated, and to red as historical plots ended in slaughter. History itself was being slaughtered, Fin mused, every night, in ten different languages, blasted across the desert to thousands of half-interested tourists who would later bore people across the world with their flimsy tales.

'Farouk, I came here looking for something. To find something.'

'You think you have not told me? One hundred times you have told me.'

'I don't even understand what I'm looking for, not fully. It's like there's something missing. I've spent my life yearning to find it so I'll wake up and be part of everything.'

'Come, English, don't talk of such things. Taste the desert air; it's so pure you can smell the farts of the camels.'

'I just want to feel right. Farouk, I never have . . .' Fin's voice tightened.

Farouk put his hand on Fin's shoulder. 'I am sorry, my brother.'

Fin gulped a breath of air.

Farouk was behind him, his voice low and serious. 'Put it in the Pyramid,' he whispered.

'Just tell me the story. I've got to kill this feeling.'

'Kill? You cannot kill what is not alive. Put it in the Pyramid, my friend. Take out love.' Fin let his head fall back. The stars throbbed and ebbed.

'It is finished?' Farouk asked as the son et lumière exploded into another crescendo of music and lights.

If only it were so simple.

'Yes,' Fin lied.

'Good,' replied Farouk. 'Then we can drink.'

Farouk took Fin back down into the kitchen and assembled glasses, a bottle of whisky in a plastic bag, and a can of Coke on the kitchen table.

'Drinking,' he explained, pulling the whisky from the bag and pouring Fin a quadruple, 'is for celebration and

233

for revelation. It is never to be used for the vanquishing of an evil spirit, especially not an *afreet*.'

Fin refused the Coke, but Farouk pushed his hand aside and splashed it into the whisky.

'For two reasons, infidel, you must take Coca-Cola with your whisky,' he insisted. 'First, whisky is poisonous and must be smuggled into the body in the same way as the great hero Haroun was smuggled into the harem of the caliph Mehmet II. And second, whisky is haram and must be disguised in case that drunken policeman Wahib passes by and wishes to sit with us.'

Fin smiled and breathed the warm night air from the window. He felt the sadness in his eyes uncoil and the tightness in his throat loosen. Perhaps he could detect the faintest tang of camel fart ... Fin sipped the warm black drink – sweet, fragrant, strong and delicious. Farouk was right again, he thought. It was good with Coke. Fin drank and sighed as he gazed through the window, beyond the floodlit desert and into the darkness beyond.

23

'The Zar are musicians,' Farouk said looking down into the dense blackness of his drink. 'But they are more than musicians, more than entertainers. They are magicians, priests, half-mad men who call on *afreets* to rise up and be gone for ever. If you want the greatest of all the Zar, then you call for the Zar of the South, and this is what Skinhead did.'

For Farouk, the timing could not have been better. His much-loved first cousin Mister Khaled was possessed by a fearsome *afreet*. Mister Khaled had visited the imam and spent fruitless hours at the mosque trying to conquer the troublesome *afreet*, but nothing had helped. He had passed a day and a night buried up to his neck in sand behind the Khafra Pyramid. He had even followed the advice of his mad Aunt Mir (either a prophet or mentally ill – no one was sure) to capture a live scorpion in the ancient step pyramids of Sakkara and then deliberately sting himself on the buttock or thigh on the night of the new moon. None of these measures had any affect on the *afreet* that grasped Mister Khaled in such a terrible way.

As everybody knows, *afreets* come in many guises and

enter through weaknesses or wounds of the heart. Once within, they suckle the life force, as a camel tick drinks blood, making the possessed dry and dull to the beauty of Allah's creation. Mister Khaled walked about with eyes as wide as his heart was asleep, and all who knew him were concerned. No one can entice an *afreet* like the Zar, and none like the Zar of the South. So that was why, even though Farouk and Skinhead Saïd no longer exchanged salaams, Farouk knew he must attend the party.

Fin interrupted Farouk with his hand. 'Mad Aunt Mir – she was the mother of the little girl, your niece? The one we visited a few miles north of here?'

'No, no,' Farouk replied. 'That is my sister Sayeeda. You think she is mad? She is not mad. She has three children. How can she be mad?'

'So was it the older woman with enormous earrings who sang the song about love and oranges?' Fin wanted to know.

'Yes,' Farouk said, 'that was Mir.'

'But there was nothing wrong with her. She wasn't mad.'

'She was completely mad ... You want to hear your story or you wish to talk of my family?'

Fin acquiesced.

On the night of the party it was clear that Skinhead Saïd had prepared a festival beyond all expectation. Fires burned and hundreds of coloured flags flickered in a warm desert breeze, reaching out on either side of Skinhead Saïd's house like welcoming arms.

People arrived in groups, women and men separately. The women settled themselves on carpets on the beaten ground, the men walked about holding hands and chatting. Everyone was in their finest clothes.

Mister Khaled, who Farouk had led to the party like a blind man, had once been a respected horseman and great teller of tales. He was often called, before the time of his possession, to sing poetry to the elders or into the ears of a dancing horse. Now, Mister Khaled wandered about without feeling like ... like that which he was – a man whose spirit had been compressed into the base of his spine by a troublesome *afreet*. He was not confused like Mumbling Iqbal, or mad like Aunt Mir. He could do the essentials: work, pay his respects, keep himself clean. But to feeling, to excitement, joy or sorrow, he was like the waterskin of a Bedouin lost in the desert, empty and dry, containing nothing.

'Mister Khaled is my cousin,' Farouk said, lighting a cigarette, 'and I longed for his smile and kindness, his flirtatious way with women, his magnificent appetite for roast lamb and hashish and his singing of the *Rubaiyat of Omar Khayyam* at a desert fireside in Sakkara. So even I had no eyes for the food or the horses – it was the Zar I sought. Only the Zar.'

Farouk's eyes were full of tears, but it could have been the pungency of the smouldering olive wood. Fin reopened the front door, which, despite Rana's actions, had been closed again by a passing neighbour. Farouk attended to the aubergines, removing them carefully from the fire and placing them side by side on a wooden board, each now perfectly covered in a wafer shell of charred blackness. Farouk waited for Fin to sit down.

'Although auspicious beyond all other places that are not mentioned in the Holy Koran,' he began with characteristic hyperbole, 'Mena village is not rich, and parties like the one given by Skinhead Saïd had never before happened, not even in the memory of Old Man el-Had, who had lived for one hundred years or more. Yes, a wedding; yes, the birth of a son; yes, a funeral – but a party for the new Saïd? This was confusing.'

Nevertheless a party it was, and having inspected the horses and greeted many of his relatives Farouk sauntered over to the food, which was laid out on embroidered cloths and was, he could assure Fin, better than any food in Fin's country. Farouk could guarantee this, swear on it. He described strips of roasted lamb so delicious and full of the flavour of aromatic cumin and smoky wood that he had felt himself drunk with the taste. He had forced Mister Khaled to eat but did not waste the finest delicacies on him, knowing that all flavour would be lost to the *afreet*. When he was satisfied, Farouk relaxed on a carpet, awaiting the Zar.

'Of course, the Zar cannot just begin,' Farouk insisted, topping up Fin's glass with whisky. 'You do not turn it on like your BBC World Service. No. It is like a stone cart in soft sand. Great effort must be made to make it move; gently it must be rocked back and forwards, back and forwards, and then the wheels turn slowly and you must push and push and, *insha'allah*, you will come to a slope and then it will roll. On and on, no longer in your control. The Zar is like this.'

Farouk had searched for the musicians, scanning secluded spots in the sand as if, he said, seeking a herd of cattle who had broken into a field and eaten a month's grass in a single afternoon. Of course he had found them lying around under Skinhead Saïd's famous Anbara date palm. Where else would they be with their profound understanding of history and magic, coupled with their extreme laziness? Where better to rest than under the date palm planted more than a hundred and fifty years ago by Skinhead's great-grandfather Yousef al-Zaki?

'Are you aware of this tree, English?' Farouk asked.

'No.' Fin confirmed, he was not.

'Of course you are not aware,' Farouk said with a broad smile. 'Your infidel head is too full of questions to hold any real knowledge, but I will tell you . . .

'A sheikh from Dakkar had crossed the desert with fifteen coloured mares and a magnificent stallion to improve the line of his bloodstock. When the sheikh arrived in Mena he glimpsed Yousef al-Zaki's youngest daughter Zelenka, a girl whose skin was mixed with liquid pearls and whose every word was a Sufi poem. And of course the sheikh fell desperately in love with her. The sheikh, a great mathematician, a famous warrior and a breeder of magnificent horses, immediately approached Yousef and offered him a beautiful chestnut-and-white mare in return for Zelenka's hand. Yousef refused. The sheikh went away and reappeared the following day with three mares – two chestnuts, and a black beauty with a patch of white on the flank like a celestial cloud on a moonless night. You have seen such a horse, *habibi*?'

Fin dutifully shook his head.

'Very few have seen such a horse, but still Yousef refused. The sheikh spent days walking through the orange orchards of the village – where the tourist coaches now park – mumbling and praying. After many days he returned to Yousef's house leading his mighty blue-grey stallion Isra, which he offered as dowry for the old man's daughter.

This was an astonishing price for Zelenka, who although beautiful was the youngest daughter, but still Yousef was not moved and again he refused the Sheikh. This was too much for the sheikh. Never had a stranger who had crossed the great Sahara with good intentions and some of the finest horses in the world been so insulted. The sheikh drew his sword, blue-grey like the stallion and made of *wootz*, the secret metal that defeated the hordes of barbarian crusaders, as you know, and he prepared to behead Yousef.

'The old man did not run away but calmly bowed before the sheikh, entreating him to understand that had he the right to give away his daughter, the first of the sheikh's mares would have been more than fair. Indeed, so noble was the bloodline of the sheikh's horses that Yousef would have asked Allah's forgiveness for accepting such an exchange. There was no question, the old man went on, that the horses of Mena village would be forever improved by the attentions of the sheikh's stallion, and the citizens of Mena were filling the tea shops of the village this very minute, he assured the sheikh, discussing nothing but the beauty and Bedouin purity of his horses. However, the old man had said that, more than horses, he, Yousef al-Zaki, loved God, and God was manifest in love. Zelenka his daughter was already in love with Karin the bee-keeper, who had called on Yousef only a week before with a honeycomb the size of a lamb and a tiny phial brimming with the essence of the queen bee. Karin had asked for the hand of his daughter and Yousef had accepted. Many would say that Yousef was a soft old man for accepting, but, he explained, he knew what he saw and felt, and he saw that God had pitched his tent of love in his daughter's heart and who was he to tear it down? The sheikh threw down his sword and embraced Yousef, and they sat down in the sand and began a conversation which, it was said, went on for three days and three nights. They talked of women, of God, of poetry and of course, horses, and when the sheikh left for his homeland, Yousef planted a date palm whose fruit cures baldness and inspires love, and under which the musicians of the Zar now sat.'

Most of Skinhead Saïd's guests, Farouk explained, had been enjoying the party for some time before their host was even seen. People were more interested in the food and their friends than Skinhead's absence and assumed that he must be somewhere. Guests by the tea stall, discussing their neighbour's wealth, thought he was by the roast meats inviting people to eat. People breaking up tobacco for a water pipe imagined Skinhead would be by the date palm, hearing or telling a story.

That he was not present, Farouk explained, only became apparent when one guest, full of food and having just finished a pipe of apricot tobacco, turned to another guest and said that he had not seen Skinhead Saïd. At that very moment, with a sense of timing that was later to desert him, Skinhead appeared.

Knowing, as Farouk and most of the village knew, that Skinhead Saïd had passed most of his life attempting to gain people's attention and admiration without achieving anything in a field of virtue or action – unless one considers the smoking of unusually large quantities of tobacco a feat worthy of respect. Knowing this, Skinhead's quiet arrival at his own party was ... Farouk could not find the word. 'What is *irtiyaab* in English?'

'Why do you ask me, Farouk? You know I speak little Arabic.'

'Of course you know.' Farouk insisted. 'What is it when the policeman says there is something in your action more than your action?'

'Suspicious?' Fin offered.

'That is it!' Farouk cried triumphantly. 'Suspicious. *Irtiyaab* is suspicious. It is a good word, no? Sssssssss like the cobra's song, or the wind in the reeds of the lower Nile. You see, your Arabic is very good. You should have more faith in the mind Allah gave you.'

Skinhead's quiet arrival was, he went on with a sibilant flourish, 'sssuspicious' to all who knew him. He bowed to his elders, greeted his friends, kissed his relatives and darted from one group to another avoiding all but the most essential 'empressements'. Farouk pronounced the word with great deliberation. He then described how he observed Skinhead from a sufficient distance to avoid the necessity of embarking on a greeting that could well be rebuffed, as he had heard that Skinhead was still angry with him. Had it not been for Mister Khaled's *afreet*, he would have avoided the party altogether.

Skinhead Saïd seemed to be spending his time looking over the shoulders of his guests and using the brief moments between – Farouk paused – 'empressements' to scan the crowd.

Fin stopped Farouk. What, he wanted to know, were 'empressements'?

Farouk raised an eyebrow. 'Do you not speak your own language? It's an English word.' He had learnt it at his school many years before. Fin must know it.

Fin said he had never heard of it.

'On my mother's life, it is a true word,' Farouk vowed. 'It is the word for the salaams and the enquiring after the health and prosperity of your guests and their families, the offering of tea and food – all these things that we do.'

Fin wondered if Farouk had made the word up, or perhaps the word had died, but he did not want to divert Farouk from the story.

It soon became clear to Farouk when he saw Skinhead Saïd making his way towards the Anbarra date palm that the target of his search was the Zar. They of course had not moved since Farouk had last seen them – except to lie down, half asleep and slippery with lamb grease. When Skinhead spotted them lying around like houris in a harem he did not wait for them to finish resting, as would be respectful, but marched into their midst and addressed them with harsh and angry words: 'Surely you have filled your large and slippery bellies with enough lamb and *foul medames* by now?'

One of the musicians replied by rolling over and unrestrainedly breaking wind, to the great amusement of his colleagues. But Skinhead was not put off and asked them, with a wit that was unusual for him, if such a noise was the only music they intended to make. There was no answer, and Skinhead walked off commenting that the musicians were as useless as his grandfather's digestion.

Skinhead should have known better, Farouk explained. Most musicians are keen to perform, but the musicians of the Zar take pride in their laziness. They know that the longer they keep people waiting, the greater the gratitude they will receive and the better access they will have to those stubborn *afreets* that are the foundation of their livelihood – as a disease is the foundation of medicine, a rat, the reason for a rat catcher and bondage the heart of liberation. Skinhead would have known that the gradual goading of the Zar was a valued if not essential part of the magic but on this day he was not, as the English say, 'playing the cricket'. Such behaviour proved to Farouk that Skinhead had no interest in the quality of magic, and yet this was a service that he must have paid for.

Such questions had crossed Farouk's mind during the party, but he had not pursued them; not asked himself how they related to other things he knew. Of course, he had been troubled by Skinhead's behaviour, and it was true that he had at times observed him closely, but he did nothing. He might excuse himself, saying that it was his concern for Mister Khaled that made him blind to the events before him, but it was more than this. Bountiful Allah had given him a strong mind and he had failed to use it, preferring to be lost in the excitement of the evening, the coloured lights, the food, the people and above all his anger towards Skinhead Saïd. Perhaps this anger had hardened his brain, for had he been a better man, he could have seen what was going on and stopped it all before it was too late.

'Should have seen what?' Fin asked.

Farouk replied that he did not know. This was what he was trying to explain to Fin. He might have known if he had looked beyond his anger, beyond Mister Khaled, or even if he had just asked himself what was happening, but he did not ask.

Farouk picked up the now cool aubergines and forked out the parchment-coloured flesh.

When the Zar stood upright for what must have been the first time in many hours they decided the time had come to play and shuffled unhurriedly to a chosen spot amid the people of the village. These people were men who spent hours in the shadowless sun cajoling angry pink tourists into buying postcards, or taking a camel ride, or visiting an empty tomb. These people were women whose every hour was full of carrying and caring, protecting and feeding. These were the people of Mena village, who had been chewing and laughing their way through the warm desert night, enjoying the horses and each other's company. They had noticed neither the musicians' arrival nor the absence of their host, but each one heard the solo drum of the Zar when it began its slow beat.

Farouk had been watching out for the musicians, and as soon as he saw them stir he took Mister Khaled by the hand and guided him through the throng of people until they were standing directly in front of the Zar. As the pipe, tabla and finger cymbals joined in with the drum, the air filled with music, just as the space around a jasmine plant is filled with the scent of jasmine.

Conversation drifted into nothing as people caught the music; a sandalled foot tapped in the sand; a woman's fingers curled slowly into her palm; shoulders began swaying like feluccas in the Nile. Soon people were dancing, hands stroking the night air, pulling the music towards them and their neighbours. Some shuffled, waving their hands as if calling to lost souls, some took great steps as if creeping into a lover's room or stepping over hot coals, some looked from side to side as if they were following a ball thrown between children. Had Skinhead been there he would have tucked his fingers under his arms and moved his elbows like the wings of a Fayoumis hen. The drum *b-boom, b-boom, b-boomed* its way across the desert, and everyone's mood was lifted because there was no room for anything but happiness.

When Farouk looked behind him he saw that Mister Khaled had slipped away and after searching for some time found him walking towards the great emptiness of the desert, deaf to the music and drifting with empty eyes. After that Farouk held him by the hand and sat away from the crowd waiting for the Zar to begin their magic. They played without stopping for an hour or more, and people danced until they were weary and then took some tea or a strip of lamb, a spoon of rose-scented *mihalabeyah* pudding or a sip of something stronger from a foreign bottle in a brown paper bag.

Farouk did not share the crowd's joy. Any musician could make rhythm, he said, and if you felt easy or you wished to forget your troubles you would dance, but these were the Zar of the South, and they had the power to open your heart and make you feel God and only they could call on the troublesome *afreet* that was dragging Mr Khaled into the dust. So it was natural, Farouk said with the certainty that accompanied all his feelings, that he should be displeased with the Zar's playing and with the villagers stamping their feet like excited teenagers.

When the musicians took a short rest to tighten the skins of their drums by the fire and sip some tea, Farouk approached them and demanded to know if they were indeed the famous Zar of the South. Of course, they replied. Who did he think they were? Farouk replied that at first he had thought they were the Zar of the South but now he wondered if they were someone else and had they not come to the wrong party? Perhaps they were musicians for a goat herder's wedding or a circumcision, or for the tourist banquet out in the desert. One of the musicians quipped to the others that he wished he were playing for the tourist banquet as the pay was good and they would not be disturbed by men with no more appreciation of music than a lizard. Farouk replied that even if he were the most stupid and hard of hearing lizard in the Great Western Desert, their music would still be fit for nothing. The musician turned to Farouk and spoke the most terrible insult that it was possible for one man to say to another, at which Farouk spat on the man's feet and said, 'Ummak,' which, of course, diverted the insult to his mother. Then, Farouk remembered, there was shouting and cursing and terrible threats. The musician vowed he would cut out Farouk's tongue; Farouk promised to burn the man's house to the ground; and so on until the villagers tired of the interruption and demanded their argument cease.

'The people of Mena village are the greatest peace-makers in the world,' Farouk said with pride. Did Fin not think this was so?

Fin said that he had never encountered people who argued so much, who would pick up on the tiniest insult and would discuss, debate and shout it with as much passion. He knew of no other place, he said, where so many people would participate with such enthusiasm in other people's arguments. If this were the same as what Farouk was saying, then he agreed.

'It is exactly the same,' Farouk replied.

'So you forgave the musicians?' asked Fin.

'Of course not,' Farouk said. How could he when they had insulted him in such a way and Mister Khaled had such need? So as the music began again he pulled Mister Khaled before the musicians and banged a metal tray with a stick until the music was forced to stop. The villagers became angry and ordered him to leave, but Farouk would not move. He shouted that everybody knew of Mister Khaled's *afreet* but they did nothing. They pretended that something so terrible could not have happened in their village. He reminded them that Mister Khaled had been born in the village, as was his father and grandfather, and that Mister Khaled's *afreet* was therefore their *afreet*. There was some murmuring and discussion at this point because, as Farouk assured Fin, there was great and rare wisdom in what he was saying. Farouk had closed his speech with an ancient poem from Iran describing how the desert yearned for life and knowledge so that even the stones longed for what people knew. As a finale he had reached into his galabeya and took the wad of Egyptian pounds that he had been saving to wager on the horses and threw it in the air above the musicians so that it fluttered on them like falling blossoms.

'Poetry and cash,' Farouk explained to Fin. 'A magic combination with the Zar.'

The Zar stood as the money settled and opened their arms out to Farouk like the strings of coloured flags welcoming the guests to the party. Farouk embraced each one, and as he stepped back into the crowd the drumbeat began with the secret and holy rhythm. Over and over again it played, rising and falling like a heartbeat, silencing even the faintest whisper. Mister Khaled, as if drawn in by invisible forces, presented himself before the Zar, his arms crossed in front of his body.

Simple merriment had long disappeared and each person, man and woman now watched Mister Khaled, who had become like stone, his eyes tightly shut. The heartbeat drum continued '*dumm tek-a-tek, dumm tek-a-tek*', for four or five minutes, rising and falling, calling for the lost Mister Khaled. The finger cymbals crept into the rhythm like the lightest caress, giving birth to a thousand new worlds, seeking the angel who could wake Mister Khaled's soul, but he remained closed, the *afreet* shaking within his body like oil trapped under the thinnest crust of rock. People were clapping, praying, egging on Mister Khaled, shouting at the spirit to move, praising the Zar. But Mister Khaled's *afreet* was stubborn. The tabla entered, bursting into the rhythm with spiralling trills, and the three instruments spun around each other like wisps of smoke, each taking turns to call God. The drumming grew louder and slower, drawing all the people around Mister Khaled into a creature of many arms and many heads but one being. And suddenly the beat stopped, and where there had been sound, there was now nothing, a space carved out of the air, like the black of the Great Pyramid at night, a place where yearning must be. At that very moment Mister Khaled's *afreet* stirred, attracted to the emptiness as a man to a woman. The crowd understood and turned as one to the spirit who was causing Mister Khaled's head to sway from side to side and his eyes to bulge. He lurched to one side, falling into the space woven by the Zar, and before the crowd's eyes the *afreet* rose up, throwing open his arms and thrusting out his chest so that his heart could be nearer that emptiness.

Then, guided by the Almighty Conductor, the reedy wail of the *mizmar* curled its way into the emptiness, embroidering the delicious pit of longing with a seductive chant, like a restless virgin, calling and calling. Mister Khaled began to spin, uncurling himself from the clasp of the *afreet*, and as he whirled his face took in a holy light, his body drawing itself up until he glowed with the smile of a man beholding God's love. Mister Khaled's head shook as he whirled, as if his mind could not contain the beauty. Such power in each turn, throwing him this way and that, with a force that was not of man. Such heartbreaking delight, taking Mister Khaled like a child, like a lover, and Mister Khaled, shaking his head and hands as if what he saw was beyond sense, beyond words, until he was toppled over with a drunken joy.

Now all silence disappeared and the crowd was shouting and cheering, banishing the *afreet*, sending it into the desert, into the Great Pyramid, anywhere but around the heart of poor Mister Khaled. All were jumping and spinning in the love of Allah, and after longer than anyone could remember, the music wound itself down and except for the panting of the crowd there was only the silence of the desert and the radiant smile of Ali Khaled bin Sahmi, freed at last from his troublesome *afreet*.

Farouk stopped talking, rubbed his eyes, pulled his delicate fingers through his wiry hair and looked through the window. The silence was palpable, like the end of beautiful music. Fin had forgotten himself for a moment and then in the silence, he remembered what he wanted and cleared his throat tightly.

'What about Skinhead?' he asked.

'Skinhead?' Farouk replied. 'Why should they remember Skinhead? People did not think of Skinhead.'

Farouk's name was called from outside and a flash of concern crossed his face. He rose, pouring his whisky into Fin's glass. 'My wife is here,' he said, folding three sticks of chewing gum into his mouth and pushing his head from left to right until his neck cracked. Again, he tugged his sleeves over his wrists. 'Please, I must talk. Samar, she knows nothing of this day or that you are here. Perhaps ...'

Fin blinked, uncomprehending, then he understood and turned away irritated at the interruption. 'Of course,' he replied. 'Shall I go to the roof?' When he turned back to his friend, he found that he was already alone.

24

Fin gazed at the Great Pyramid, no longer lit for the tourists, now a thick black absence like an unfinished picture. He lay on his side, his head supported by one arm. He knew he was near the story's end and was determined that it must give him what he needed. It had to hold something, otherwise why would he desire it? He must trust that everything would fit together when he discovered what was under Skinhead's house. Perhaps later he might meet Skinhead, venture into the tunnel himself. Fin felt a kinship with the protagonist of the story, or at least with the man's ambitions, and he suspected this was an empathy that Farouk lacked. Farouk's grudging telling of the tale seemed coloured by prejudice, envy. If the narrative reflected as well on Farouk as he would have Fin believe, then why was he being so evasive about it? Perhaps it was just that Farouk lacked curiosity, the peculiar curiosity that Fin and Skinhead shared – that made them special.

A spark caught Fin's eye far in the distance, a tiny dot of yellow like a fallen star. Fin sat up and peered into the darkness. It was there and then not, a glimmering speck swelling to a golden mark, a shape, approaching, shimmering like fire. He heard noise, activity, shouting and braying. It was a torch, a man on a horse with a burning torch, galloping out of the darkness. Soon a dozen others appeared bobbing over the shallow ellipse of dunes, each rider's form softened by flowing muslin.

Crossing the line where the light of the village touched the floodlit shadow of the desert, the first rider produced a communication device from inside his robes and spoke into it. Fin rushed to call down the stairs for Farouk.

'There's something going on. Quick, come and look,' he shouted.

Fin ran back to the edge of the roof and stood gaping, his hands clenching and unclenching by his side. The noise increased as a line of fifty or more camels appeared out of the darkness, their pilots shouting and whistling, the night wrenched apart with the aggressive bray of males on the rut and pierced by ululating cries.

Fin rushed down the stairs and burst into the kitchen. 'There's something going on, a tribal war party or something,' he exclaimed.

Farouk was with his wife. They were holding one another, Farouk's arms around her waist, her hand cupping the back of his head. They pulled apart at his arrival and she backed away. Embarrassed, Fin thrust out his hand in greeting and then withdrew it too quickly. It was impolite to offer physical greeting to a woman. Farouk said a few words to his wife in Arabic and she extended her hand to Fin. He shook it and exchanged salaams. Her voice was at odds with the limpness of her handshake. She flinched at his nervously enthusiastic clasp, not from timidity but an intense sensitivity to the intimacy of touch.

She removed her hand and spoke to Fin in quick warm Arabic. He looked at her cheeks smooth and full as an infant's, her eyes large with thick perfectly sculpted eyebrows tapering to a fine point. She turned away and left the room. He knew she had welcomed him but the rest he could not understand.

'Please give us some time ... I will come up ... in one moment,' Farouk said.

Fin noticed Farouk's eyes were watery with emotion. Perhaps he knew about the riders already.

'What's going on? Is it serious?' Fin asked.

'It is nothing,' Farouk answered quickly, turning away. 'Go up. I will finish the baba ganoush.' He gathered the garlic, lemon juice, olive oil, tahina and cumin, and folded the mixture together with the now-soft threads of aubergine. 'Please,' he said to Fin, who was still behind him, 'I will follow you.'

Fin ran back up the stairs to the roof.

When Farouk joined him, Fin was leaning on the low wall at the roof's edge, observing the mounting activity with breathless interest. 'Something's happening, something big,' Fin intoned.

Farouk seemed unconcerned. He was carrying the earthenware bowl of baba ganoush and a bundle of pitta bread. 'The lemon must whisper to the tahina; the cumin must sing songs of love to the aubergine; the garlic must be given time for her seduction. Only then can the dish be eaten.' He balanced the bowl and pitta on the low wall and went back into the house, appearing moments later with two wooden chairs, which he placed side by side at the edge of the wall.

Fin was riveted to the goings-on below. The riders

seemed to be taking orders from the identically dressed figure with the walkie-talkie. 'The one over there is in charge. He's telling them something, giving orders. What do you think's happening? Are they extremists, tribal warriors?' Fin whispered breathlessly.

Farouk settled himself on one of the chairs. 'Two, three years in Egypt and you are still in a movie. What is it today, Fin? *Lawrence of Arabia*? *The Cursing of the Mummy*?' Farouk shook his head scornfully. 'There are five million mobile telephones in Egypt; we are the centre of culture for the Arab world; we have civilisation longer than any place on earth; we make more films, music and books than your country and you think we are from the past, that we are nothing? Look at yourself, Fin. You sit in the dust; most times you wear clothes that are old, with holes, and dirty. No man in the village would wear the clothes you wear. It is *zibbala*.'

Fin was shocked. 'What are you talking about? My clothes? I am sorry if I'm not up to your standards. I've spent the day—'

'No. Now, *habibi*, you wear a galabeya like an Egyptian. This is good, although it is not clean, of course, because you sit in the dirt like a child and it is cheap imported cotton. Tomorrow I will buy you one – top-quality cotton from Egypt. You clean, you shave, then you will get a job and a wife, *insha'allah*.'

'If I want another galabeya, I will buy one,' Fin snapped. 'I ask for nothing from you. I can pay for myself – and usually for you as well. I paid for the vegetables, the whisky . . . I saved your life, Farouk! Now there are Bedouin warriors beneath the house and you criticise me for getting excited?'

'They are tour guides, you fool,' Farouk replied, 'waiting for tourists who eat a Bedu banquet in the desert. It is the same meal they eat in their hotel, but in the desert.'

Farouk chuckled at this idea and tore off a swathe of bread which he plunged into the baba ganoush. 'Let me tell you, *habibi*, you should forget when you pay or not pay, but to keep money in your heart . . . this is not how a man should be.' The camels neared and Fin could see that clinging on to each beast was an uncomfortable tourist longing for the sanctuary of his hotel, the novelty of the expedition worn off long ago.

Two gleaming luxury coaches with enormous wing mirrors like insect antennae roared to a halt and confirmed Fin's surging embarrassment. The hydraulic brakes of the coaches popped and hissed, spooking the arriving camels and awakening the glorious memory of the power of stampede as they bolted back towards the open desert, dragging with them whoever was holding on.

A tremendous scene of shouting and confusion played out in front of the house, with camels being dragged back from the desert by furious Bedouin and shaken tourists cautiously snaking into the air-conditioned buses, or fanning around taking pictures or buying unlikely antiquities from rapidly appearing traders. Both men watched, Farouk leaning back on his chair, scooping up the smoky baba ganoush with crisp slivers of pitta, Fin pacing along the edge of the roof and kicking away tiny stones. It took the horsemen twenty minutes to round up the camels and the tourists were heaved off them with plaintive moans of 'Oh boy' and 'Get me down, Harold,' echoing incongruously across the desert. Finally the ungainly caravanserai was loaded into the coaches, which roared back towards Cairo. The horsemen remained, counting their wages, chatting and laughing.

Fin sat down next to Farouk. 'I am sorry. I am not myself . . .'

'It is nothing, *habibi*,' Farouk replied, extending the earthenware bowl.

Fin dug into it with a scoop of bread.

Farouk stared at the men below and then stood up, inspired. 'Tell me, in your country are there horses?'

'Many,' Fin replied.

'In all of your country, your England—'

'Republic of Ireland,' Fin corrected.

'Yes, yes. Ireland, England, Republic of . . . In all these places are there any great horses?'

'I'm sure there are,' Fin replied, 'some of the best horses in the world.'

'No,' Farouk informed Fin. 'The greatest horse in the world is the Arab, the Egyptian-Arab. It is true, I swear on my mother.' Farouk had not been to Fin's home, he said, but he knew with absolute certainty that if there were good horses in his country, it was because they had Arab blood. No other line of horses was so pure, bred for centuries by the desert Arabs, and the greatest of the Arabs were *al-khamsa*, the five bloodlines. Did Fin know this?

Fin assured Farouk that he did not really care, but he suspected the Irish had possessed fine horses for hundreds of years. Farouk ignored him.

'Did Jesus or Moses, peace be on them, breed your horses? No, of course not. And yet you say you have good horses. The Prophet Muhammad – blessings upon his name – chose *al-khamsa* himself – do you know of this?'

Fin said he did not know, and before he could stop him,

Farouk recounted how the Prophet, after many days in the desert, saw an oasis and released his horses to run ahead and drink. Before they reached the water, he called them back, wishing to test their obedience. Only five returned, and these the Prophet called *al-khamsa*, from which descended the finest of the Arab breed. The very shape of the Arabian horse reflected nothing less than the love of Allah. Did Fin know this? The large forehead encompassed Allah's blessings, the broad chest reflected power, the arched neck, courage, and of course the tail held high like the staff of a king, this was the pride of the Arabs. From these very horses came every horse of quality throughout the world.

'It's an opinion, Farouk,' Fin said, yawning. 'It's just an opinion.'

'Opinion?' Farouk asked.

'Arab horses, Egyptian horses – in fact everything you say.'

Farouk ignored him. 'Before Arabs,' he snorted, 'your horses were donkeys.'

'Sure, Farouk, but what about Skinhead Saïd?'

'Skinhead? He loved horses, of course, there were many horses at his party,' Farouk answered. 'Each of *al-khamsa* was present. The *Kohailan, Saklawi, Hadban, Dahman* and *Obeyan*, they were all there and standing like kings, tended by grooms who wove old Bedouin silver into their manes while their masters whispered poems and praise into their ears.'

Farouk closed his eyes in nostalgic rhapsody. 'Such horses as a king would trade his kingdom to own,' he whispered. 'Horses bred for thousands of years in an unbroken line longer than the written word, longer than history. And these, *habibi*, were the artists of their breed – not your racing animals, bred and sold for speed by your queens of England, but artists, magical dancers who, if it suited them, would reveal to the eyes of man the soul of the horse.'

'But why all the horses? Fin asked.

Farouk insisted that they were vital. Although food was important at a gathering, more important even than food were the horses, dancing horses in particular, and it was rumoured that villages as far as Sharayya had brought their horses to Skinhead's party. From the moment the festivities began it was clear to all but Mumbling Iqbal that whatever problem people had with Skinhead Saïd – and everyone had at least one – he had organised the party with admirable style.

'You cannot pay horses to come,' Farouk explained. 'The owners must believe that the event is important and that they would be foolish not to arrive with their best animals, and then people will bring as much money as they can afford.'

Perhaps it was the confusion around the purpose of the party, perhaps it was the descriptions of Skinhead's preparations, which had grown larger with each telling. Who could tell how the excitement was born? But what was certain was that the greatest dancing horses of Egypt had arrived at Saïd's party.

But there was more, Farouk explained. Not only were there at least thirty great horses, but two most extraordinary and prized animals were present – Izeah from Balan and Noor from Tal' Shiid. Both horses were exquisite dancers, he said, combining grace and complete unexpectedness in their movement. Some said they were the greatest horses Egypt – and therefore the world – had seen for fifty years. The problem, and it was a great problem, was that when the two animals danced, they danced with the same spirit, in the same manner. Noor was a night-black *Hadban* mare with three white socks, Izeah an *Obeyan* stallion, golden bay in colour. Although it was known that their bloodlines had not crossed for two hundred years, when they danced it was like watching a single horse dance in the reflection of still water.

Each of the owners, Farouk went on, had spent years combing the gossip from the other's family or servants so as to monitor the movements of the rival horse and keep the two apart. This unspoken agreement had maintained a natural balance for many years. If it were known that both horses were present at the same event, he explained, then honour, the foundation of all that is valuable, would have demanded that they compete, and this of course would have been a dark day for one of the owners. To bring two such horses together was a terrible thing, Farouk said, terrible and wrong. But now at Saïd's party, through accident, fate or the will of the Almighty, it had happened. A great excitement possessed the crowd, like the promise of a fist-fight between twins in the schoolyard.

Farouk leant back on his chair, more confident than Fin would have been about the support of the spindly legs eaten into honeycombs by the rapacious woodworm of the desert.

Throughout the Zar's inspiring performance Skinhead Saïd had not even been glimpsed, and despite his name floating somewhere in the mind of every guest, nobody even noticed his absence. Perhaps they had all been drawn in by the quality of the food, by the banishment of Mister Khaled's *afreet*, or by the quality of the horses. Farouk did not know. In this, Farouk explained, he may have misjudged his old friend's cunning, for it may have been part of his design. If this was true, and Skinhead had deliberately plotted such excitement to divert people's attention from his absence, then the plan, however brilliant, was soon to fall apart.

As Saïd left his house and made his way towards his guests, people who saw him screamed and shouted, 'AFREET! AFREET!' For a moment everyone believed that Mister Khaled's *afreet* must have reappeared and taken over the body of Skinhead Saïd. An *afreet*, Farouk explained, must go somewhere, and to anyone with eyes Skinhead Saïd had the look of a man possessed.

Skinhead was walking as he had always walked. He was even smiling, Farouk remembered, in the way that some people do when they are nervous or embarrassed, not sure if they should be joining in with a joke or if they are the joke. This should have shown those who were close enough to see that Skinhead could not be possessed with an *afreet*, as an *afreet* will never smile. No, it was not these things, it was something much more revealing. From the top of his hairless head to his large bony feet Skinhead Saïd had turned white.

'From shock?' Fin asked.

Farouk agreed that there were shocks that could turn the skin white, and even the hair, but what shock was so terrible that it would also change the colour of a man's clothing? For not only were Skinhead's face and hands white, but his clothes were now as white as the great wide dome of his head. To make matters worse, Skinhead's eyes were red, red as fresh blood, which, Farouk explained, was a sure sign of possession.

Skinhead had no idea how he looked nor that people assumed he was a demon spirit. He imagined their staring and pointing was a new form of respect. And how, Farouk asked himself with sympathy, would he have known the difference, since no one had offered Skinhead Saïd respect since he was a child? But when people started to throw stones, Skinhead began to suspect something was wrong. He looked down and, seeing the whiteness on his body, began slapping and shaking his clothing, making tiny clouds appear around his person. This made people scream even more and run in terror.

'We are a brave people,' Farouk added quickly, 'braver than all other nations, but there is nothing Egyptians fear more than an *afreet*.'

Skinhead had snatched a bucket of water from next to his well and tipped it over his head.

'This,' Farouk said, 'changed everything.'

'Everything?' Fin asked, stretching out his bruised leg and changing position.

'Paff!' Farouk replied, slapping his hands together. 'As light changes darkness.'

Skinhead's *afreet* was a trick of dust, no more than that. The front of his body was covered in fine white powder, as if he had stepped halfway into the world below.

'And his red eyes?' Fin asked.

'Dust, of course.' As soon as the water washed away the dust, people understood and began to laugh with the relief of those who have been more afraid than they would care to admit. Skinhead, finding himself a joke once more, was furious. He turned and ran into his house, throwing the bolt across the door and refusing to come out or answer.

People at the party now talked freely of Skinhead's curious behaviour, but not as if it pointed to some sort of mystery. Had the inhabitants of Mena village known what was to happen later, they would certainly have tried to find meaning in his strange actions, but of course they did not. Had it been someone else in the village, they might have asked themselves questions: Why is he acting this way? What does it mean? But as it was Skinhead, they asked nothing; he had always acted strangely. The only conclusion people allowed themselves on this occasion was that Skinhead's behaviour must be the result of an overindulgence in the fine ochre kif that had been making its way over from the Levant after a much-mourned absence of many years.

Farouk confided in Fin that he had never believed that Skinhead's behaviour was connected to the Levantine hashish. He and Skinhead had been smoking kif in great quantities since they were twelve and then mixing what was left with camel dung to sell to tourists. He knew it was not kif that had caused Skinhead's behaviour and so had approached Skinhead's house and banged at the door, but Skinhead did not answer, so Farouk had returned to the horses.

Incense and the rich fragrance of cooking crept up to the roof during Farouk's tale, and soon, as if she too had floated up on a sweet smell, Samar appeared from the stairs and invited them to eat.

When his wife went back down, Farouk retrieved the whisky from a time-worn plastic bag and refilled Fin's glass. He replaced the bottle and carefully tied the bag shut as if the whisky might try to escape and rampage through the village. He stretched and looked at the stars. A light banging was coming from the rooftop where Fin had seen the pigeons, audible only in the pauses between the story. Farouk jumped up and walked towards the noise, shouting at the boy next door to stop.

'Banging all the night, he has no respect. Every night this boy builds his tower up into the sky, higher and higher for his birds. You have seen these birds?' Farouk asked.

'The pigeons?'

'No, not pigeons. They are loves.'

'You mean doves.'

'Yes, of course, doves,' Farouk replied. '*Gamila*, no?'

'Yes,' Fin said. 'Lovely. Very *gamila*.'

'I will not forget what you have done today,' Farouk said quietly. 'This story, it is what you want?'

'It's what I want,' Fin replied.

25

They went to eat in a room above the kitchen where a low wood and leather table was surrounded by cushions of different sizes. Fin sat on a cushion and seeing Farouk recline on his side, he followed his example.

Samar appeared in the doorway. She held a paper-thin metal bowl stamped with tiny crescents and an antique jug with a long exotic spout. Farouk smiled and threw up his hands. 'We are honoured, *habibi*. My wife brings water,' he said, placing his fingers under the deft stream as she poured.

Farouk washed carefully, rubbing away the grime of the day and digging out the sand beneath his nails. He dried his hands on a folded damask cloth exchanging affectionate words with Samar. Fin watched her smooth movements. She wore an indigo material embroidered with silver flowers, her deep blue scarf tight around her head, framing her round and beautiful face. Fin found himself wishing that he could hold her in his arms or perhaps that she would hold him. It was not a sensuous yearning, he told himself, but he looked away when Farouk caught his eye.

Samar turned to Fin and trickled the warm water over

his hands but, ill at ease, Fin splashed the water onto a delicately embroidered silk cushion beneath him. She passed Fin the damask, which he pressed into the damp stain. Samar tutted in dismay, whisking the cloth away from the stain and placing it firmly over Fin's hands, before tossing the cushion out of the room as if it were of no concern.

Rana squeezed through the doorway laden with bowls of deliciously pungent food. Now that she could not run away, Fin complimented her warmly. Rana blushed through her white scars and hastened from the room.

'Rana has been with you a long time,' Fin said pointlessly.

'Where else would she go?' Farouk replied.

Samar heard something she did not like in Farouk's tone, or perhaps she understood more English than she admitted. She complained to Farouk while she moved the low table to one side, spreading a cloth on the floor and arranging the dishes before him.

Farouk looked at Fin as Samar left the room. 'She loves Rana,' he said by way of explanation.

Farouk guided Fin through each of the dishes before them – chicken with preserved lemons, hummus, chicken with garlic and olives, chicken livers grilled on wooden sticks, fava beans and lemon – all with a reassuringly thick mantle of Egyptian olive oil which, Farouk assured Fin, was the finest in the world. Fin ate, tearing and dipping and scooping, while Farouk seemed to take more pleasure in ensuring that Fin ate the best part of each dish than eating himself. When Fin's eating slowed, Farouk tempted and cajoled him to more food, and when Fin could eat nothing more, Farouk dared him to taste the end of a vermilion chilli the size and potency of a sniper's bullet.

Fin picked up the tiny gauntlet and chewed confidently. He enjoyed chillies and was proud of his ability to weather their storm, but after a deceptive lull a brimstone heat exploded in Fin's mouth, scourging his throat and making his face throb. Fin tried to remain calm, remembering that it would pass, but the heat kept building beyond what he had ever experienced until, close to panic, he reached for the water. Farouk was observing Fin's suffering with a certain degree of amusement and whisked away the glass before Fin could drink, passing him a whole cucumber instead. Fin lay back on the cushions, taking crunching bites out of the cucumber and panting until the fury of the chilli died down.

'Good, no?' Farouk asked, grinning.

'Bastard,' Fin replied through teary eyes.

Samar returned and sat down by Farouk. As the fire in his mouth dissipated, Fin watched her hennaed fingers elegantly form balls of rice and gracefully extract meat from pools of oily liquid. He looked down at the scatterings of rice and crumbs in front of him and flushed at the clumsiness of his eating. Samar spoke into Farouk's ear.

'She wants to know what it is about this story that you desire so much,' Farouk said. 'We are your friends and we can help you in many ways. Samar, she has unmarried cousins – almost as beautiful as her. Also, her uncle works for *Al-Ahram* newspaper.'

Samar cast a sideways look at Fin and whispered something else. Farouk laughed. 'At least let us buy you a better galabeya. I told her I'd offered this and many things. But you wish only this story – nothing else. She does not understand why you want to hear about Skinhead Saïd. He is nothing.'

Fin shrugged.

Samar watched Fin. She yawned, rose to her feet, whispering a few more words to Farouk, and moved to leave.

'What does she say?' asked Fin.

'Oh, she is tired, she wishes to go to bed,' Farouk replied. Samar stopped and looked at her husband.

'Is that what she said?' Fin demanded.

'No, she says . . . she knows what it is you want,' Farouk replied. 'But it can never be found.'

Samar left the room.

'What does she mean?' Fin asked quickly. 'What do I want?'

'How can I know?' Farouk shrugged. 'She did not say.' He laughed, yawned and lay back amid the cushions, closing his eyes.

Fin coughed and, as there was no response, he leant over Farouk and gently shook him. 'Can you finish the story?'

Farouk raised himself on one elbow. 'Oh, yes, of course . . . Where was I, *habibi?* Skinhead, yes, he is in his house but the horses . . . I remember of course.' He sighed and continued.

The discussion between Hamid and Fibir, owners of the magnificent horses, like all conversations held beneath Yousef al-Zaki's date palm, had proceeded very well. Both men accepted that fate had brought their horses together and honour demanded that they dance. The question to be decided then was the precise nature of their agreement.

'Agreement?' Fin asked.

268

The fine that the loser must pay, Farouk explained. Normally a fair sum could be agreed on in equal barter, but Hamid, owner of Izeah the stallion, was considerably less wealthy than Fibir, who was a man blessed with riches. It was important, Farouk said, particularly in a battle of honour such as this, that the agreements and penalties must be fair and equal.

'When you say "agreement", you mean "bet,"' Fin insisted, adding that he was aware that gambling was forbidden in Islam, but since they were friends, and Allah was presumably everywhere, could they not just call things what they were?

Farouk sat up indignant. Fin had again confused everything and twisted the truth with his Coca-Cola brain. Of course gambling was not permitted in Islam, but this, Farouk was adamant, was not gambling. Gambling was haram. Perhaps Fin was not aware of the Hadith spoken by the blessed Prophet to Abu Hamsa? 'When a man puts his mare against another horse unknown to him and the winner is a matter of chance, that is not gambling. But if he knows his mare will win, that is gambling.'

Fin accepted that he had never heard these words but supposed that the Prophet, peace be upon him, meant that it was acceptable to compete but not to cheat. Yet there was no mention of money being exchanged.

Farouk stood up, throwing a cushion to the floor.

'Money! Money! Everything is money to you. Did I say to you that Hamid and Fibir wagered money on their horses? Did I? No, I did not. There was no money.' He crouched on his haunches shaking his head wearily. 'Now you are an interpreter of the Hadith? And you try to trip me up like a schoolboy in my own faith! You have no god and so perhaps you envy mine. Let me tell you something, Fin. I invite you to join us, one hundred million Muslims and myself invite you to Islam. Allah can be your god, Fin, but there is only one and Muhammad, peace be upon his name, is his Prophet. If you accept Almighty Allah, you will know that he alone is the judge. He alone.'

Fin did not know what to say, so he was silent and, as always with Farouk, his wrath passed quickly and was forgotten.

Arabs, Farouk said, rarely agreed with one another but were masters of debate and in the time it took the Zar to banish Mister Khaled's *afreet*, the two men, Hamid and Fibir, had reached an agreement.

It was Hamid who had unshakable faith in his stallion and was certain he would win. If he was not the winner, he vowed to give Fibir whatever possession he asked for. If his horse did win, then Hamid could demand whatever possession he desired. Oaths were made and the horses were brought before the crowd.

Not since the time of the great Mameluke sultan Ahmed ibn Tulun had two such horses stood face to face. Izeah's colour was like ripe apricots; his mane was long and the lightest shade of amber; his tail, even when held in a graceful arch, reached almost to the ground; his shoulders were round with muscle, his head small and fine with a strip of pure white between the eyes as if touched by the Almighty's paintbrush. The mare Noor – Farouk waved his hands before explaining that Fin could never understand the beauty of such a horse until he stood before her – Noor was more than perfection, Farouk said. Her blackness was like filtered oil, like all the colours of the universe concentrated into eternity, her neck so long, curving like el-Nil, her head held upright as if she were the rider of her own delicate back. He explained how the horses' quality was clear to everyone in the village and described how the people sat in a wide circle while the musicians stood ready with their drums. On each horse sat a rider chosen by the horses themselves but, Farouk added as if it need not be said, no one had eyes for the riders.

When the oldest of the musicians began his thirteen-beat cycle with the two-sided *nahrasan* the animals were eye to eye, motionless. But on the eighth beat, both beasts reared up on their hind legs and landed together as if they were one. Each horse picked up its legs as if trotting in the air, their heads held high, nostrils flared, tails swishing in the night. When the *mizmar* pierced the darkness with its mournful wail the horses stepped sideways crossing their hooves, moving away from each other, turning in circles with the music and then moving together until their muzzles were touching and they became still, exchanging each other's air. They remained like this until an old woman called out an ancient *dkhir* with the words, 'The way of love is not a lane: once entered you cannot pass through.' At this, both horses reared up, clambering at the air, twisting and whinnying until they had unseated their riders, who scrambled to the safety of the crowd. No one dared approach the horses, who were pawing at the packed sand like Nubian bulls, looking as if they meant to fight to the death rather than dance. Noor suddenly reared and spun round, presenting her hindquarters towards the stallion. With a whinny he leapt up and covered her, shaking his head, his mane flicking like flames of fire as he entered her with savage thrusts that sent ripples through her muscular flanks. The crowd gasped as one and the music stopped, so that until the horses had exhausted themselves, there was only the sound of bestial mating.

Such a thing had never before happened in a dance, and the people of Mena village were silent with awe and wonder. As the horses were led away, the question remained: Who had triumphed? After long and noisy discussion the village agreed that there could be no actual winner. However, as Umm Attallah, a woman with six sons and three daughters, much respected for her wisdom, pointed out, Hamid, the owner of Izeah, should pay the penalty since he had sworn that his stallion would defeat Fibir's mare. The truth of this could not be disputed and Hamid accepted the judgement. All eyes now turned to his wealthy adversary Fibir to see what penalty he would demand. In a few words he could ruin Hamid, demand his house and land or even his great horse. But Fibir showed the wisdom which had been the source of his great wealth and the courtesy that made him so admired in the village. What he demanded, he announced to the village, was the foal from the horses' coupling, no less and no more.

Suleiman the Magnificent could not have chosen better. The men cheered, the women ululated, the *mizmar* wailed and the *nahrasan* throbbed, and the village knew that for this night they were part of a story that would never be forgotten.

'In Mena village life is difficult, full of suffering. Perhaps it is the same in all the world? But at such times we understand how blessed we are to be living in such a village, that long after our death our stories will be told in the cafés of *al-Kahira* and on roofs and around fires across Egypt – who knows, perhaps further.' Farouk said no more and stretched out with his hands behind his head.

'This cannot be the end of the story, Farouk. I want the real end,' insisted Fin.

'*Khalas*, it is finished. This is what you wanted, *habibi*?'

'Farouk, I don't care about horses; I don't even like them. I don't care about camels, about musicians, about *afreets*. It's like a joke to you, but to me it's different. Can't you see? What I want is what Skinhead wanted. What was under the house?'

'You are an ignorant man, Fin. Always hungry even after a rich meal. It would be better if you had some pride,' he said, 'some dignity, then perhaps you would find satisfaction . . . You do not like horses?' Farouk asked.

'It's not the point,' Fin insisted.

'But do you fear them?'

'No, no . . . Yes, a bit.'

Farouk was astonished and demanded to know how a man could be afraid of a horse when it did not speak ill of you, curse, lie, steal your money, sleep with your wife or give you disease.

Fin answered that he did not care for them. Up to this point in his life he had deliberately kept a distance between himself and the entire equine family. It wasn't that he was scared of horses, he explained, it was just that he felt they were uncontrollable and strong. They were unpredictable and they could sense the fear in him – the fear that he would be trampled, hurt.

'A horse,' Farouk said with passion, 'can free a man.'

'Well, free me then! That is all I ask. Tell me what happened, what really happened.'

'If the story had finished there, all would have been well,' Farouk said. 'Please, it is enough,' he implored. 'Skinhead took the story and made it his. You are the same. You break off the blossoms of the fruit tree because you are in love with their beauty, but you will weep when there is no fruit.'

Farouk stared into Fin's adamant eyes. 'The Zar, the village, the horses, the desert ... to Skinhead they were nothing. He believed he was separate from these things, separate from everything but the dark place beneath his house, and he tried to mend this wound with dreams as you do, Fin. You dream there is a treasure richer than the song of birds, richer than the love of your friends, than your health. Trust me, on my mother, on my precious Samar, on the children we will have, *insha'allah*, it is better that the story ends here.'

Farouk stood up. 'I am tired. Let us sleep; your room is—'

'No, Farouk,' Fin hissed, grabbing his wrist and pulling him back. 'Just tell me what he found.' Fin's whisky glass slipped from his other hand and smashed on the floor.

Farouk stared at Fin's hand gripping his lean wrist until Fin let go.

'I will tell you,' he said quietly. 'But once it is told, you will see there is nothing. You should have left your emptiness under Skinhead's house and not carried it into mine.'

Farouk sat down and began speaking with his eyes downcast.

'While the celebrations, the dancing and wailing were still full of life, Skinhead Saïd was seen running out of his house as if chased by all the *jinns* of hell. Before he had passed the moon shadow of the roof there was a great explosion which tore the house apart and threw Skinhead into the air like a child's doll. Night became day and everybody was thrown to the ground. When the explosion passed, a storm of rocks fell from the sky, striking the ground with a thousand blows. By a miracle only Skinhead Saïd and Mumbling Iqbal were hit, but the horses Izeah and Noor broke free in the panic and ran into the Great Desert, never to be seen again.'

'What about Skinhead?' Fin demanded.

'He woke after three days, also Iqbal,' Farouk said. 'They were in full health although Iqbal no longer mumbles.' Farouk yawned deeply.

'What about the vault,' Fin demanded, 'under Skinhead's house?'

Farouk got up and moved towards the door. 'Too much dynamite,' he said over his shoulder. 'Everything was destroyed, everything. Dust and rubble, that is all.'

Fin jumped up and ran to the door, blocking Farouk. 'You are hiding something. There's got to be more! I don't believe you. Skinhead would not give up. I know he wouldn't. There *must* be more! I want to ask him myself. Take me to him,' demanded Fin, his voice cracking.

Farouk looked up at Fin. His eyes were heavy and tired, his voice low. 'I cannot. Skinhead was taken by the police. He is in prison, five more years.' Farouk stepped around Fin and ascended the stairs. 'This is all. It is finished. *Khalas.*'

'You don't know that,' Fin called out to Farouk's back.

Farouk turned, his eyes twitching in irritation. 'Is it because you fear the ocean that you seek a pearl in an orchard?' He shook his head and walked away. Fin watched him leave, engulfed by blackness as he climbed the stairs until only his white shoes were visible, and then nothing.

Fin had no choice but to go to bed. He opened the door

Farouk had pointed out to him and walked into a room which was empty but for an old iron bed. He lay on his back looking at the ceiling, struggling to comprehend the information. It was late. He should try to sleep. Fin patted the mattress around him: it was stuffed with tinder-dry straw or horsehair. He ran his palm over its gradients, impressed for a moment by the significant dune that rose up at one end. No part of the mattress was flat but it would not be the topography of his bed that would keep him from finding peace.

Fin lay accelerating with the roaring speed of his thoughts. He did not, dared not, believe that there was nothing more, that the discovery he had been waiting for did not exist. He steadied himself, palms pressing the mattress flat on either side of his body. His mind whirred like a gyroscope, drilling downwards, spinning and spinning. He squeezed the iron bed frame until the rusty edges cut into his skin and anger replaced confusion. He had been close to death on this day, and for what? Rubble and dust. Farouk was hoarding the truth, hiding it. Lying.

Fin did not hear the infant cry for its mother, did not see the two mice scampering along the rough edges of the wall, did not smell the wafts of roasted meats, sewage and washing powder carried in the light breeze of the night. He did not know how long he remained or when it was that he leapt up and ran into the darkness. He did not feel the stairs under his feet or his shoulders smashing through doors, his hands beating walls, his voice bellowing for Farouk. He ran through the house, fleeing from nothing behind him, until he found the line of light leaking under the door and burst into the bedroom where Samar sat astride her husband, both naked and lost in the act of love.

Startled, she dived down next to her husband with a shriek as Farouk roared at Fin to leave. Fin froze, could not move. Farouk leapt up and charged him through the door, where he fell onto the stone floor.

'Get out. Tomorrow, when the sun rises, you will leave my house.' Farouk spat the words at Fin, his eyes cold with fury. 'If I see you again . . . I will not see you.'

Fin lay in the dark corridor, shame replacing the madness. Farouk took a step towards him, and Fin hoped that Farouk would strike him like the American had done. Strike him down. Flood his body with a pain that would drive out shame. But Farouk turned his back and stepped into the bedroom, slamming the door behind him.

Fin struggled to his feet and stumbled away, mortified, exhausted. He limped to his room and fell upon the bed, not even bothering to brush away the crumbling debris of plaster that had fallen from the ceiling.

26

Fin still sleeps.

Hardly sinking into the mattress, a slight body print on the tucked-in bed. The corner of the blue-covered pillow is flattened, a dark stain from his leaking mouth; faults in the cotton cover filled with crumbs of rubble from the ceiling. Hardly an imprint, as if even in sleep he is absent. Fin dreams, caught for a moment in a child's slumber, an innocence that offers no resistance to gravity, that sinks, contouring where it lies. The door crashes and clatters. Fin tenses, wakes, holding himself, gripping against consciousness, against the ceaseless earthward force. His first thought is Waled, come to take him somewhere, begin his day again. A light flicks on. There is a man, a Bedouin, a white cloth wound round his head, his face a skull through the thin fabric, the desert night now cold, the cold clinging to him.

'Get up,' he orders, throwing a headscarf at Fin. It is Farouk, Fin hears this. The scarf floats onto his face.

'Come, desert side,' he says as he leaves. Fin remains on the bed, looking through the cloth, a shroud which sucks and billows against his mouth.

Fin has slept fully clothed – no rituals of dressing to allow a pause; even his shoes are on his feet. He stands up and grunts as the bruise on his thigh bites like an old dog. He tugs the scarf off his face and, winding it round his neck, stumbles through the door and makes his way down to the street.

The front door is open and the alleyway still and empty. Fin pulls the door closed and as it creaks he hears a call. He follows the voice until he finds Farouk standing where the thick shadows of the houses meet the grey moonlight of the desert. There are two horses.

'Take the horse,' Farouk commands.

Fin retreats into the darkest moonlit shadow of the house, his palms up in front of him.

'They are Arabs, pure bred, of *al-khamsa*.' Farouk tosses the reins at Fin.

'I can't ride,' says Fin, picking up the reins. 'It's dark and my leg—'

Farouk mounts his horse. 'Why speak of injured limbs?' he says from the saddle: 'Come, let us go.'

Fin steps back. He can ignore his leg, it is true, but he cannot ignore the beast in front of him, pawing at the sand and shaking its head impatiently, so full of unstable power that it looks ready to burst. The desert stretches out before him like a threat.

Farouk spins his horse round. 'Come,' he demands in a whisper. 'I will show you.'

There is comfort in the shadows but no escape. Fin steps out. He approaches the horse, guiding the reins over its head as he has seen others do, silently imploring it to remain still. He places his hand behind the pommel, feeling its felt and cold metal studs against his palm. It gives a little as he leans against it, and the horse steps towards him. Fin looks to Farouk for help, but he is not there. Fin lifts his foot and places his toes gingerly in the deep leather cup of the stirrup. Feeling Fin's weight the horse shies away swishing its tail and Fin is forced to hop into the air, his foot in the stirrup, his injured leg clawing for purchase in the cold night. With a grunt Fin twists his hips and falls astride the saddle, kicking at the empty stirrup until his foot finds its place. The horse sidesteps and shakes its head, shivering through its muzzle, impatient for the desert.

Farouk rides over and holds up Fin's reins. 'Like this, long. In one hand, one hand!'

Fin takes the reins, moving as little as possible in case the horse should interpret movement as provocation.

Farouk walks his horse round Fin, adjusting straps and commenting on his posture. 'Head up ... Foot down, down! No, back of the foot! Do you have ears?'

'Heel?' Fin suggests weakly.

'Heel, heel, yes. Point down the heel. Good. Up, up, your back, make it straight. You are a man, no? Straight, good. Now, be comfortable.'

The last order is a cruel contradiction, but Farouk is already disappearing into the desert. Unbidden, Fin's horse follows, and he lurches forward into the void of its first step. He grasps the pommel as his body weight plunges towards the ground. The horse takes another step and the space is suddenly filled, allowing Fin to find his balance. A few more steps and he infers that there is a pattern which he can predict and even move with. A chink opens up in his fear, wider with each rhythmic step, and through it he can for a moment glimpse the great breadth of the desert. Fin rests his hand on the thick neck of the beast, admiring the muscle and heat, swaying slightly to its step.

They turn and skirt the village, life and lights to one side, dark silvery emptiness on the other. Farouk slows his horse until Fin is by his side.

'Good?' he says, regarding Fin for the first time.

Fin nods.

Farouk turns away and on some invisible signal his horse breaks into a canter. Fin's horse, impatient for such a sign, leaps in pursuit, following the other horse's moon shadow as if it were its own. Fin shouts, grasping for something to hold, his legs flailing. Finding the pommel, he clings on, working every muscle into his saddle. The lights of the village become a jagged line in the corner of his eye, the ground rising and falling, hooves thundering across hard sand. Fin shouts and grips the horse. His spine is battered and jangled; his muscles tear with strain. Every step is a promise of injury.

Without warning, Farouk halts. As Fin's mount stops beside him, Fin carries on alone, moving with unhindered velocity, released from the saddle and horse, flying through the air until sand breaks his fall with a brutal breath-seizing *thud*.

Fin gasps until his breath catches him up. He raises himself, moving each limb experimentally. Nothing is cracked or fractured, but an even imprint of pain marks where he has met the ground. He rubs the stony sand off the side of his face. His horse has bolted into the desert with Farouk in pursuit. Fin hopes it has gone a great distance and Farouk with it. The ground is hard, but it is a relief, like land to the seasick. He sinks back into it waiting for the jagged memories of the horse to give way to stillness.

Farouk returns, leading Fin's horse. 'Is this what you want?' he shouts down to Fin, sweeping his arm across the empty desert. 'Look around you; is this what you seek?'

Fin looks. All he can see in the moonlight is piles of sand. 'I don't see anything.'

'Of course you see nothing, but this is what you wanted, no?'

Fin's gaze follows Farouk's arm to a pile of rubble on one side of what might once have been a wall. He stands and takes a few steps. On the other side of the wall is a ridge of wind-blown sand. Another Mena house that has given up its struggle against time.

'It's a ruin, so what?' Fin says.

'This ruin,' Farouk replies, turning his horse, 'is the house of Skinhead Saïd.'

Fin leans against the jagged stump of a collapsed palm. He walks stiffly to the crumbling wall and scans the piles of rock for a sign, a clue. Anything will do – a hole, a strip of carpet, an artefact. There's nothing, or perhaps it's only that he can see nothing because of the monochrome light on the layers of rocks and rubble.

'The roof is scattered across the desert,' Farouk calls to Fin. 'The walls and floor fallen where you stand. There is nothing more.'

'But beneath it, Farouk' – Fin sinks to his knees – 'Beneath must be the tunnel, the vault. Don't you want to know?' Fin begins pulling at the rubble. 'We can dig until we find the alabaster wall, then ... who knows what we might find.' Fin sweeps away stones and pulls up armfuls of sand, but the debris tumbles into the depression, filling it faster than Fin digs.

'Dig. Dig if that is what you wish. It does not matter.

Everywhere we walk there are tunnels, some with treasure and some not.' Farouk is behind Fin. 'We live above tombs on ground no stronger than a crust of sand. Choose anywhere, Fin, and dig if that is what you wish. Choose Mena village, choose Cairo, your own country, anywhere. It does not matter.'

Fin scoops deeper, pulling armfuls of sand and rubble towards him, damming the leaking sand where he can, pushing it back as it flows around him and sifts through his fingers, filling every hole. He digs faster, scooping with his hands, sweeping with his forearms, scratching at rocks till his nails break and his fingers bleed, but everywhere is sand, moving as he moves, filling the spaces he creates, unruly as water, irrepressible as time. Fin keeps digging until he knows that his treasure cannot be found, until he knows there is nothing there for him, and exhausted, without hope, he crumples into the sand.

'We go,' Farouk says from above, riding up to where Fin lies and dropping the reins of Fin's horse by his head. Fin does not move.

'Pick them up,' Farouk orders. 'I will not search the desert for your horse again.' He turns and rides off.

Fin raises himself, struggling against a heaviness in his chest, and as he heaves himself into a vertical position, pushing against gravity, it seems that a part of the weight that holds him down remains in the shallow hole he has dug. He picks up the leather strap of the reins and scrambles onto his horse. Tolerating Fin's uneven weight, the horse follows the path Farouk has taken. Fin slumps in the saddle, lost in the space of his vacated dreams, wondering if there ever had been anything to hope for.

Sunk in the saddle, his heart full of falling, Fin does not

notice that they are moving further away from the village until he draws alongside Farouk.

'Let's go back,' Fin says.

Farouk raises the palm of his hand to silence Fin.

Fin looks around him. His body aches but the sky is boundless, a faint wolf tail of light on the horizon.

Farouk winds his scarf tightly around his head and face, leaving only a gash for his eyes. He signals to Fin that he should do the same, but Fin is gazing up, wondering if the transformation he is sensing is the lightening of the sky. Farouk says something to Fin, his voice muffled by the cloth. Fin looks over and can see only the two glints of moon caught in his friend's eyes. Farouk flicks his reins over the neck of his horse, and as the leather cracks on the strong damp muscle, the horse hurtles into the desert.

Fin's horse charges forward in pursuit and Fin remains in the air. He grabs at the pommel like a man grappling for the edge of a cliff. With each leaping stride of the horse, the metal-studded pommel rams into him. He tries to tug at the reins but it only loosens his grip.

Fin screams as the horse gathers pace, its muscles pushing ever harder into the ground as if trying to free themselves from the earth. Fin clenches, clutches at the horse's mane, clinging on with his legs, squeezing the animal's ribs, inadvertently urging it on. He burrows his face in the animal's mane and cries out screaming with determination to hang on, to stay attached. His world is now fear and the thick hay-piss stench of the horse's sweat.

Somewhere through the panic and thunder Fin hears a voice shouting his name. He snatches a look to his right, where Farouk is galloping beside him, leaning back on his horse as if it were a deckchair, the reins cradled in a half open hand. Fin buries his head back in his horse. Farouk keeps calling and shouting until Fin looks up.

'Stop, make it stop,' Fin begs.

Farouk unhooks his scarf and leans towards Fin. 'A man does not ride this way,' he shouts. 'Let go!'

Fin cannot. Letting go is destruction, is smashing into the ground, is iron hooves on his soft body, pain, perhaps death. Fin grips harder.

Farouk leans further in, shouting at Fin, demanding that he free his grip. Every leap of the horse smashes through Fin's spine, shreds his legs on the sharp buckles and rough leather. Exhaustion and fear twist around him like a tourniquet until, exhausted, he lets go. Fin's chest is thrown open as he smacks into the saddle, his thighs lock, his calves latch behind the pounding forelegs. As Fin's hips swing, meshed into the movement of the horse, he knows that he will not fall, that the terror is behind him.

Fin is flying, flying through the night. Underneath him, steady air, his eyes open, exalting. The darkness that surrounds him becomes colours – blue, each moment deeper, as they fly on. Ahead a hill, a dune, the curving line where ground and sky meet rising before him as if sand were filling sky. Farouk is in front, his horse bounding up the slope, vaulting until it reaches the cresting edge of the dune. It halts, caught then ablaze in the pink-gold light of the rising sun. Fin's horse follows, its powerful legs loaded with leaps, each stride a body length higher until in a breath they too are at the crest. Fin's horse halts beside Farouk. Fin sinks deep in the saddle, a cloud of sand bursting before him like gold dust, like a glorious ghost shimmering into the first light of the sun, loosing his wordless fears into the morning sky.

Irresistible, the sun breaches the horizon, catching the tip of the Great Pyramid, and the *Salaat el-fajr*, the prayer that follows dawn, drifts over the distant city, banishing the last blue-grey shadows of the night in its golden blast. Vivid, aglow, Fin urges his horse on towards the new day.

FIN

Glossary

afreet	evil spirit
al-khamsa	'the five' great bloodlines of Arabian horse
al-Kahira	Cairo – literally, 'the Triumphant'
Allahu akbar	God is great
araa'	bald
asseer manga	mango juice
ba'dein	later, afterwards
bissm al-saleeb	in the name of the (Christian) cross
cus	female genitalia (very crude)
dhikr	a devotional act including its repetition of the names of Allah
Eid	festival at end of Ramadan
el-Nil	the Nile
fayn	where
felucca	traditional Egyptian wooden sailing boat
ferenghi	foreigner

foul medames	cooked mushy brown beans
gamila	delightful, beautiful
gazma	shoe
habibi	my dear, my darling
Hadith	collection of Islamic traditions containing sayings of the Prophet Muhammad
hajj	the great pilgrimage to Mecca
haram	forbidden by Islamic law, what a shame
El-hamdelillah	praise be to God
Ellei faat maat.	What is past is dead.
insha'allah	if God wills
irtiyaab	suspicious
jinn	spirit (genie)
Kayf haalak (m), *haalek* (f)	How are you?
keffiyeh	headscarf (for males)
khalas	finished, enough
khamseen	hot wind from the Sahara
khasi	eunuch
kif	hashish
la'	no
madrasa	school
Ma'alesh.	Never mind.
Medjool	large sweet date
mizmar	wooden reed instrument
nahrasan	two-sided drum
rahgel	man
Sabah / Masaa' el-khayr.	Morning / Evening of goodness (Good evening).

Sabah/Masaa' el-noor.	Morning/Evening of light (reply to *Sabah/Masaa' el-khayr*).
sharia	Islamic law
sharmoota	woman of easy virtue
shish	small cubes of meat on skewer
shokran, shokran gazilan	thank you, thank you very much
shwarma	sandwich of shaved lamb or chicken from turning spit
shwayya	a little, a bit (misused by Fin to mean small)
sitt	woman
sura	term used to denote 'chapter' of Holy Koran
tabla	drum
teez	arse (slang)
Teezak hamra.	Your arse is red (insult).
torshi	pickles
wootz	Damascus steel
Ya, besh!	Hey, boss!
Yallah.	Let's go.
Yallah imshi.	Go away.
za'atar	thyme
zibbala, zibbaleen (pl.)	rubbish, rubbish collector
zobra	penis (slang)

the end of sleep

Reading Group Notes

In Brief

The number of drinks are critical for Fin. If he gets it just right then sleep will welcome him. If not . . . The giant bruise on his leg is not helping – a souvenir of the fight with the American. Still, he sleeps on. He can afford to sleep now, as his boss fired him the previous day – apparently the fight was the last straw. How many bars had he visited?

When Fin came to Egypt three years ago to take up the post of senior reporter on the *Cairo Herald*, his mind had been full of linen suits, shady meetings in souks and vintage typewriters. The reality had been something of a let-down. Expat cricket matches were some of the more interesting stories making up his bread and butter, and he wasn't sure why he was a 'senior' reporter when there were no junior ones.

Before collapsing into bed Fin had telephoned his friend Farouk. When Fin had come to Cairo Farouk had shown him the delights beneath the dusty surface of the extraordinary city. But Fin had not kept the contact up – and a post-scuffle drunken telephone call may not have been the best way to rekindle the friendship. But hadn't Farouk said something about sending a cab? So when the insistent ringing of the doorbell drags Fin from sleep at 5.30 in the morning, the appearance of Waled and his cab isn't a complete surprise – but so early?

After Fin had known Farouk for a while, his certainty had worn Fin down. Farouk would tolerate no other view than his own as all his views were right – even if they contradicted each other. Fin just couldn't take it any more – but Fin had telephoned him nonetheless. Why?

Waled drives Fin to Farouk's village of Mena, and leaves him outside Khayam's tea house with the assurance that Farouk will be along soon. Fin's tea arrives and he settles down to wait . . . and wait . . .

When Farouk finally arrives Fin tells him of the lost job and Farouk plants a dangerous seed. He tells Fin of the fortunes of Skinhead Saïd to illustrate the importance of having a job – for you never know what will happen. Apparently the houses of Mena were built upon ancient tunnels, and one day Skinhead Saïd's cellar had disappeared. This story has an unusual effect on Fin – perhaps it's the possibilities such an occurrence might bring – artefacts, treasure? What had Skinhead Saïd found? But Farouk will not tell him.

And it takes a long time, a car accident, an abduction and some detective work before Fin hears the end of the story. Fin believes that he and Skinhead Saïd are similar, that as Skinhead Saïd struggles to unearth treasure, he is a kindred spirit – that he will find what he is looking for, which is somehow the same thing that Fin is seeking – but Fin's freedom appears in an entirely different guise in the end.

About the Author

Rowan Somerville was born in the West End of London in 1966. He was educated by Jesuits and took an honours degree in Literature from the University of Edinburgh. He has worked in film, television and radio and he now lives in rural Ireland. *The End of Sleep* is his first novel.

He welcomes comments on his novel, and you can email him at rowansomerville@yahoo.com.

The Story Behind *The End of Sleep*

One Christmas a dear friend gave me the mildly eccentric present of half a trip to see a fortune teller. Half a trip because this particular urban seer was expensive and my friend was, like me, sufficiently committed to the arts so as not to be able to afford the whole price. But half a trip? What use is half a trip of anything? Put simply, I had little interest in seeing a fortune teller and less in one that I would have to pay for. So it had taken me three months to book an appointment and then only because my friend, although small in stature, has a fearsome temper.

I'll tell you precisely what happened. I walk in, and the fortune teller is a gold-bedecked Irish woman with hennaed hair and big laugh-at-you eyes. We'll call her Noor, the Arabic for light. She's smoking long cheap cigarettes and drinking tea. All seems normal, two adults at a kitchen table in West London. She looks away, looks back at me with big actressy eyes and begins to laugh until tears roll down her face. In between a belly laugh and nicotine wheeze she manages to say, like it's the most obvious thing in the world: 'Your problem, ha hah hah … your problem,' her face becomes a high gradient map of laughter lines for a second, 'hah hah hah, is that you need someone to love. If you can't find a girl or a boy, get a cat.'

I found this rather irritating. It's just I'd prefer to be more sophisticated in my problems, have a more grandiose complex, but she'd hit the nail on the head – and this was before she'd even got out her tarot cards. When she did produce the finger-worn deck, wrapped in an old cloth, and settled her extravagantly skirted self and me in a dusty sitting room, she spread the cards out, took one look at them at them and told me with unshakable confidence to forget the cat because I would meet a girl within the week.

Great. Didn't believe her, of course, but it was so heart-warming to hear something positive and em-pirical from the world of the paranormal and 'within a week' too – so ballsy.

There was a point in Noor's confident and flowing reading of the cards where I became aware of a shift in her demeanour – like the pressure change when the last window in a speeding car is closed. An almost invisible difference, but undeniable. Her gaze had scanned down to the final row of cards and there was a flinch, no more than a couple of pairs of ears flicking up in a herd of grazing antelope. I asked her what was going on and she seemed perplexed for a moment, saying it wasn't clear to her.

'Go on,' I said, 'just tell me.'

'No,' she said and scooped up the cards.

She re-shuffled them and instructed me to lay out another row of six. Now here's where you believe me or not – but five of the six I selected were the same as before. My thoughts and expressions were the common expletives that buffer us when slammed up against the paranormal – and hers, God knows, but she quickly regained composure and told me that she could now reveal with greater clarity what the cards were saying. What she saw, she said calmly, was violence. Dramatic, unexpected violence. I shouldn't be overly concerned because violence could be an intense change of attitude – or a violent opinion … anyway, it was a long way off – more than a year.

We finished the session pretty quickly and I left her house genuinely fearful about the impending doom and totally forgetting the love she'd promised. Of course, ninety-six hours later when I met a beautiful moon-faced girl in a mobile phone shop, I fell for her and forgot about the violence.

A year passed.

And yes, I got attacked, jumped – a random act of violence, no words, no robbery, just a few moments of brutal self-expression from three young men. It happens all the time. I was lucky in a way, no knives, no death, just seven fractures to the face and jaw. It felt personal but it wasn't personal. It felt meaningful, but it had no meaning – other than pain, fear and anger – and of these, only pain is real.

A couple of weeks after leaving hospital, I was lying on the floor of my apartment feeling miserable – in truth, crying like a child, the kind of bawling you can only do if you are alone. I'd had a spectacular series of operations, resetting all the bones in my face – accessing tricky areas through the roof of my mouth and eye socket, fusing shards of bone together with Meccano-like titanium bolts. I was lucky but I didn't feel lucky. Gradually, like stunned fish, the memories of the tarot woman's predictions floated into my consciousness. I leapt up and realised that I must find the fortune teller again and tell her what had happened.

As life has it, rather than living in West London, she had moved to Mena village outside Cairo – just opposite the Great Pyramid.

So I went to Egypt.

What happened in the book is another story, and it is a story – fiction – but how it all started you now know.

Rowan Somerville

For Discussion

- The novel begins with Fin in a drunken sleep – in fact, Fin is no stranger to the bottle. Why do you think he drinks? What does Farouk have to say about booze?

- Cairo is a bustling chaotic metropolis – what is it that attracts Fin to this city?

- Fin's love affair with Egypt begins with an invitation to a wedding. Discuss the place of hospitality in the novel.

- When Fin reconnects with Farouk he is in exceptionally bad humour. Fin thinks this may be his fault – is it? How does the slaughter of a rabbit help?

- 'Fin did not know where the women went.' Why are there so few women in the novel?

- How is time marked in the novel? What are the differences between Fin's Western sense of time and Farouk's?

- 'Dawn does not come twice to waken a man.' The action of the novel takes place within a 24–hour period – is this important? What other novels, films or TV series are set in this space of time – and why?

- After his plunge into the Nile, Fin creeps into an ancient mosque and washes himself. What is the significance of this?

- How is food important in the novel?

- 'The American' is never given a name – why do you think this is?

- Discuss the portrayal of Islam and the Arab world in the novel. How is this relevant in respect to Western views?

- Is it possible to draw any parallels between Fin's journey and mythological tales of the West such as the Holy Grail legends?

- 'It had to hold something, otherwise why would he desire it?' Fin cannot quite identify what attracts him to Farouk's story – what do you think it is?

Can you see any similarities between Fin's hunger for the story and Skinhead Saïd's obsession with treasure?

- Can Fin's treasure be found?

Suggested Further Reading

The Yacoubian Building by Alaa Al Aswany

The Cairo Trilogy: Palace of Desire, Sugar Street and *Palace Walk* by Naguib Mahfouz

Cairo: The City Victorious by Max Rodenbeck

Playing Cards in Cairo by Hugh Miller

A Partisan's Daughter by Louis De Bernières

The Enchantress of Florence by Salman Rushdie

Big Fish: A Novel of Mythic Proportions by Daniel Wallace